I0761842

SKETCHED

SKETCHED

ROSE CARVER, BOOK TWO

DAVID ALAN JONES

Cover Design by S.H. Roddey

PROLOGUE

The girl led them on a merry chase. Alice hadn't run like this in months. Neither had the lads. Alice found it exhilarating.

They crashed through a series of narrow alleyways and crowded sidewalks west of Times Square, garish shop lights illuminating their path while simultaneously sending their shadows scuttling ahead of them on the mottled cement. They jostled New Yorkers, the offended Americans sending expletives chasing after them on the crisp October air. The humans liked to talk. That was their way. They thought themselves alone on the Earth—masters of the land and sea.

Alice pitied them their hubris. It kept their eyes shut to the truth.

The girl dashed into a car park, taking the chase away from the city center, probably hoping to jump the high fence ahead of them and slow their pursuit. That was good. Alice liked overconfidence.

Barney, the fastest of Alice's lads, streaked across the macadam, his footfalls like gunfire, and managed to leap just before the girl. He took her at the waist and slammed her into the chain links. They rattled like old bones.

The girl didn't cry out as Alice expected. Instead, she twisted in Barney's arms and smashed an elbow into his temple. He melted off her, his eyes rolled back in his head, his considerable muscles rendered useless.

In other circumstances, that might have been good enough. The girl clearly had more votaries than average, coupled with a keen sense of drawing. She was fast and strong and determined to get away, but the lads had captured many a slippery fox in their time, and they knew they'd be paying Saint Peter's price if they let this one escape.

Fig tackled her before Barney hit the ground. Shifty seized her legs to keep her from kicking free and Fig got an arm about her throat. If he had been an ordinary man, the girl would have ripped that arm from its socket, and possibly from Fig's body altogether, but try as she might, she couldn't budge the incubus's steel grip. The pressure on her neck turned her already flushed cheeks ruddier. She locked eyes with Alice.

Alice favored the girl with a nod: a master hunter acknowledging her prey's near escape—the cunning moves she had employed during their chase.

The girl's eyes rolled back.

"Ease off." Alice flicked two fingers, and Fig relaxed his grip, though he kept control of the girl.

Barney sat up, rubbing at the welt rising on his head. "Goddamn. The little minx hits like a mule."

"She should," Alice said. "She's got the fear draw in her blood. Haven't you, girl?"

The girl sneered, but said nothing.

Though the hour was late, nearly 3 a.m., humans still walked the streets. Alice gestured, and the lads hauled the girl away from the bright carpark to a short alley behind a TGI Friday's and some coffee shop Alice had never heard of. America abounded in those. The air smelled of rancid food and old lattes. Fig leaned against a refuse bin, his meaty arms encircling the girl.

"Your name is Melody." Alice fished her phone from the back pocket of her jeans and snapped a picture of the girl. "Your sister is Anna Rose Carver."

Melody's nose flared at the sound of her sister's name. Good. If

Alice's intelligence was right, the girl hated her sister with a murderous passion.

"What do you want?" Melody no longer struggled to free herself from Fig's grip, but Alice knew she remained dangerous. Now was the critical moment.

Alice leaned forward, close enough to smell the reek of hard living on the girl. Despite her many votaries, and the power they entailed, Melody had been living rough for months, sometimes on the street but almost as often in fleabag motels or whatever hostels would take her. She knew the American slinkers were after her. Vampires, too. Raising herself, even for a day, might be enough to let them catch her. Therefore, she had been living low—well beneath her considerable means.

She deserved better.

Alice met the younger woman's eyes. "I want to neutralize your sister, destroy every vampire on this continent, and overturn American Society. Are you in?"

1

SOCIALITE

Rose Carver leaned forward to see past the crowd of people dressed in evening finery. "Is that her? The redhead?"

"Yep." Matt gently drew her back by the elbow. "Best not stare, hon."

Leading up to this night, ostensibly a fundraiser for Gloria Torres's Senate campaign, Matt had continuously warned Rose to keep herself in check. Some of the richest and most powerful of the American elite occupied this room. That sort of thing meant nothing to Rose, who had grown up a slinker, her family on the brink of poverty her entire childhood. And even if it had, she possessed other reasons to dislike the people gathered here. Some of them, perhaps most of them, had tortured members of her immediate family in the last six months.

The venue they had rented, rather haughtily named *The Rake's Regret*—the owners blanched whenever Rose referred to it as an auditorium—rang with voices, not one of them human. Black-tied and evening-dressed partygoers mingled in stratified groups based mainly on their political clout and who might be trending on the latest social media outlets. Some of these people had answered Rose's invitation out of a legitimate desire to help the campaign. Most had come to goggle at the upstart slinkers who had thrown succubus society into turmoil these last few months.

"She doesn't look like much." Rose took a sip of sparkling grape juice. Others about the room imbibed the real stuff; she could smell the alcohol fumes pouring from their champagne glasses. Good for them. Rose would keep her edge, thank you.

"Maybe not, but don't let her grandma charm fool you. Barbara Griffith ran Society from the turn of the last century right up to my father's coup ten years ago. She's tough, and a lot of the old guard like her." Matt tipped his head to encompass the spacious room. "Some of the succubi in here have known her—known her leadership—for a century."

"Why didn't your dad take her out when he took power? Seems like his way of dealing with people."

"Dad might be a scoundrel, a grifter, and a conniving son of a bitch, but he's no fool. Harming Barbara would have ended the Indrawn Breath in an instant. Besides, she gave him no reason to attack her. She stepped down when she saw things swinging his way."

"But now that we unseated him, here comes Barbara."

Matt's right cheek twitched with that patented half-grin of his. "She isn't all that old, just a hundred and fifty or so. She probably figures we'll lose favor within a few weeks, maybe even days considering the state of the world."

"And once that happens, she'll step right back in as the undisputed leader of American Society." Rose swirled what remained of her juice around in her glass, her lips pressed into a hard line.

"Definitely. Slinkers don't go in for politics. Yeah, we won a victory, shut down the fear factory, but we're not the sort of people you call on for long-term governance. Not in the minds of people like Barbara Griffith, at least."

Rose, who knew next to nothing about government, whether the regular human variety or her own shadowy succubus kind, understood Matt's point. Slinkers, a nomad class of succubus who lived ever on the move, couldn't be trusted to manage Society's affairs.

Rose would know; she had been a slinker all her life.

"That's going to change." Rose daintily finished the last of her drink and placed the empty glass on a passing waiter's tray. Not so long ago, she would have been one of those carrying away the dirty dishes.

Matt met her eyes. "Yes, it is."

When Rose turned back, she found Barbara Griffith heading her way, a young incubus on her arm. Succubi, who aged far slower than humans, whether by some caprice of evolution or divine providence, tended to be gorgeous. Both sexes exuded sensuality as part of their raw charm, a glimmering influence possessed by every member of their kind. Barbara was no exception. Even at well over one hundred years old, her flat stomach, curvaceous figure, and flawless posture afforded her the appearance of a human woman enjoying her sexy forties.

"You're Rose Carver." It wasn't a question. Barbara lifted a coiffed eyebrow at Rose. "You're the woman who overthrew Kraft's house of horrors." She proffered her free hand.

"And you're Senator Barbara Griffith of Arkansas." Rose shook as graciously as she knew how. "You're the woman who successfully ran Society for nearly a hundred years."

"Ran is too strong a word, dear. Guided might be better." Though slight, Rose thought she detected something of Dixie in Barbara's accent. The older succubus looked askance at the man holding her arm. They shared a smile. "Or perhaps, haphazardly played maidservant, cleaning up every mess I could. It's not an easy job, leading American Society."

"I imagine not," Rose said.

Silence fell between them despite the burbling crowd. Barbara watched Rose with keen interest, her gray eyes like a pair of drills spinning their way into the younger woman's head.

"I thought I should take your measure now, while you're atop the world."

Uncertain how to answer, Rose nodded.

Barbara took Rose's silence as some sort of victory. The Senator's eyes crinkled with mirth, and she spun about to scan the crowd. "Is that your girl? The one running for Senate?"

"I would never call Gloria Torres a girl," Rose said, trying in vain to keep her temper. The way Barbara spoke reminded her of how self-righteous bigots talked about minorities, with a clear sense of superiority. "She's my friend, and yes, she's running for the Senate seat out of Georgia."

"A slinker in office," Barbara mused as if speaking to herself. "It's a frightening thing if you ask me."

"You're afraid of slinkers, Senator Griffith?" asked Matt, and Rose's heart filled with pride.

Barbara regarded him with an expression that bordered on disdain until it settled for mild pique. "Matthew Kraft."

"Snow."

"Right. You took a bastard's name. How literary of you." Barbara glanced again at her unnamed companion. "I don't blame him, really. His father's a powerful incubus, a true leader, though I, of course, abhor and repudiate his methods. Still, Jason at least made something of himself. This one? A born flunky. All he's ever done is his father's bidding and then his mother's after that. Kraft might be a bastard, but at least he has some chutzpah."

Rose squeezed Matt's hand. She expected him to stiffen in anger, maybe even spit a few choice words Barbara's way. To her everlasting surprise, he smiled.

"You always know when an elite's back is up because they start saying the quiet things out loud."

Barbara's young man bristled as though he might say something hot, but she stopped him with a gesture. He quelled like a trained dog, leaving Rose to wonder if the old Society leader had him charmed out of his wits, but his eyes appeared clear, his expression animated.

Probably just a gold digger.

"I heard you were arrested when the fear factory came down." Barbara twiddled her fingers, and a nearby waiter hurried to serve her a glass of champagne.

"I was."

"But you weren't, Rose?"

Rose shook her head. Three hours of campaign fundraising, and she had had her fill of Society. More than ever, she congratulated herself on demurring to run for political office. Thank God, Gloria had stepped up.

"Why is it then," asked Barbara, looking between them, "that everyone's talking about Rose Carver, the hero of the fear factory? The woman who single-handedly put down Kraft's Indrawn Breath in a matter of months."

"There was nothing single-handed about it." Rose loathed discussing the fear factory. It brought back too many painful memories. No, that was a lie. That wasn't why she hated remembering the place. She had to be honest. It brought back her craving for fear.

"I think you're overmodest," Barbara said. "It's your name I hear again and again any time someone brings up the topic. And they bring it up often."

"Because they're happy it's gone, or are they jonesing for the votaries they lost?" Though the smile hadn't left Matt's face, his eyes grew cold as he spoke.

"No one's pleased about what your father did there, Matthew. Don't be boorish. Frightening people out of their minds is abhorrent. This world is better without that disgusting place."

"I'm glad to hear you say that."

Barbara inclined her head to him. "So, exactly how did you escape after the fall and your subsequent arrest? I heard there were those in the state department who wanted to pin the entire enterprise on you."

"I didn't escape. I was set free."

"Because of your father's influence?"

Matt's jaw grew tight, but he maintained a civil tone. "I honestly don't know, but if I had to guess, I'd say he had something to do with my release, yes."

Barbara gingerly placed a hand on his shoulder in a faux sign of comfort. "To think, after all that's passed between you—so many betrayals and lies and ill uses—that the man still loves you enough to flout the law on your behalf."

"I'll be sure to nominate him for father of the year."

"How long were you in custody?"

"Three days." Matt barely opened his mouth when he spoke.

"Imagine that. By that time, the attorney general was already hounding your father for his involvement in kidnapping and torturing innocent Americans. Embattled and soon to run for his life, he thought to save his only son. That's a father's love."

"I doubt it. He probably wanted me out of the way so I wouldn't testify against him." A slow grin tugged up the corners of Matt's mouth. "I did anyway."

Barbara scrunched up her nose as if she smelled something foul, her attention suddenly diverted.

Rose followed her gaze to find Olivia Crown, a vampire in Rose's care, sauntering toward them in a sleek red evening gown. Silver tassels danced across the mid-line, hips, and shoulders as she moved, playing up her lithe form.

There had been a time, not so long ago, when Rose would have been anything but pleased to see a vampire coming her way. Her experience with their kind had been tainted during last year's invasion of Mexico. Subsequent experiences with Olivia's mother, her many sisters, and one brother had laid those fears to rest. After three months of spending most nights in Olivia's company, Rose had come to view her as a dear friend. Though circumstance had thrust them together, commonality and mutual respect brought them close.

It didn't hurt that most of the rich, snooty, upper-class succubi in the room hated vampires even more than they hated slinkers.

Olivia, no doubt aware of those feelings and yet blithely unimpressed, opened her arms to give Rose a hug. The show of affection surprised Rose. They had arrived together before all the schmoozing began, yet Olivia embraced her as if they had been parted for days. At first, Rose took her friend's gesture as a way of tweaking the crowd's collective noses, but there was genuine feeling in Olivia's tight embrace.

As it turned out, that feeling was fear.

"We have a problem." Olivia whispered the words sotto voce into Rose's ear.

Rose gave her the barest of nods before gesturing. "Olivia, this is Senator Barbara Griffith."

"A pleasure to meet you." Olivia's deep southern accent had softened during her time living amongst succubi, but her charm, even in the face of enemies, had not. She and Rose had discussed this woman many times during late-night planning sessions for the Torres campaign. She knew the threat Barbara posed for both of them. During the senator's previous tenure as head of American Society, vampires had been relegated to second-class citizens in the States and Canada: a minority to be tolerated, put in its place, and forgotten.

"Indeed." Barbara pointedly did not offer her hand to Olivia as she had Rose. "Do excuse me, I believe Ms. McAleese of the Irish delegation is being ignored over there in the corner. I think I'll go see she doesn't get too bored with your little soiree."

The haughty succubus pivoted like a clockwork soldier and marched across the room to greet a short, blond woman surrounded by oversized guards. She did not look back.

"How'd that go?" Olivia asked, watching the senator and her escort.

"About as well as could be expected." Matt snagged a grape left over from dinner on an abandoned table and popped it into his mouth. "She's here to reclaim her spot at the top, and we're in her way."

"Did she say that?" Olivia lifted her eyebrows.

"Not in those words," Rose said. "But she made it clear where we stand in her estimation."

"Where's that?"

"Under her $2,000 pumps," Matt said.

"What's the trouble you mentioned?" Rose asked. "Is it Piper?"

Olivia nodded. Her mother, not a natural mother, but the woman who had transformed Olivia from human to vampire, was named Piper Ross. Unlike most of her kind, Piper had little trouble creating offspring. In fact, she had spawned so many daughter vampires in the last two decades, others of their kind had, against their usual natures, prohibited her from leaving her home state of South Carolina. Had she fewer children, they might have attacked and killed her for her sheer fecundity, but they dared not. No one, not even Rose, knew exactly how many children Piper had created, but Rose had met twelve of them. While that number sounded small, compared to the average vampire who might create one full-blood child in a century, it made Piper the leader of a veritable army. Worse, at least for her enemies, Piper also commanded scores of wights, vampires who had failed to make the full change from their human form. Like drones in a beehive, the wights followed their mother's every order for lack of personal internal drive. Less intelligent than a human, vampire, or succubus, wights were nevertheless formidable warriors that, once unleashed on a foe, would gladly walk into a meat grinder at their sire's behest.

Rose drew discernment from her votaries, and her breath caught. She knew at once, Piper had broken her agreement to remain in South Carolina, at least until Rose and Matt could get a foothold within succubus Society. By the set of Olivia's jaw, her controlled breathing, and the concern in her eyes, it was apparent her mother had gotten herself into some sort of trouble with vampires outside her domain. Equally obvious, she needed Rose's help right away.

"This is not a convenient time, Liv."

Olivia nodded, her lips pressed together, no doubt to hide the fangs extruding from her gums due to anxiety. "She's in real danger, Rose. She needs us."

"This was our chance to open talks with some of the Societies from other nations. We need allies right now, not more enemies."

Olivia said nothing. Her eyes pled her case.

Rose heaved a sigh. "Where?"

2

AT ODDS

Rose sat in a darkened van, twisting a piece of rawhide in her hands. "How much longer?"

"Five minutes." Matt swerved into the left lane to pass a sedan and floored it to make the next light. He didn't. The wail of a siren and the flash of blue lights bouncing off encroaching apartments made him curse. Though traffic was light along North Washington Street in Alexandria, Virginia, none of them had spotted the hidden motorcycle cop.

"We don't have time for this." Rose twisted to face the team she and Matt had hastily gathered at the fundraiser. "Everyone draw charm. Make this guy forget he ever saw us."

As one, the four turned to the rear window. A palpable, at least to a succubus, wave of charm rolled off them like heat from a blast furnace, all of it aimed at the cop. He immediately switched off his siren and lights. Slowing, he performed a tight U-turn and headed back the way he had come, his bike's rear tire kicking up a fine spray of water from the wet asphalt.

"Damn, I need you guys with me on my next Disney trip," Tanner Watts said, grinning in the light provided by passing cars. "Got a two-hundred-dollar ticket in Florida last year, and the wife won't let me forget it."

"Pay my way, and I'm there," Myra Hanks said from the farthest rear seat. The former math teacher-turned-prognosticator had aged significantly in the year Rose had known her. Despite her relative youth for a succubus, just seventy-eight, new strands of gray decorated her otherwise auburn hair, far more so than when Rose first met her the year before. That, coupled with the worry lines etched along her eyes, created an odd sort of juxtaposition with the sensual, low cut evening gown she wore. Not that Myra wasn't pulling it off. She was pulling it off in spades.

"Any updates from Piper?" Garrett Timmons asked, a rarity considering his usual quiet nature. The young guardsman had volunteered to serve on the security detail at Torres' fundraiser. Most of his peers remained behind to protect their charge, but Rose insisted on bringing Garrett along. Quiet or not, the man was a hell of an operator in the field.

Olivia shook her head. Rose couldn't feel the vampire's emotions, not the way she could with humans or her fellow succubi, but she had no trouble reading the worry on her friend's face. Her mother's call for help had come more than thirty minutes ago. Rose knew from experience that thirty minutes could be an eternity in a fight, especially between vampires. Even unarmed, they were nearly unstoppable.

"What was she doing in Alexandria anyway?" Matt asked as he slewed the van into a tight left turn, following the directions broadcast by his phone. He had loosened his bow tie and unfastened the first two buttons on his white shirt but still wore his tuxedo jacket.

Olivia gazed out the side window, silent for a long moment, her pale skin white under passing streetlights. "Waging a turf war, I think."

Rose felt her eyebrows shoot up. "She came here looking for a fight?"

"She came here looking to make allies. She wants more of our kind, especially the old-world vamps, to join her."

"But if they don't join, she goes after them?" Garret asked.

"Of course, she does. She's forming her own coven kingdom." Matt glanced at Olivia in the rearview mirror for confirmation.

"Yes. She is."

"That wasn't the agreement." Rose turned to catch Olivia's gaze. "She's supposed to be back in South Carolina biding her time."

"I know that." Olivia couldn't meet Rose's eyes.

"So does Piper," Matt said. "She's showing an incredible lack of patience for a vampire."

"She's been locked up in one state for more than half a century," Olivia said, but with little vigor.

"We promised we'd help her fix that, but only after we get a handle on our own affairs," Rose said. "This sort of thing will piss off every succubus in the nation. We're having a hard enough time convincing them to accept the fact we've allied with her. Now she goes and picks a fight? Who's it with, anyway?"

"Felix Dietrich."

"Shit." Matt twisted around to glance at Olivia. "You're not serious."

"Who's Felix Dietrich?" Rose asked.

"First off, he's one of the oldest vampires in the States. Probably nine hundred, maybe a thousand years," Matt said.

"More like seven, maybe eight." Olivia sounded ill.

"Point is, he's old and powerful." Matt signaled another turn and gunned the van up to seventy miles an hour along a small, two-lane road lined with large brick homes, apartment buildings, and small shops.

"He's also one of the top enforcers responsible for keeping my family locked away all these years." Olivia sat forward against her seat belt. "Whenever Piper broke coven law, it was Felix who came south to deal with her. He once executed three of my sisters and seven wights because Mother took a trip to Bermuda."

"So, they're old enemies," Rose said.

"Mother loathes him."

Matt took a hard right to pass through an open gate in a fifteen-foot high cement wall. He brought the van to a hard stop, its wheels sliding on the wet drive. Though the storm that had earlier swept across the city and into DC had passed away, everything remained shiny under the city lights.

A large home, at least for this part of the greater DC metropolitan area, where housing prices would make a real estate tycoon blush, loomed ahead of them. Surrounded by majestic trees completely out of place this deep in the city, it looked like an eighteenth-century manor house transplanted from its proper time to the present. Several ornate lampposts spilled light across its manicured front yard.

"Is this—" Rose began but was interrupted by a series of muted bangs accompanied by flashes in the bottom story windows.

"Yes." Olivia flung open the van's door and, moving with preternatural speed, headed for the manor house's front entrance.

"Dammit, Liv," Rose cursed as she and the others trailed after Olivia along a brick walkway. "Slow down."

A shadow detached itself from behind one of the lampposts as Olivia climbed the front steps. Rose's heart lurched at the figure's sudden appearance, but just as quickly settled when she recognized the vampire hurrying Olivia's way.

"Liv!" Grace, Olivia's teenage sister—truly teenaged, since she had been turned only a scant two years before—threw her arms around the older vampire. Her light blond hair fairly glowed in the wan light.

"What's happening?" Olivia endured her sister's hug for a moment before pulling back to look Grace in the eyes. "How long's Mother been inside?"

Grace shrugged. "Thirty seconds? She made Stephanie and me stay out to charm the neighborhood."

Like their cousin succubi, vampires could innately control their charm, the ability to manipulate the thoughts and emotions of other people, especially humans. Piper wouldn't want any nosy neighbors or, God forbid, police showing up to ask bothersome questions, so she had left two of her youngest daughters to quell curiosity about the sounds emanating from the house.

"I thought you said she was in trouble and needed our help?" Matt gestured toward Olivia.

A long screech originating somewhere inside split the night in two, followed by several shotgun blasts and what sounded like splintering furniture.

"She is, and she does."

"But she didn't less than a minute ago. She waited for us to show up before she attacked this Felix character." Rose mounted the house's front steps to peer inside. The storm door had been shattered. The steel door behind it lay on the entranceway floor.

Olivia bit her lip, no small feat for a vampire with her fangs out, and let go a heavy sigh. "I can't argue, except to say I didn't know. She made it sound like she was in the middle of a fight when she called."

"So we'd come running," Rose said.

More sounds of battle shook the old house, and a vampire, female by the sound, screamed inside.

"I guess you can refuse to help if you want, but I'm going in." Olivia didn't wait for an answer from her succubus escort; she charged inside.

Matt glanced Rose's way, and she nodded. They had made a covenant with Piper and her brood. The vampires kept up the first part of that agreement when they aided Rose and her cohorts in destroying Jason Kraft's fear factory. And while Piper might be blowing the second part by extending her coven before the agreed-upon time, she was their only ally.

"I knew we should have brought guns to the fundraiser," Rose said as she stepped inside, drawing speed, strength, and discernment.

"That's not what you said when we were packing yesterday." Matt crouched to come in behind her, his gaze roaming the interior.

"What have I said about listening to me?"

Overturned tables and broken chairs lay strewn across the foyer and a large living area. Olivia stood in the midst of them, hands splayed at her sides, scanning the room. Though the lights were out—Matt tried a switch the instant he entered the room—ample illumination came through the windows for the succubi. Rose drew vision from her votaries, which, while it couldn't make the room appear as bright as noonday, at least pushed back shadows and sharpened colors.

"Everyone grab something to fight with." Matt stooped to pick up a heavy table leg, and the others followed his lead.

The sounds of battle emanated from deeper within the house. Rose stomped a foot, drawing hearing while simultaneously amplifying the sensitivity in her feet and legs. "There's a basement level."

"Bet that wasn't part of the original house," Tanner said as he strode across the room to a darkened hallway. He played the beam of a small, powerful flashlight along the wood paneling. He banged the wall a few times before grunting in satisfaction. "Got it."

A concealed door swung open before Tanner, and the sounds of fighting intensified. He shone his flashlight down a long set of dark wooded stairs.

"Tell me that's not creepy," Myra said. "Stairs leading down into perfect darkness inside a vampire's lair."

"Lair? Really?"

Rose twisted in surprise to find Grace trailing after their group. "Aren't you supposed to be shielding the house?"

"Stephanie's got it. She's our best charmer. I was just there because Mom thinks I'm too young to fight."

"She's right," Olivia said.

"Yeah, well, we can argue about that later. Right now, it sounds like Mother needs help." Grace pointed toward the secret door. "Besides, you think I'm going to pass up the chance to fight next to Rose Carver?"

Olivia grumbled something under her breath but said aloud, "Fine, stay behind us, and if things get out of hand, run."

"You got it. Now let's go. We're wasting time." Grace headed for the door as she deftly tied her long hair in a bun.

Stealthily as they could manage, the two vampires and four succubi negotiated the darkened stairwell, Tanner in the lead. A stone room opened at the bottom of the stairs, incongruent with the rest of the house and its wood paneling. The air here was cooler than above and laden with the scent of dust, neglect, and spent gunpowder.

Three figures, two male and one female, stood opposite the stairway, their backs to Rose and her people. They wore mismatched, dated clothing, frayed and threadbare in the flashlight beam. The female, who stood eight inches taller than the men, turned to reveal a pair of eyes glowing red in the reflected light. She bared her teeth, an impressive double row of fangs, the envy of any shark, and hissed.

Wights. The bastard children of the vampire world. Nearly mindless but as powerful as any full-blood vampire, the creatures relied on their progenitor's commands to make decisions. These three must have been told to protect the door and kill anyone who tried to enter. Like predators on the hunt, they spun to face the succubi, pale hands spread out at their sides, nails like claws splayed for battle.

"I take it these don't belong to your coven." Tanner stepped forward to shine his flashlight in the monsters' faces. They cringed and squinted but didn't falter.

"Felix's pets," Olivia said.

The wights hissed in unison, the female leaning forward, her chasm of a mouth open wide.

Charm like a bucket of frozen water hit Rose. Though the wights lacked sophisticated control over their own powers, this one came as naturally to them as flying came to a sparrow. Sleepiness threatened to shut Rose's eyes. She stumbled back a step, as did Tanner, Garret, and Myra. Gritting her teeth, Rose drew charm to match her foes and spread its enveloping bubble to everyone around her.

Just in time, it turned out. The female wight launched herself at Tanner, clawed hands aimed for his throat. Drawing speed, he sidestepped her attack, and she barreled into Rose with the force of a small car.

Rose struggled to maintain her balance, drawing strength, speed, and dexterity to match the attack. The wight growled, producing a sound like a whistling teapot mixed with a coffee grinder. She swiped at Rose and even managed to tear a chunk from her dress before Rose could dance away.

"This cost seven hundred dollars!" Rose kicked the female wight in the face, the blow so powerful it snapped her head back with a sound of cracking bones and tearing ligaments. The creature stumbled to the cement floor and sat there, facing the ceiling, seemingly unable to bring her head down for the damage to her upper spine.

Not to be outdone, Olivia plunged the sharp end of a splintered table leg through the wight's chest. The wight howled in pain as she writhed on her back, leaving a bloody smear in her wake. In seconds, her screaming ground to a warbling groan and finally nothing as her pale eyes lost their spark of life. Popular fiction and movies had gotten one thing right about vampires: a stake through the heart killed them. Of course, a stake through anything's heart killed it.

Tanner and Garret dispatched the male wights in the same manner and withdrew their weapons once satisfied the creatures were dead.

Rose felt little sympathy for the wights. They were rabid animals, hardly capable of human-level thought. They would have killed her people given the chance. If she had any remorse for them, it was for the humans—or possibly succubi—they had been before some vampire attempted to change them. Had that been a decision on their part, or a choice forced upon them? Many humans romanticized the idea of becoming a vampire. Of those who got the chance, most died. The majority of the rest became these hapless, thoughtless killer minions chained to their master's will. Rose could think of little else to better define pure hell.

An open hallway led off the main basement room. Garrett entered it, flashlight held steady before him. The others followed in a staggered V formation, their makeshift weapons at the ready. Sounds of struggle mixed with god-awful screams and warbling hisses grew louder as they traversed the shadowed hallway. A set of double doors, the rightmost askew, its wooden face split nearly in half, opened into what Rose took for a spacious meeting room illuminated by soft overhead lamps. Somewhere nearby came the incessant chug of a generator. The room reminded Rose of an audience chamber in a movie castle. Tanner kicked the damaged door off its hinges and marched inside, obliging the others to follow or get left behind.

A dozen vampires and wights engaged in a fierce battle occupied the far end of the stone room. Some fought on the floor, others on a raised platform where a throne stood under a burgundy velvet awning. The sweet yet fetid reek of vampires filled the air.

Piper Ross, the self-styled vampire queen of South Carolina, stood before the throne, menaced by an aged man dressed in chinos and a Grateful Dead t-shirt. Two wights fought by his side, their clothes moldered nearly to the point of decomposition. Piper moved with unnatural grace and speed, but though she could have easily bested any one of her attackers, the three together were getting the better of her. A shotgun lay on the ground near her feet.

"The old one is Felix, I suppose?" Rose asked.

Olivia nodded as she took in the sprawling battle.

Four of Piper's daughters were likewise engaged with wights or one of the five full-blood vampires, or both. Though they put on a good show, Rose could tell Piper and her girls were on the losing end of the conflict. They lacked the numbers to survive this battle.

Without warning, Olivia sprinted across the room, emitting a banshee wail, a splintered coffee table leg brandished in both hands. She fetched the nearest wight a blow to the head, and the creature flew ass over crown into the raised platform where her mother fought.

Matt met Rose's eyes, brows raised.

She grimaced but nodded. "We promised we'd help Piper. We can't stand here and let her die."

Rose and her people threw themselves into the fray. While Matt, Tanner, and an older op named Landis joined Olivia by slamming into the rearmost rank of wights attacking Piper's daughters, Rose, Myra, and Grace jumped onto the platform.

Though he appeared wizened, Felix moved with almost as much speed as Rose.

Almost.

He spun about, letting his wights continue their attack on Piper, and hissed as he attempted to punch Rose in the jaw. Infused with speed and discernment, she saw the blow coming and rocked back enough to let him swing wide. Drawing strength to bolster her speed, she smashed Felix's jaw with a looping left hook and followed up by clubbing him on the back of the head with the table leg. The wood made a satisfying CRACK when it connected, but the concussion split it in half and sent the top portion flying.

To Rose's surprise, her successful attack had little effect on Felix. He staggered a step, regained his balance, and, baring blood-tinged teeth, flew at Rose with all the melodrama of a low-budget movie bloodsucker. She expected another rake of his claws. Instead, he got a hand about her neck, his grip like a great white trying to crush her larynx, and dove for the side of her neck with his double row of serrated teeth. The vampire's frail appearance masked his incredible strength. It was all Rose could do—all she could draw—to keep him from sinking his fangs in her unprotected flesh. His breath smelled of blood and rancid coffee. The stench made her gag.

Felix's teeth scraped the skin where Rose's shoulder became her neck. She cringed, bracing for the inevitable puncture, when a shaft of wood speared past Rose's face to pierce the vampire's eye. He screamed, his steel grip gone from her throat, and fell against the throne at the center of the platform, one hand plastered to his face, hot blood gushing between his thin fingers.

Rose turned to find Grace behind her, the young vampire baring her fangs. Her savage expression softened, replaced by doubt and worry. "Was that good?"

"That was perfect."

Grace beamed, sharpened teeth gleaming.

Rose spun back to Felix, heart singing in her chest. Sometimes, though she would never admit it aloud, she loved a good fight. It had been months since she had last drawn this much from her votaries—last pitted herself against enemies out to take her life. Not since the night she and the others overthrew the fear factory had she felt this alive.

Felix, hissing and groaning, withdrew the long splinter from his eye. Vampires could absorb a lot of damage. So long as their hearts kept beating, they could recover from incredible injuries. But doing so took a toll, both on the vampire and his votaries. Tied by blood, the vampire's victims provided him access to myriad talents, much like a succubus with her acquaintances, friends, and lovers. Except a vampire's blood ties, so far as Rose could tell, delivered a lot more bang for the buck.

As she watched, Felix's damaged eye transformed from a gaping hole surrounded by rapidly swelling flesh into a pale blue orb free of injury. He dropped the makeshift weapon by his feet in a splatter of blood before looking down at his shirt.

"That," he said in a faint German accent, "was my favorite Dead shirt, you succubus whore."

Felix attacked again. This time he feigned a blow at Rose to get her attention and throw off her balance. Instead of striking her, he caught Grace with a kick to the ribs that sent her sprawling. She fell with an audible "oof," and slid a couple of feet on her back. Felix used Rose's momentary surprise to smash her with an elbow, followed by sweeping her legs out from under her. Apparently, with thousands of years to live, some vampires learned to fight.

Felix slammed Rose to the ground and was atop her before she could think to defend herself. He obviously meant to make short work of her, and with his incredible strength, she wasn't certain she could stop him. A moment of genuine fear washed over her, whether from the vampire's charm or originating inside her, she couldn't tell. And, in the end, did it matter?

"Felix, you son of a bitch, get off her!" Piper shouted her war cry at top volume, an earsplitting sound incongruent with her petite frame. Like her volume, her strength also contradicted her short stature and alluring curves. The vampire queen possessed a huge votary count, and her physical prowess proved it.

She seized Felix by the ankles, arresting his attack before he could get his feed on and, with a guttural scream, whipped him away from Rose as if he weighed no more than a bed sheet. The hapless vampire sailed over Piper's head to collide with the stone floor behind her. His head made a sound like a bowling ball hitting the pins.

He struggled to rise, but Piper was already there, scrambling across his body like a spider. Before Rose could utter a word, she sank her fangs into his neck with a squishing sound that turned Rose's stomach. Felix struggled the way a gazelle might once the lioness has set her teeth, but his feeble attempts at pushing Piper away, or even gouging her with his nails, gained him nothing. In less than ten seconds, his limbs fell still, his life's blood drained from his corpse.

Piper rolled off the body onto her knees with a satisfied groan of pleasure, her chin covered in crimson gore. Head leaned back, fangs exposed, she stared at the ceiling without moving. Her eerie stillness reminded Rose of the first vampires she had met in Mexico, the ones who made a show of freezing in place like terracotta warriors.

Rose shivered and shared a glance with Matt, who shrugged and shook his head. He had never seen this sort of behavior before either.

The battle below them had come to a similar end. The full-blood vampires—distinguished by their clean clothes and proper hygiene—lay dead on the floor with their wight cousins. Piper's daughters, including Olivia, wore fresh bloodstains around their mouths. Two of them bore gashes on their cheeks and arms, but the wounds were rapidly disappearing.

Piper shuddered and jerked forward like a woman snapping awake from a deep slumber. Her green eyes roamed to Felix, and she nodded once, her lips curving up in a crimson grin. "That old shark almost had me there for a moment."

"I know the feeling." Rose rubbed at the spot on her neck where Felix had nearly made a meal of her.

"Thank you for coming, especially when you did." Piper turned an intense gaze on Rose. This was a side of her Rose had never seen, not even the night of the fear factory battle. The otherwise diminutive vampire looked more than lethal; she looked like a sentient killing machine hunting for a new target.

Drawing calm, Rose met Piper's eyes and steeled herself for what she would say next. She didn't relish an argument when the vampire's blood was up but now was the best time. "You should have waited."

"I did." Piper's expression showed not an ounce of remorse or even concern.

"No, I mean you shouldn't have attacked Felix at all." Rose couldn't say for certain if Piper deliberately misunderstood. Vampires put the dead in deadpan. Either way, she wasn't about to let Piper slide. "We had an agreement: no fighting the other coven kingdoms until we've established our place in Society."

Piper pushed effortlessly to her feet. "Your place in Society is at the top. I don't see why you haven't established that already."

"Society doesn't work that way," Matt said, his tone guarded, though Rose could hear his irritation buried within. "There are thousands of succubi in this town, all of them running their little piece of the whole. We can't barge in and expect them to step aside. We have to win approval."

"Strength needs no approval." Piper wiped her mouth with the back of her jacket sleeve, which did little more than smear the blood. "Look at Felix here, almost a thousand years old, and he spent the last fifty keeping me chained up in a little corner of the world. Now he's dead, and I'm free. Why? Because I was the stronger between us. You're stronger than the rich bitch phonies who lord over the regular succubi. There's no reason to let them put you down—put them down instead."

Matt started to say more, but Rose placed a restraining hand on his arm.

"You might be right, but we're not looking to start a war. That would cost lives, and in the long run, it would delay the help we've promised you. I know you want revenge on the vampires who've held you back all these years, but Society's going to take notice if you go around executing them like this. That sort of scrutiny will make things harder for us."

"Because you're slumming it with bloodsuckers?" Piper's southern drawl held no heat. In fact, she smiled when she said it, an expression that might have been sweet in other circumstances—her fangs had retracted into her gums after all—but instead struck a gruesome chord for the bloodstains on her teeth.

"The only thing worse to Society thinking than a slinker succubus is any sort of vampire," Rose agreed. She put a hand on Piper's shoulder. "Can't you cool it just for a little while? We're doing everything we can to secure our place. Once that's done, we'll help you any way we can, just like we promised."

Piper gave Rose's hand a squeeze, her face all but human now. "Yes, okay, but hurry. I have family to protect."

"Don't we all."

3

THE DISCARDED

The sound of a roaring engine and the monotonous drone of tires on asphalt threatened to lull Rose to sleep. She drew alertness to stave off her doze, and her eyes popped open. Better than two cups of coffee, and it wouldn't leave her spazzing out later when she went to bed.

They had departed Washington at nightfall more than seven hours ago, following I-85 South and lately turned onto US-77 headed through Charlotte, Matt at the wheel the entire time—the man loved to drive. In a few minutes, they would enter Sharon Woods, a nice, but not too nice, neighborhood on the outskirts of the city, where Rose had placed her parents and brother, Troy, after their harrowing stint in the fear factory.

"Any sign of Piper's car?" Rose twisted about in her seat, scanning the road, though all she saw were headlights.

"Nope. I wish she would share locations with us on the phone, but you know her," Matt said.

Piper and her daughters, each driving a different super car, had followed close behind the van for a couple of hours out of Washington. One by one, however, they had passed or else dropped away until Rose and her people lost sight of them. That hadn't been the plan.

Their little caravan was supposed to remain close for mutual support. Piper had assured Rose and Matt she and her daughters were close by at all times, but somehow Rose doubted the vampire's word.

Not that they could do a thing about it. In general, America's old school vampires didn't have it out for Rose so far as she knew. That may have changed after helping Piper defeat Felix, but Rose doubted they viewed her as a bigger target than Piper. By going it alone, Piper split their combined forces and weakened her position. Should some five hundred-year-old bloodsucker with a vendetta against her and a slew of minions at his back go after Piper, she would have to face them alone until Rose could find her.

Fool.

"How are you feeling?" Matt asked, dragging Rose out of her reverie.

"I'm a little nervous," Rose said. "Isn't that stupid? Nervous to see my own family."

"It's been three months," Matt said. "And the last time wasn't exactly pleasant."

"No, it was not."

They turned onto a wide two-lane road lined on both sides with modest houses, most built in the late nineties or just after the turn of the century. Even after nightfall, Hinsdale Drive struck Rose as a respectable, safe place, the sort she rarely lived in growing up. Some of the lawns even sported white picket fences. The Carver residence, a split-level home with a brick first story and siding up top, looked no different from any other on the street. Never mind the insane succubi inside.

Matt woke Tanner, who would set up a perimeter guard to watch the house for the night. Though Matt and Rose alike had argued he and his security team should find a hotel and get some rest, Tanner had refused to leave, and Matt seemed disinclined to renew the argument.

"I'll join them for a bit," Olivia said as she climbed out of the van. "Sun won't be up for a few more hours."

"We'll be glad to have you," Tanner said as he set about unlocking a weapons safe in the back of the van. He offered her a pistol, but she shook her head.

"Thanks for helping out." Rose gave Olivia a quick hug. "You don't have to, you know. It's not your job."

"What else is there for a vampire to do in Charlotte besides guard her succubus overlords?"

Rose rolled her eyes.

Floodlights affixed to the carport blinked on, and Troy came out to give his younger sister a hug. "How are you? How was DC?" Troy had put on weight, a good sign considering his emaciated state last summer. At 6'1" and probably 170 pounds, he still looked like a stick figure.

"Not great," Rose said. "Torres got some backers, so that was good, but we didn't have time to make any alliances during the fundraiser."

"I thought you were going to see all the high rollers? Schmooze, eat caviar, drink wine, all that sort of thing." Troy took Rose's heaviest bag as they headed for the front door, not that he could hope to match her strength. It was a big brother thing. She knew better than to argue.

"That's a long story," Matt said with a huff. "We got called away and couldn't get back before the event was over."

"How are they?" Rose asked as she mounted the steps.

Troy, his hand on the door, paused. "Good. They get antsy at night sometimes, but things have been better these last few days. Mom's quiet—watching a lot of movies. Dad...I can't tell with him. Lately, I feel like he's been charming me, even though he swears he hasn't."

Rose tensed. "I knew I shouldn't have let you take care of them alone. I told you we could get someone, one of our kind, to help you."

"It's not as bad as all that. You'll see." Troy pushed the door open and held it for Rose and Matt to pass inside.

The house smelled of fresh-baked cookies and something savory—pot roast? The combination created a surprisingly alluring scent. Rose's mouth watered.

Rose's father, Graylen, stood from the couch, his weathered face splitting into a wide smile that made his dark eyes twinkle. "Anna!

Troy said you were coming and I—" Graylen glanced at Troy before throwing his arms around Rose for a stiff hug. "I didn't believe him, but here you are, and with that young man of yours."

"Matt Snow, Mr. Carver." Matt stuck out his hand as he had the last two times he had met Rose's father.

"Matt, that's right." Graylen shook enthusiastically, smiling all the more.

"Hi, Mom," Rose said.

Rose's mother, Sarah, gazed at her daughter, blinking once slowly before something seemed to click behind her eyes, and she perked up. "Anna. Is that you?"

"It's me, Mom." Rose drew calm to combat the lump in her throat. She bent and hugged her mother but kept the contact brief. Touch had a tendency to drive Sarah Carver into fits of hysteria.

"What are you doing here?" Sarah asked.

"Just came for a visit. We're staying until tomorrow night."

"I'll take your bags to your room if you want to sit and chat," Troy said, reaching for Matt's overnight luggage.

"I'll help you," Matt said. "Rose, you have a seat."

"I made...I guess it's dinner, even though it's almost three in the morning," Troy said.

"Sorry about that." Rose took a seat on the couch next to her dad. "One of the drawbacks of traveling with a vampire: nighttime travel only."

"Vampire?" Graylen's salt-and-pepper eyebrows shot up.

"Yeah, Dad, you remember me telling you, we're friends with a vampire named Piper, right?"

"I remember her," Graylen sounded peevish, as if Rose had challenged his memory. "I thought she was in that comic book of yours. Those two gay fellows drawing that still?"

Rose suppressed a sigh. "Yeah, they are. But it's not nice to call them, 'those two gay fellows,' Dad. Their names are Luke and Brendan Pruett."

"I thought gay was the right term. What? Are we supposed to call them faggots again?" Graylen scrunched his eyebrows. "That doesn't seem right."

"Definitely not."

"But they're still making your comic?"

"One a month."

"I was reading them for a while, but I got busy. Troy's probably got a stack around here somewhere. You still get votaries from them?"

Rose shrugged one shoulder. "Not as many as I used to."

"Life is busy these days. Readership dropping off?"

"No, Drawn's still popular, but the boys have had to diverge the story quite a bit from my real life. They say it's to protect me from people discovering I'm a real person, but I think it's because my life's gotten boring. It's all campaign management and office work now. A lot more calling people and stuffing envelopes than going hand-to-hand with bad guys."

Rose avoided mentioning her recent fight with a vampire coven. No reason to upset her dad or, worse, excite his conspiratorial mind.

"That's good," Graylen said. "Not the paperwork part, but the hiding your identity. You don't want some crazies tracking you down, especially folks from Society. They've got to be pissed at you for breaking up that fear factory. They'll be gunning for you sooner or later. You know that, right?"

"So, how have you been, Dad?" Rose asked. She considered drawing charm to woo her father away from his favorite subject but nixed the idea. He was no slouch when it came to that particular trick and would probably notice. "How are the Timberwolves doing this year?"

"Anna—sorry—Rose, I am not insane." Graylen stared into her eyes, his own intent.

"I didn't say you're insane."

"I get confused sometimes since the factory. But that doesn't mean I don't know what's happening all around us, okay? I know."

What would her father think if he knew Rose had traveled to Washington solely to network with members of Society? He would probably run, just light out and get the hell away from her as fast as possible. From messages she traded with Troy several times a week, Rose knew their father often spoke of leaving. He yearned for his old slinker ways but refused to leave their mother alone in her shocked and damaged state.

"Dad, I don't think you're crazy. Something I never told you—all those lessons you taught us as kids—they're the only reason I'm free right now. If it wasn't for sparring in the backyard, learning about burner phones, and—" here Rose smiled, "—always wearing sensible shoes, the Indrawn Breath would have thrown me in that fear factory with you. We'd be there right now."

"I wouldn't." Graylen's brows drooped. "I'd be dead, honey."

Rose couldn't argue.

"You guys want dinner?" Troy asked as he and Matt descended the stairs.

Her brother looked wan, his skin too pale, his eyes still sunken all these months after his time in the fear factory. Rose didn't have to guess what he had experienced there. Members of the Indrawn Breath, one of them her own sister Melody, had socked her away in the place for several days before Matt launched an effort to save her. Serving as an unwilling votary bound to gluttonous succubi by chains of pure horror and fear had been more than a nightmare. How Troy endured nearly a year of such treatment and come out a functional human being defied all logic. Not that he bore zero scars from the experience.

Growing up, Troy had been outgoing, gregarious. Despite his lack of powers in a family of succubi, he had always been the heart of the family, the boy who made everyone laugh, even through the hard times. Now he suffered panic attacks whenever he left the house. He couldn't hold down a job; the stress of dealing with other people sent him into spasms of fear. He should have been out in the world, living his life. At twenty-seven, he ought to be dating, or even married. Instead, Troy lived with his broken parents in a house paid for by his younger sister.

Rose put on a smile she couldn't feel. "Dinner would be great."

They ate in the impeccably clean dining room under a cheap chandelier the home builder had probably bought at Lowe's. The house wasn't expensive, but Troy kept it tidy. Rose doubted either of her parents helped out in that regard. Neither of them had been clean freaks when their kids were young. Why bother cleaning up a house or apartment, or a car for that matter, when you might abandon it at a moment's notice?

"This is delicious," Matt said as he heaped a second portion of Troy's pot roast onto his plate with a generous scoop of mashed potatoes and gravy.

"You know, I never cooked as a bachelor." Troy looked delighted at the compliment and Matt's healthy appetite. "It was all takeout back then. But I'm finding I really like putting together a meal."

"It's an art," Graylen said as he refilled his own plate. "Troy's become a first-rate cook. Your mother and I would be starving without him."

Sarah lifted her gaze when Graylen referenced her but didn't smile. Her intense blue eyes, eyes Rose remembered as far more animated in the past, bore into her husband. Rose worried she might be on the verge of a manic tirade. She had seen her mother scream and claw at her own skin for half an hour while Troy, Graylen, and she struggled to calm her. It wasn't pretty. But the moment passed, and she returned her gaze to her plate. Her graying blond hair fell across her face, some of it cascading into her gravy, but she didn't seem to notice.

"Mom, is something wrong with the food?" Troy asked.

She shook her head.

"I made chocolate chip cookies for dessert. Want some?"

"Melody's coming to visit," Sarah spoke to her plate, her voice hardly more than a whisper, but everyone heard.

Hearing her sister's name sent a jolt of anger wending its way up and down Rose's spine. She bit down on a curse and reminded herself that her mother wasn't in her right mind, nor had she witnessed the things Melody had done. She remembered her little girl, not the monster Melody became.

"Honey, Melody's not coming here." Graylen put a hand on his wife's arm. "Not ever."

Sarah nodded vigorously, but Rose couldn't tell if she was agreeing or arguing.

"I hope we're not keeping you up when you'd rather be sleeping," Matt said.

Rose favored him with a grateful smile for his valiant attempt at a subject change. She was on the verge of suggesting they would take care of the dishes while everyone else went to bed when her phone rang.

"Hello?"

"Rose," Myra, who generally served as Tanner's second on the security team, sounded concerned. "Somebody's headed for the house."

Rose felt her eyes widen. "Who?"

"I don't know. We haven't seen anyone out here, but my head's buzzing." A gifted succubus, Myra's most potent draw originated from borrowing discernment from her votaries. Her ability to prognosticate the future was scarily accurate.

"Any idea where they are? When they'll get here?"

Matt lifted his eyebrows, a frank expression of worry on his face.

"We've got movement. A person just came around the side of the house. Fast. I'm guessing it's a woman by the silhouette."

Someone knocked on the front door.

Troy's brows knit. "Who could that be at three in the morning?"

"No one good." Graylen, his face drained of color, seized a steak knife from the table and stood, gaze locked on the door

Rose placed a hand on his wrist, gentle but firm. "Dad, there's no reason—"

Sarah shot upright on votary drawn speed, beaming with sudden delight. Her chair flew across the dining room to crash against the wall, one of its legs broken. "Melody!"

"Mom, don't!" Troy reached for Sarah's wrist to forestall her, but without powers of his own, he stood no chance of catching a determined succubus. Sarah danced past him like a professional basketball player and opened the door before her son could even turn to find her.

Melody Carver, the youngest of the Carver children—twenty years old as of April—stood on the threshold dressed in boots, jeans, and a button-down shirt of checkered blue and white. Her auburn hair, turned raven by the night, hung loose down one shoulder.

"Hi, Mom," she said as if she was a college student come home for a holiday weekend, and not a murderer responsible for the death of Rose's closest friend.

"Melody." Sarah threw her arms about her daughter, crying and shaking. "I missed you! I missed you so much."

Rose couldn't move. For an instant, she feared Melody had somehow charmed her into inaction, but no, this was pure, natural shock. She stared at the sister who had become her worst enemy in a state of utter disbelief. How could Melody come here? Why would she? Did she think her family would forget how she betrayed them?

Perhaps Sarah had, considering her state of mind, but Rose would never forgive Melody the evil she had perpetrated on them and, judging by the looks on Troy's and Graylen's faces, neither would they.

"What the hell are you doing here?" Seeming to find himself, Troy surged to his feet, knocking over his chair though not with the force Sarah had managed.

Melody, who had made no move to hug Sarah, pushed her away, albeit gently, but with intent. She pointed at Rose and Matt. "I came for them."

Whatever stupor of thought had been holding Rose vanished under Melody's pointing finger. Drawing speed, strength, and agility, she came around the table to face her sister, Matt instantly at her side.

"I don't know what you were thinking, coming here like this, but I'll be damned if you're leaving." Energy surged through Rose like gasoline exploding in an engine. A small part of her worried about what fighting her sister would do to her already fragile parents, especially her mother, but she wasn't about to let that stop her.

Melody sauntered into the living room as if Rose hadn't spoken.

She glanced around, taking in the tidy American decor. She appeared wholly unimpressed. "You couldn't buy them something larger? And for God's sake, why didn't you at least spring for a gated community? We rolled in here like it was nothing."

"We?" Matt, already tensed for a fight, stiffened and craned his neck to peer out the front door.

A petite woman, shorter than Melody, entered. Slim yet curvaceous in all the right ways, Rose knew her for a succubus the instant she appeared, not merely by her striking beauty, but by the wash of charm that flowed from her like water from a fresh spring. This wasn't an attack. It was an aura of succubus charm the small woman created by the simple fact of her existence, like the scent of a flower.

For a moment, Rose didn't recognize the newcomer, then it clicked. She was the woman Barbara Griffith had hurried over to at the fundraiser after growing uncomfortable around Olivia—a delegate from the Irish contingent.

Three incubi, one large and the other two gargantuan, strolled into the house behind the blond. Each bore scars and a smattering of lurid tattoos on their necks, faces, and hands. Dressed in casual sport coats, they looked like either undercover cops or the sort of meat shields crime bosses kept around for protection.

"My name's Alice McAleese," said the woman, who smiled prettily at Rose, her voice sultry and lilting. "I represent the Irish. I've come to talk business."

4

CONDITIONS AND COALITIONS

Rose?" Myra's voice sounded clear on the phone Rose held limp at her side. "We've been compromised. There's too many of them. The entire neighborhood's surrounded. Olivia got a call in to Piper, but—"

"—but your vampire friend isn't here," said Alice in an Irish brogue. She shut the door behind her. "Me and the lads have you all to ourselves for now. Ain't that grand?"

Rose switched the phone off and delicately placed it on the table so as not to trigger one of Alice's guards. The oversized men watched her every move with scrupulous attention. The one on the right, who was easily six-and-a-half feet tall and bore a star-shaped scar on his chin, nodded his approval.

"Melody? Who's your friend?" Sarah appeared to have only now noticed the strangers in the house. She peered at Alice, her head on one side. "I've never seen her before."

Alice ignored the older succubus to focus on Rose. "I won't insult you by asking if you've heard of our coalition."

"Yes." Rose figured keeping her answers short might buy her some time. She had no idea how many people Alice had outside, but if they were enough to neutralize Tanner's perimeter team, they had to be formidable. With any luck, Piper could take them unawares. Between her daughters and Rose's people, they could handle nearly anything.

Graylen's gaze darted from Alice to Rose. "What's this about? Melody, why are you with this woman? Who is she?"

Melody said nothing. She heard Graylen just fine, Rose could tell that much, but she appeared unfazed by either his voice or his question.

"If you wanted to speak with us, you could have arranged it anytime," Matt said. His eyes roamed to the men who had taken up strategic positions around the room. Any one of them made three of Matt, but you would never know it by his calm, determined expression.

"That's not the point," Rose said. "She's showing us she knows where my parents live, and her people can sneak up on us any time they like."

"I'd heard you had a fair amount of discernment." Alice's smile never wavered in the slightest. "And you've a good head on your shoulders, too, I see. Makes sense. You wouldn't have overthrown the breathers otherwise."

"If you're here to talk shop, let's go outside," Rose said, keeping her voice deliberately cool. "My parents have nothing to do with this."

"No, we'll talk here, girl."

Sarah, rocking back and forth on her heels, put a hand to her mouth. Her dry hair waved with her movements, and she angrily brushed it aside. "You're not Melody's friend."

"Shut up, Mom," Melody said without rancor.

More than anything, her sister's offhanded, peevish reprimand sent paroxysms of anger through Rose's chest. She wanted to fling herself across the room and punch Melody in the mouth. She longed to do worse than that.

She did nothing.

"Like I said, you're a smart one, Rose Carver." Alice moved to stand within arm's reach of Rose, her perfect skin and hair glowing in the light thrown by the dining room chandelier.

"I don't understand." Sarah twisted one way and then the other like an animal caught between two panes of glass. She turned beseeching eyes on Melody, who ignored her and pulled at her own hair with both hands.

"They're Society, aren't they?" Graylen asked. He shook all over, his eyes wide and shining. Despite that, he strode to his wife's side and tried to comfort her. Sarah appeared not to notice.

"You're upsetting my family," Rose said, her tone clear and calm though her heart pounded in her chest.

"I'm sorry for that. Truly," Alice said, and Rose believed her. She looked genuinely pained, but that could have been an act. "I'll make this brief. I want you to join the Irish Coalition. How is that for succinct?"

"No. Now, get the hell out of my parents' house."

Alice sighed. It was a put-upon sound, one that expressed her expectation of just such an answer, her resolve to see it overturned, and no small amount of authentic disappointment. "Look, we could go around in circles like this for years. I could explain the advantages of marrying American Society with the Irish counterpart. I could offer you incentives—money, power, that sort of thing—and I could eventually make a more overt threat against you and yours than my simple appearance here tonight, but why go through all that? Rose Carver, we Irish are in the process of conquering the world. You could be a part of that. If not, then you're a hindrance to us."

"Why are you talking to me about this?" Rose asked. "I don't run American Society. I'm a slinker, not some Washington elite."

"You're the slinker who destabilized the foundations of succubus rule in this nation. No one's in power here at the moment, all because of you."

"And that's why you've come sniffing around." Matt had slipped an arm around Troy, who appeared faint. Her brother's face shone with sweat, his hands shook as bad as Graylen's, and his breathing had shortened to a pant.

"There are plenty of outside forces, as you put it, 'sniffing around,' in America. Your succubi are weak right now. Leaderless. They need a regime change."

"They're not leaderless," Rose said, though the words rang false even to her ears. Rose had destabilized American Society to a dangerous level. In her heart, she knew it was true and hated herself for it. But if destroying an abomination like the fear factory led to infighting, then so be it. She couldn't conscience such a place to exist.

"Is that right? Who do you credit for leading your Society right now? Barbara Griffith? That woman hasn't been relevant in half a century. She's hapless. Doesn't know the first thing about the modern world. You really expect her to lead your people during these perilous times? The humans have eyes and ears everywhere now. They're encroaching on our power bases around the world. How long will it be before our kind and our cousins, the vampires, are found out? No, she's a lost cause, girl."

Rose was surprised to hear Alice refer to vampires as their cousins. Most succubi wouldn't admit such a thing. "Doesn't matter. Someone will step up. They always do."

"Why not you?" Alice leaned forward, head cocked to one side, and hooked a thumb at Matt. "The two of you could have seized American Society the day after his father ran for the hills. Instead, you're playing their game, running one of your people for Senate. That's a queer choice if ya ask me. What were ya thinking?"

"Senate?" Graylen pushed Sarah behind him as if the invocation of government held more danger for his wife than Alice's thugs.

"I'm not discussing this with you now," Rose said, her voice menacing. "Get out of my parents' house."

"You see, I know what you're thinking. You never wanted power, nor even fame, but you got those things thrust upon ya. And when flint met metal, you sparked right up. You put together a gang of slinkers and took Jason Kraft's fear factory apart, all because they left ya no choice. That's potential, that is. But it don't mean you want to lead now, does it? 'Cause deep down, you're just a frightened girl in too deep to turn back. Tell me I'm wrong."

She wasn't.

After Rose and her team had brought the fear factory to light, dozens of politicians, most of them succubi, saw their careers ruined during the ensuing media frenzy. That included the President and most of her cabinet. That had been unfortunate, not simply because President Judy Hershel-Smith wasn't a succubus and knew nothing about the succubi who secretly ran DC and therefore the United States, but because the subsequent chaos had left Society in turmoil.

Without an organized, targeted campaign of charm to keep them from asking too many questions, some reporters came perilously close to exposing succubi kind to the world. While the news cycle gloried in how government officials, some at the highest levels of power, knew about secret experiments performed on innocent citizens, a handful of journalists uncovered the shadow conspiracy at the core of the American experiment: namely that succubi had, from its inception, commanded positions of power and influence in the United States. While they set policy for the humans, they likewise ruled succubus Society. If not for a last-minute effort organized by several prominent legislators and civil servants to charm those reporters into rewriting their stories, the world would have known the truth.

Rose wasn't ready for that sort of change. Who knew what regular people would do if they discovered much of modern life was a sham perpetrated on them by beings they considered mythological creatures? It wouldn't be pretty.

And she had almost caused it.

Alice, scrutinizing Rose's face, gave a decisive nod. "You can't call me a liar because everything I've said is true." She turned to Graylen, who flinched under her gaze. "I'm sorry for what was done to you. The fear draw is severely policed in Ireland and all our coalition nations. Those who use it without permission, and strict adherence to the law, are put to death. When we're in control here, we'll find everyone associated with the fear factory, and we will end them. You have my lawful word on that."

Where the hell was Piper? Given the right incentive, the vampire could run nearly a hundred miles an hour. That aside, she was driving a Lotus the last time Rose saw her. Any second now, Rose expected to hear a commotion outside—the sound of Piper's daughters attacking whatever force Alice had brought with her. But even with draw-enhanced hearing, Rose heard nothing besides the incessant chirrup of crickets and muted roar of distant traffic.

Briefly, she contemplated attacking Alice. What could her goons do with their mistress in the middle of a fight? Would they risk harming Alice to get at Rose? By the looks of them—the one with the scar appeared more ape than man—Rose worried they might not care. Alice's confident expression gave her pause as well. Rose had no idea what abilities Alice might possess, but she doubted the Irish leader would have waltzed into the house without tremendous personal power. She had to be a sime, a succubus capable of drawing more than one ability at a time from her votaries. Given her position as a leader in one of the world's most powerful Societies, she could be nothing less. What would that mean for her votary count? It had to be high. Could it rival Rose's own? And did Rose want to find out here in her parent's living room?

Definitely not.

But neither was she about to join some foreign Society just to appease this stranger. Asking Alice to leave hadn't worked. Perhaps it was time for a new strategy.

Rose turned to Melody. The sight of her filled Rose with a loathsome, burning hatred she had no reason to feign. What she planned to say would upset her parents, she knew, but it was better than an all-out battle that might get them hurt or killed.

Rose pointed at their parents. "You see what you did to them?"

Melody frowned, her first real sign of emotion since she had arrived. "Me? I did nothing to them. I was in the fear factory, too."

"What? For a day?" Rose had never gotten the full story of her sister's rise from a factory votary chained to a bed to a member of the Indrawn Breath, the succubi responsible for placing people in that hellhole.

"Want someone to blame? Start with him." Melody pointed at Graylen, who looked momentarily incensed before cringing back against his shuddering wife.

"You blame the victims?"

"I was a victim!" Melody's face flushed scarlet, her eyes wide. "I was a goddamned teenager—a child. I relied on my father to protect me, and what did he do? Nothing! He moved us from town to town, spouting nonsense about how it would protect us from Society."

"No!" Graylen wailed, his hands over his ears, his expression broken. "I kept us ahead of them. I made you safe."

"You made me vulnerable!" Melody's voice, strengthened by a draw, shook the house's windows in their panes and rattled knick-knacks on the coffee table. "You knew about Society. You could have been teaching us, showing us how to grow strong. Instead, you stuck your head in the sand. You want me to feel bad about that, Anna? I should get all teary-eyed because Dad bloodied his nose shoving his head in the ground?"

Sarah, crying like a heartsick child, collapsed and would have hit the floor had Graylen not caught her. Her horrified expression, matched by his, reminded Rose of their gaunt visages the night she located them in the fear factory. How like skulls they looked, their mouths open, their dark eyes streaming tears.

Yes, you should feel shame, Melody, you should feel remorse, but you never will. You care about one thing in this world, and that' s yourself. Well, sister, I'm not going to feel any remorse either.

"You want me to join your coalition?" Rose turned back to Alice. Her voice shook with anger, and she could feel hot tears wanting to well up at the corners of her eyes. She drew calm to beat them back and huffed out a heavy sigh. "Give me my sister, and I'll join tonight."

"Rose, don't." Matt might have been a man witnessing a bus crash. He had eased a near-catatonic Troy onto the couch but now sprang to his feet.

"Don't be making sudden moves like that, mister," said the goon leaning against the bookshelf. Though he remained still, his ease somehow punctuated the menace he posed.

Alice, her green eyes far away, tapped her chin with two fingers as she stared at Melody.

"You can't be considering this bullshit." Melody, whose expression had morphed from rage to questioning fear, watched Alice like a mouse who has found herself under a lion's gaze.

"You would kill her? Your own sister?" Alice's tone remained as mild as a woman discussing the price of butter.

Sarah screamed and cried harder at the mention of Rose harming Melody. In vain, she struggled to escape Graylen's hold on her her.

"I'd see her turned over to someone who can judge her crimes. I'm not that person."

"She would do that?" Alice focused her question on Matt.

"She would."

"You can't be seriously considering taking her up on this. She's lying. She'll kill me the second you leave; she's threatened to before."

That much was true. Rose had promised to kill Melody once for executing Rose's best friend, Leslie. Could she follow through with that promise? Maybe. But she liked to think she wouldn't stoop so low, especially with Matt there to help her see the moral way of doing things.

"It's a tempting offer," Alice said, "but I can't do it. Melody's made an oath to me—she's one of mine now. What sort of leader would I be if I broke my word?"

"It's that or nothing," Rose said. She drew strength and speed, preparing for a fight.

"Oh, I doubt that. I believe you'll see things my way before the year turns, though I'm sad you're unwilling to make that decision now."

"I might not know much about world politics, but I know you don't have the power to threaten us. The elites in Washington might not like me all that much, but nothing would galvanize them faster than you making a martyr of me. You can't touch us. Any of us."

"You might be surprised."

"I doubt it." Rose stepped closer to Alice so they stood nose to nose. "No one wants your meddling here. We have plenty of Americans doing that already. Now kindly get the fuck out of my house before things get messy."

For an instant, Rose worried Alice might react physically, but then a slow smile turned up the corners of her mouth. She backed away a couple of steps, gave Rose a nod like a fencer acknowledging a touch, and exited the house. Melody and Alice's thugs followed close on her heels.

"Melody, no! Stay with us!" Sarah cried as she struggled to run after her departing daughter, but Graylen kept her from leaving the couch.

"I feel like we just got served a subpoena," Matt said.

"No, you can ignore a subpoena, and the worst that happens is you go to jail." Rose leaned on the table, her heart beating hard. "If we ignore this, we'll end up dead."

5

TIES THAT BLIND

The scent of homemade, or at least handmade, biscuits and gravy, roasted pork, and snap peas filled Rose's nose. The caterers she hired specialized in upscale southern cuisine, and they had put on quite a spread. The succubi dignitaries in attendance, most from right here in the United States, others from far-flung parts of the world, seemed to enjoy the stuff.

Rose didn't know. She was too nervous to eat.

"It's a good turnout." Renni Rogers surveyed the crowd from their spot at the back of the room. The elderly succubus, who had become like a grandmother to Rose, wore a sequined black dress and a pleased grin. "Wouldn't have said it before, but I was worried—thought we'd probably entice five, maybe ten people to show up."

"Even that would have been better than nothing," Rose said. This crowd wasn't a patch on the one they managed to wrangle back in DC, in numbers or sheer political might, but it far outstripped anything Rose, or even Matt, could have put together on their own.

Renni and her husband, Lee, had retired from public service as FBI agents and later security consultants nearly fifty years ago. Despite that, they retained several contacts within Society, due to their friendly natures and ability to schmooze like pros, but also owing to succubus longevity. Many of the youngsters they had worked with in the mid and late twentieth century held positions of power in the government today. Not a few of them owed their lives, either politically or literally, to the aged couple. When Renni and Lee invited them to Atlanta for a formal dinner and discussion about Society's way forward, those in the know donned their best evening wear and came running.

It didn't hurt that one of the couple's daughters, a succubus named Emily Walsh, happened to work in Washington as well. Emily served as executive secretary to Sheila Isaacson, a junior senator out of Ohio. Though Emily's position carried little clout with this set, she had nonetheless helped her parents reach as many Society elites as they could for this rally, and Rose appreciated it.

"I had hoped the Kennedys would at least send one of the lesser-known cousins." Lee, who cut a dapper yet remarkably uncomfortable figure in black tie, munched a finger sandwich. "I guess they've forgotten how we helped make that little car wreck disappear from newsrooms back in the day."

"I'm pleased we got so many foreigners." Renni leaned heavily on a cane with a floral print, her smile tired but satisfied.

"I'm not," Rose said. "I don't see what good they'll do. The Order needs ties here in the States if we want to remain relevant. How are German or Malaysian or Egyptian succubi supposed to help American slinkers? We need strong ties in the American government."

"Oh, I don't know. You might be surprised what a coalition can accomplish." Lee popped the last bite of sandwich into his mouth and dusted off his hands, either unaware or unfazed by the haughty eye rolls some of the guests leveled on him. Though he, unlike Rose, had been born into Succubus Society, he nevertheless exuded an uncouth air disdainful of popularity. Anyone who might frown at Lee for his lack of manners was beneath his notice. That brought a smile to Rose's lips. Renni smiled too but also shook her head at her husband's lack of decorum.

Matt, who had been chatting with a succubi delegation from Italy, sauntered over in time to catch Lee's words. He wrinkled his nose.

"That's what the Irish are offering us: a coalition. No thanks. They're scarier than Breathers. I don't want any part of them."

"Harry Drake—" Lee waved a hand to indicate a slim, bearded incubus across the room chatting with several DC bigwigs, "—he tells me they've been approaching most anybody with power and influence outside the mainstream leadership. I guess they don't want to deal with the likes of Barbara Griffith and her usual crowd."

Though Rose rarely recognized the power players in Succubus Society, which had led to some awkward situations since her rise to fame, she knew of Drake. A financier and major stockholder in several of the world's largest banks, Drake commanded considerable influence in American Society. There had been talk the last several months that he might take a leadership position, perhaps even seize the reins altogether during the power vacuum left after the Indrawn Breath collapsed. He hadn't. Like so many of Society's elite, he appeared content to sit by while others vied for dominance.

For Rose, as much an outsider to this world as would have been a regular human, the situation made no damned sense. Rule within Society was next to impossible to quantify. It had no particular offices of leadership and no votes to fill them. While many of the most powerful and respected succubi held positions in the US government or governmental agencies, those seats had little to do with an individual's political clout. The FBI chief might hold more sway over Society than the president. An undersecretary in some state cabinet might have the standing to give the Speaker of the House orders. How such things were determined remained an ineffable mystery to Rose, an enigma as opaque to her as fashion trends or the whims of internet taste makers.

Was money the determining factor? Yes, but also no. Each of the elites in this room possessed more money than a single person could spend in a lifetime. A million more here or there made no never mind to them. Jason Kraft, who had managed to install his own governing body and subsequently rule Society for more than thirty years, had never been as wealthy as many of the succubi who had followed him.

What about votaries? If that was the yardstick, then Rose could have counted herself somewhere near the top. She wasn't even close. Her win over Kraft, and the subsequent fall of the Indrawn Breath, made her a curiosity to the upper crust, as had her legion of votaries tied to her by a hungry fandom. None of that meant she could walk into a leadership position. Succubus elites might be vague when it came to allegiances—they certainly marched to the beat of their own EDM machines—but Rose had no doubt they'd come together against her instantly should she make a play for the ethereal throne, no matter how many votaries she claimed.

Not that she had any inclination to do that sort of thing. All she wanted was a place at the table for the Order. Otherwise, she wouldn't be standing here, willing herself not to sweat and trying to think of ways to woo people who, frankly, made her ill. Slinkers had long been the downtrodden masses of the succubus world. It was time they got a fair shake. If that meant Rose had to give a few speeches and glad-hand a bunch of snobs, so be it. No matter who eventually came out on top, she was determined they recognize her people and make a place for them at the proverbial table.

A chime toned, and conversation ceased. Gloria Torres, a woman who had once been Rose's sergeant in succubus boot camp, and was now a true friend, mounted a low stage set up in front of the tables as the crowd took their seats.

When Rose and Matt had put out the call for volunteers to enter public life, Torres had traded in her tac gear and boots for conservative dress suits and pumps. Though in no way enamored with the idea of becoming a senator representing Georgia, like a good soldier, Torres had thrown herself into the role. To her astonishment, though not Rose's, Torres was a natural.

"Ladies and gentlemen, succubi and incubi, thank you for joining us tonight." Torres stood straight-backed and confident, her dark eyes roaming from face to face amongst the crowd. "For those of you who don't know me, my name is Gloria Torres, and I am running for Senate. I do so not merely to win the seat and represent the people of Georgia, though I plan to serve honorably, but also to stand up for a long-unacknowledged and oft-disenfranchised sector of our kind, those known as slinkers."

Though they had written Torres's speech together and practiced it several times on stage and at home, this portion still sent a shiver through Rose's belly. She felt somehow the shock of stating their intentions outright might send the audience scurrying for the exits. To her relief, no one left. In fact, a few even nodded.

Torres kept her talk short. She stuck to the basic facts of her history and that of the Order, the countermovement founded by Robin Ambrose, Matt's mother. The Order had given Torres, and Rose as well, a place in the world of succubi. They, and many other slinkers, had united under the Order's banner to combat, and eventually defeat, Jason Kraft and his illegitimate rule. Now, the Order was seeking representation in Society, a chance to make their plight known, and even the playing field between them and those who would keep them oppressed. Gaining that sort of recognition wouldn't come easy. The Order needed allies within Society to plead their case and make it understood they had support in joining the succubi ruling body.

This last statement led to whispered conversations and head shaking amongst the Americans, but not as much as Rose had feared. The international guests showed almost no reaction. Rose couldn't decide if that was good or bad.

"After Robin Ambrose's untimely death, leadership of the Order fell to my good friends, Rose Carver and Matthew Snow. They are the reason I'm standing before you today. Without them, I might well have ended up in a fear factory instead of campaigning for the Senate. I'd like to invite them on to the stage to speak with you. This is an open forum. All questions are welcome." Torres gestured toward the back of the hall, beaming.

"You ready?" Matt whispered as he took Rose's hand.

"No, but let's do it anyway."

All eyes followed the couple as they made their way forward. Rose felt like a thief trying to sneak through a gauntlet of armed guards and making a hash of it. It didn't pass her notice that no one clapped. The captains of industry and government arrayed before her hadn't come here to ally themselves with the Order or with Rose in particular. Curiosity drove them more than any other factor, that and fidelity to old friends like Renni and Lee. If Rose and Matt had any hope of securing alliances here, it lay solely on impressing the crowd from the get-go, and they had to do it without using charm.

Because of his upbringing in succubus Society's limelight, Rose and Matt had decided he should speak first. He squeezed Rose's hand and took a step forward to address the crowd.

"Most of you probably recognize me, at least in passing. I was the rugrat in the background when you attended one of my parents' lavish parties. Or maybe you saw me during my time working with David Lord under my father's direction as part of the Indrawn Breath. If so, I'm sorry for that. I make no excuses about my time there. Remembering the work we did, capturing people, many of them succubi, for the fear factory, gives me zero pleasure. It took years for me to wake up and make a better choice. Once I did, I joined my mother in the Order, and we eventually brought an end to my father's tyranny.

"As Gloria stated, Rose and I are here now to ask for your assistance. My father was able to kidnap thousands of slinkers over several years, and no one tried to stop him. Not until my mother made that decision. We're here to see to it that sort of crime can never happen again."

"What exactly are you asking of us, Snow?" asked a man seated three tables to the left. Rose didn't recognize him, but he sat with Harry Drake, which meant he was probably a powerful incubus.

"Support, Tom," Matt said.

"To get Torres her Senate seat?" Tom lifted bushy eyebrows, frowning. "That's easy enough, but I get the feeling you're talking about something more than a representative in Congress."

"We want slinkers in key positions within Society."

Murmurs erupted throughout the gathering. Rose could tell the snobbish leaders hadn't expected so blunt a demand.

"You go too far," said a succubus at the center of the crowd. "It's one thing to advocate for kindness when dealing with the common sort, but this is foolishness. What do slinkers know about ruling?"

What do any of you know? Rose stifled that thought and her inclination to snap back at the woman. She instead clung to the talking points she, Matt, and Torres had put together ahead of this meeting. She stepped forward into the spotlight.

"I don't come from money or power. I had nothing growing up. Even so, I understand your hesitation. Slinkers are nothing more than a liability for succubi the world over, am I right? We're a faceless people, all living in obscurity. Any one of us could expose succubus kind to the world at any second. That's why policing us, preventing us from using our gifts, has always been the norm. I'm sure some of you might wish we didn't exist at all."

Though no one had the bad manners to nod, Rose could feel a wave of agreement wash over the crowd. It might not be the sort she wanted, but she had their attention.

"Problem is, you probably know at least a handful of slinkers. In fact, I'd wager most of you are related to some. What happens when Society starts rounding up and torturing them?" Rose stopped shy of asking what these people had done when that very thing was happening only a few months ago, though the warrior inside her yearned to pose that question and many more. The crowd's expressions had shifted to encompass a range between thoughtful curiosity on one end and plain discomfort on the other. That was when she knew she had them.

"For centuries, succubus Society has made it their business to keep slinkers like me quiet by seeing to it we rarely, if ever, use our natural-born gifts. A succubus who lives like a human is indistinguishable from a human. But that scheme is flawed. Jason Kraft proved it. Slinkers had no voice, which made them easy targets for his manipulation. But when his plans failed, there were suddenly hundreds of slinkers, many of them mentally damaged by their time in the fear factory, exposed to the bright lights of news cameras and the media's insatiable hunger for the next big story. Suddenly, we were scrambling to keep our existence hidden. And I say we because I was part of that cover-up. It took hundreds of us working around the clock to keep the secret.

"This should never happen again, and here is how I propose to stop it: allow us, the Order, to become a true, recognized part of Succubus Society in America. It will be our job to care for, instruct, and when the situation demands it, punish slinkers. No more convincing us to give up our powers, no more arresting us when we do what comes naturally to any succubus, no more silencing the hundreds of thousands, possibly millions, of voices who live and work in this country."

A reserved silence filled the room. To her surprise, Rose had managed to convert many of the skeptical expressions before her into contemplative ones. Not all, certainly, but many, perhaps even a majority. She wouldn't take for granted that meant they believed her or would toss their support her way, but she had gotten them thinking, and that was a start.

A curvy blond woman wearing what Rose took for a $10,000 dress raised a hand. "Do you have enough people and resources to manage this sort of undertaking? You're talking about a national police force."

"To be honest," Matt said, "no—not at this time."

"And that's where we come in?" asked Harry Drake tonelessly.

"We need sponsors, that's certain," Torres said. "We can't create a reliable system without money, but right now, this very instant, we need your support more. Society is in a state of turmoil since Kraft fell."

"And who's fault is that?" asked a succubus seated next to Drake. "You all took him down with no consideration for the future. I don't understand why you never came to us for help."

Rose and Matt glanced at one another. He shook his head minutely, silently willing her to refrain from verbally ripping the succubus's ears off her skull. Come to Society with grievances against Society while Jason Kraft was in charge? Was she insane? Rose clamped her jaw shut to hold back a fiery retort. Luckily, someone else spoke before she could lose her battle of wills with herself.

"Obviously, they couldn't come to you, not as what you call slinkers." The speaker was a short black woman with a faint accent Rose couldn't place. She wore a purple and gold head wrap, a matching dress, and slippers. "Could you imagine a Jew taking grievances to the Third Reich at the height of the Nazi regime?"

Several people gasped at the comment, which made Rose smile despite her best efforts to remain stoic.

"We overthrew the fear factory," Matt said. "We did it because it needed done and no one else was taking the job."

Several people acted as though they might speak, but they subsided one by one, probably after playing through the words in their heads. What defense would they give for sitting idly by while their fellow succubi tortured slinkers? Some of them might even have benefited from that horrid scheme.

"You make a good case," said one man near the back. "I like the idea of slinkers policing their own so long as they can do a competent job."

"Who's doing that job right now?" Rose asked.

The question seemed to perplex the man. He frowned until realization washed some of the color from his face. "I don't guess you are."

Rose shook her head. "Only in our organization, and that's small potatoes. The answer is, no one's watching the slinkers in America right now. They're the last thing on anyone's mind while Society struggles with succession, whatever that means."

"I like what I've heard tonight," Drake said but held up a hand when Rose turned eager eyes his way. "My problem isn't with the Order; it's with the company you keep. I've heard rumors you've already made an alliance with a vampire named Piper Ross. Is that true?"

An iron fist dropped into Rose's belly. Though she had prepared for this question—they all had—it nevertheless blindsided her. She was forced to draw more calm, more mental acuity to keep her wits and avoid flubbing the answer.

"Yes, the Order is allied with Piper Ross."

This time when the crowd erupted, it wasn't with mere gasps. Several people moaned aloud, and one couple, thankfully seated near the rear entrance, stood up and left.

Rose knew how they felt. A little over a year ago, she hadn't known vampires existed. She had thought tales of succubi who drank blood nothing but a fear tactic and movie trope. Once she met her first vampires, a family of drug dealers in Mexico, she had been convinced they were all monsters driven by their thirst for blood ties. She saw in them no redeeming qualities, only the basest of animal instincts.

Piper had changed all that. Whereas the Mexican vamps had acted otherworldly on purpose to build up their mystique, the petite southern vampire, who styled herself the vampire queen of South Carolina, was nothing of the sort. She watched prime time TV, for God's sake! Yes, she could act a bit crazy when it came to discussing her enemies, but who wouldn't after more than fifty years locked in a single place? On any other topic, Piper was the most down-to-earth person Rose knew.

"That's a no-go for me," said the blond succubus at the front. "You can't trust vampires. They're only out for themselves no matter what they say otherwise." With that, she stood, slung a toy-sized purse over one arm, and headed for the exit.

Her departure functioned as a signal for a mass exodus. Succubi all around the room stood, collecting phones and purses and other items before following that first defector.

"Will you at least let us explain our truce with Piper?" Rose stepped off the stage intending to follow the crowd outside. If haranguing them all the way to their waiting limos would make a difference, she was game.

"It won't help," Drake said, turning back to forestall Rose. "You might have wooed them to your side without the vampires in play, but even I can't go that far.

"Lee, Renni, it was a pleasure seeing you as always," he said. "I'm sorry I couldn't help your friend, but I do wish you all the best."

"We'll survive, Harry." Lee shook the billionaire incubus's hand, and Drake departed.

"That could have gone better," Rose said, turning to Matt. "I'm sorry. I think I said the wrong thing."

He shook his head, his lip curling in that half-grin of his that always made Rose feel better even on days like this. "I don't think you could have done anything to change the outcome. Those people were never going to help us so long as we're aligned with Piper."

"Why'd they even bother to show up then?" Rose knew she sounded petulant but didn't care enough to change her tone.

"Perhaps they believed they could break that bond," said a now-familiar voice behind Rose.

She spun in surprise to find the woman in the traditional headdress watching her, three guards, two women and a man, at her back.

"My name is Thandiwe Buhari. I represent an alliance of several nations, most in Africa. I came here because I heard you're looking for support. Tell me, Rose Carver, is that still true?"

6

AVATAR DIVERGED

Rose resisted the urge to adjust her skin-tight bodysuit, an outfit made to resemble combat fatigues. Mostly, it showed off her boobs and ass, which, by the stares she was getting from passersby at the Lexington, Kentucky, Comic and Toy Convention, was working. She hadn't donned the thing in months. Thankfully, it still fit. Granted, it was a bit tighter than it had been during her time at Camp Den. She had been forced to shimmy a bit to slide it over her hips, and the zipper gave her a few seconds of grief, but she won in the end. So long as she remained upright, she probably wouldn't split her pants.

As with the suit, so with Rose's convention attendance. She hadn't appeared at a con in some time. Last year, during her initial training with the Order, and even after graduation, she had spent weeks traveling to comic, gaming, toy, and book conventions to meet fans and hawk copies of the graphic novel about her life called *Drawn*. Initially, she had found these gatherings both nerve-wracking and confusing. She had no references for any but the most popular fandoms, and little enough of that. It was like traveling to a foreign market where people spoke some obscure dialect of English. She understood the words but grasped so little of the content that she was practically deaf and dumb.

That changed over time. With the guidance of Brendan and Luke Pruett, the incubus twins responsible for *Drawn*, Rose eventually came to not merely accept her duty of attending cons, she learned to love them. Week by week, she saw many of the same people, folks who adored their particular hobbies, stories, or whatever else brought them together. Mostly, they loved geeking out with their friends, and so did Rose.

The main dealers' hall buzzed with the sound of excited attendees. Most wore costumes based on movies, books, animes, and every sort of entertainment imaginable. Rose waved at several women, and a few men too, dressed as her. After a few dozen cons that had ceased being surreal and became a simple honor.

"It's like a theme park on steroids." Olivia, who had accompanied Rose to the event, had delighted in dressing up for it. She wore a black leather jacket over a black tank top with black jeans and black boots. A drizzle of fake blood decorated her lips and ran down her chin, made all the more grizzly by her very real fangs. Usually, vampires kept the retractable double row of sharpened teeth hidden, but apparently, they could expose them as long as they liked without discomfort, something Rose hadn't realized. Olivia called the look "biker vamp," and she adored it.

"It's fun," Rose said, watching the crowd with a feeling akin to nostalgia.

Olivia pulled a *Drawn* issue number one reprint from one of the bins next to her. "You know, I've never read this. I gather I'm in it?"

"You, Piper, pretty much everyone I know."

Olivia plopped down on a folding chair and began to read. Anywhere else on the planet—a bus stop, airport, shopping center—she would have appeared quite odd dressed as she was and reading a graphic novel. Here, she garnered no more notice than any other cosplay vampire.

Brendan and Luke commanded a large piece of real estate in the hall, seven tables filled with their comics, books, and other memorabilia. Sales reps employed by the twins worked the tables with gusto. Most were succubi, former slinkers attached to the Order happy for the work. The twins were delighted to have them since a salesperson able to charm rarely fails to close.

"So, this African woman wants the Order to join some consortium she's put together?" Brendan, who was busy restocking a box of comics, turned a quizzical expression on Rose.

"I guess so." Rose and the others had taken up a position at the far end of their vendor area, nearly out of sight of foot traffic. Fans could still see them, but most had taken the hint and kept their distance, a situation the boys reinforced using a blanket of charm to steer them toward the sales reps. That sort of thing might have attracted unwanted attention from Society enforcers a year ago, but with Society basically leaderless, the threat had evaporated.

"Africa? Seriously?" Brendan finished restocking and turned back to her. "What can they do for us? Hell, what does she think we can do for her?"

"I felt the same way when she suggested it, but considering the frigid winds I'm getting from Society elites, I figure the least we can do is talk. Her name's Thandiwe Buhari, and her consortium isn't all African. Mostly, but not all. She's stitched together a bunch of smaller societies from Turkey, Egypt—"

"That's in Africa," Brendan and Luke said together.

Olivia chuckled behind her comic.

"Okay. Yes. Fine. But she's got some people from Malaysia and a few island countries too. Point is, they're searching for allies, especially in the States."

"Because why?" Luke had colored his hair flaming red since Rose last saw him. It wouldn't have seemed so odd—the guy was gorgeous and could certainly pull it off—if he hadn't died his goatee acid green. The combination made him look like an insane Santa's elf.

"Because of the Irish."

"Oh," the twins said, their expressions suddenly dour.

"Those bastards are bad news," Brendan said.

"Um...Rose Carver?"

Rose turned to find a girl of maybe thirteen standing on the other side of the vendor table, holding a boxed set of the first three *Drawn* books before her like a talisman. She was shaking.

"Yeah, hon?"

"I'm so sorry, I know you're busy, but I'm only here this one day. Would you sign my books? Please?"

Rose's cheeks heated, as they always did whenever fans asked for autographs, not from embarrassment, but from pride and a sheepish sort of impostor syndrome. Odd that, since Rose really had performed most of the feats depicted in the first three volumes of *Drawn.* That made her less an impostor than some washed up movie star charging fans for a scrawled signature on a head shot taken twenty years ago. Not that rationalizing her thinking changed her feelings. Rose knew she didn't deserve people asking for her autograph, but her fans disagreed, so she sure as hell would deliver it with a heartfelt smile.

She signed all three books, personalizing them for the girl, and sent her away with a free copy of the next issue.

"That girl must have some succubus blood in her," Brendan said. "She slipped right through my blind."

"There are probably a lot more of us out there than anyone realizes," Rose said. "You make people afraid to use their powers, then they don't teach their children about them. Pretty soon, you've got a generation of kids charming people without realizing it."

"Those cost money, you know?" Luke said, pointing at the box Rose had stolen the comic from. He twisted his lips to one side like the Church Lady from that old *Saturday Night Live* skit.

"I'm sure your business will tank because I gave a girl a freebie comic." Rose stuck her tongue out at him. "But speaking of money, I never asked how things finally panned out with the IRS. Are you guys still under investigation?"

Brendan shook his head. "Nope. Audit's done. Once the Breathers lost power, it all evaporated."

"We got a notice we've been cleared."

"That's good. Maybe now you can start paying more attention to *Drawn*."

Both men gave her a scandalized look.

"How dare you!" Brendan said with faux indignation. "We slave over that storyline."

"Yeah, but it's not my storyline anymore, is it?" Rose put on an endearing smile though she knew deep down some of the accusation in her voice was real. "You've got America broken up into three parts by a civil war, succubi and incubi serving as super soldiers for all sides, and me struggling to stitch it all back together."

"You know the best part?" Luke pushed at Rose's arm the way a girlfriend with juicy gossip might. "All three think they're the only ones who know about the super soldiers. They've got vampires fighting all these midnight battles, and they don't seem to notice the other side is employing the same creatures."

"It's not my story. That's not what's happening in the real world."

Brendan, who was sometimes more empathetic than his brother, lost his grin, his face going at once serious. "You're really upset about this?"

Rose shrugged. Despite herself, she couldn't keep the disappointment off her face. "Maybe a little. I miss it, you know, seeing all my exploits in your pages. Somehow, and I know this sounds crazy, but I feel less real now without that in my life."

"Rose, darling." Brendan put his hands on her shoulders and met her gaze with his steely blue eyes. "I'm sorry for that, and for what I'm about to say next."

"What?"

"You've gone straight."

Rose slow-blinked at him. "I was always—"

"Not that sort of straight. Straight like straight-laced, dull, boring as a social media game app. We've tried to spice up your regular life, but it's all attending fundraisers for Torres's campaign and trying to convince some elite Society assholes to accept slinkers when they've been prejudiced against them for hundreds of years. You're basic, girl. I'm sorry, I said it."

Coming from anyone else, that might have stung, but Brendan's flamboyance made Rose smile. Being around him and Luke felt like a family reunion. Besides, hadn't she said much the same to Matt a few weeks ago? She *had* become basic. Without the Indrawn Breath to fight or the fear factory to track, she had settled into a mundane life, one fraught with its own sort of perils no doubt, but none so dire as combating hordes of gun-toting succubi in lonely Mexican villages.

"As for you feeling less real," Luke said, "I think some of that might be attributable to losing votaries. Our readership has fallen off a bit. That always happens as a comic matures, but there's more to it than that."

"I'm losing votaries because they no longer recognize the real me in *Drawn*." Rose shrugged. "I get that. The comic me is diverging farther and farther from me in the flesh."

Luke nodded. He made no pretense about consoling her or assuaging her feelings. Rose appreciated that.

"It's not like you're going to lose all your votaries though," Brendan said. "Hardcore fans remember the original comic, and they still love that Rose. In fact, they love both. Those folks aren't going anywhere. You'll be able to draw from them for years to come."

"Draw from who?" asked a voice from the other side of the table.

Rose turned expecting to find another fan, and she did after a fashion, but this one she recognized.

"Grace!" It was a struggle, but Rose managed to lean far enough across the vendor table to give Piper's youngest daughter a faltering hug without ripping her outfit.

"What are you doing here?" Olivia scanned the crowd. "Where's mother?"

"She's coming—said she wanted to wander around a bit. I heard you were with the twins and I wasn't about to waste time shopping. How are you guys?"

"Grace, you grow more beautiful every time I see you, girl."

Brendan pushed the table back to make space for her, opened his arms, and Grace flew into them to give him a hug.

"I doubt that. I stopped aging three years ago," she said, as she transferred her hug from him to Luke.

"What prompted a visit?" Rose forced a smile. She was always happy to see Grace, and her mother too for that matter, but Piper's blasé attitude toward their treaty irked her.

Grace shrugged as she thumbed through a box of old comics. "Mom said she wanted to speak with you. I'm not complaining. It's my first time at a con. Can you believe that? I swear, we never go anywhere fun."

Movies had given Rose a specific image of how vampires should look and act—an image somewhat reinforced by her time in close proximity with a Mexican vampire named Clemente and his coven. Clemente's people had gone out of their way to act mysterious by showing little to no emotion, standing still for long periods of time only to rush about when they did deign to move, and speaking with no expression whatsoever.

Piper and her children had shattered that Hollywood image. They acted like everyday people. They got their hair and nails done, they went shopping, they dressed in the latest fashions. Of course, they drank blood, but they did so discreetly, and rarely if ever killed their victims. Doing so would make no sense because vampires wove their networks of votaries from the blood ties they created. Biting someone tied that individual and, to a lesser degree, every member of the victim's family, to that vampire. From that moment until the victim's death, the vampire could borrow traits from their family like healing, eyesight, speed, and many more. Piper and her children cultivated vast networks of blood ties amongst their neighbors, spreading out the breadth and depth of their votary bases like farmers seeding land. And they did it without anyone in the community catching on.

Not everyone appreciated Piper's activities, no matter how clever she might be at hiding them. But like it or not, both her fellow vampires and Society could do little about Piper's unprecedented family. This was partially due to their sheer numbers, but also because of their simple ability to get along with one another. Her children remained unified long after other vampire offspring would have abandoned their mother's coven to seek their own path. Whether by design or simply love, Piper had built an army, one her peers could not match.

Allying the Order with Piper's coven hadn't been an easy choice for Rose. She did it cautiously, and only because she saw it as the best means to overthrow the Indrawn Breath at the time. It had been a marriage of convenience, and one fraught with ill consequences, some she foresaw, others that blindsided her.

Succubi tended to hate vampires, a feeling Rose shared when it came to Clemente and his ilk, but she doubted many of them knew vampires like Piper. They considered their blood-drinking cousins evil and treated them as such. Gone were the days when succubi hunted vampires like vermin, but not long gone. From what Matt had told Rose, that sort of thing had been happening well into the 1960s, a time not so far removed for vampires who could live millennia.

The vampires remembered, and so did the succubi.

"You think something's wrong?" Olivia asked.

Rose realized she must have looked preoccupied, maybe even worried. She schooled her expression and grinned. "I doubt it. I guess your mother was in the area and decided to pop by."

Olivia, who had been Rose's guest now for several months, shrugged one shoulder, a sure sign of her anxiety. She glanced at Grace, who was having an animated conversation with the Pruett twins, and bent her head close to Rose, voice low. "You think she's come here to ask for your help with another fight?"

Rose saw no reason to lie. "Could be. That thing with Felix, it wasn't right. It wasn't time."

"I know." Olivia turned away, seemingly unwilling to meet Rose's gaze. "I wish Mother would have some patience. The other covens aren't going anywhere."

"I have a question," Grace said, catching Rose's attention.

"Shoot, kid," Luke said, transforming his voice into that of a gunfighter straight out of an old western.

"Why did I hear you call the *Drawn* movie an anime? *Drawn* is a graphic novel, not a manga. You don't make animes from graphic novels. That's bad fandom."

Brendan cupped the young vampire's cheeks with both hands and planted a kiss on her forehead before backing up a step to place a hand on his brother's shoulder. "You are a precious angel, girl. Precious!"

"Okay..." Grace lifted her eyebrows. "But I'm right? The *Drawn* movie is not an anime. I mean the style is all wrong."

"Of course, you're right," Brendan said. "You're dead right. We call it an anime around plebes—" here Brendan waved vaguely to encompass Rose and Olivia. "They don't know the difference between a graphic novel adaption and anime. To them, anime is synonymous with cartoon."

"Are you crying?" Grace put a hand on Brendan's shoulder.

He whisked a tear from the corner of one eye. "It's just such a pleasure to speak with a real aficionado of the art, you know?"

"We're usually stuck with that one." Luke, grinning, pointed at Rose. "She thinks anime is something mimes do."

"I do not," Rose said, hands on her hips. She winked at Grace.

"You mean it isn't?"

Rose and the others turned to find Piper Ross standing on the other side of the table. The petite vampire wore a frilly dark green blouse matched with hip-hugging jeans. Except for her height, she might have been a supermodel straight from the runways in Milan with her silky black hair, knockout figure, and golden brown eyes.

"Mother." Olivia started to move the table aside, but Piper stopped her with a brief hug.

"I need a few minutes with Rose, if y'all don't mind."

"Only if she promises to dish later," Brendan said. "Our two alliance leaders show up at the same con? I smell story material."

Piper made a show of rolling her eyes. "It's not like you'd use anything I do in the comic anyway."

Luke feigned taking an imaginary arrow to the heart. "You wound us, lady!"

"Want to join me at the hotel bar?" Piper gestured toward one of the spacious room's exits, her dark eyes searching Rose's face in a way that set off alarm bells in her mind.

Without thinking, Rose drew discernment. Something about Piper's demeanor screamed deception. Though Rose had never known Piper to lie, her heightened senses warned her to be on her guard. All at once, she had no desire to be alone with her supposed ally. Why? Rose couldn't say, except that her gut told her Piper Ross didn't have her best interests at heart.

"I think we're fine here," Rose said, giving Brendan and Luke side eye.

"Definitely," Brendan said, catching on a little faster than his brother. "We're all friends. Besides, the last place you want to hold a private conversation is at the bar. That's where all the authors hang out. You've never seen a bigger bunch of eavesdroppers outside the NSA."

The usually unflappable Piper appeared uneasy. She scanned the crowd for a moment as if she expected some random passerby to attack her. When they didn't, she looked at her daughters and nodded.

"Is something wrong?" Rose asked as Olivia opened a gap in the tables for Piper to squeeze through.

"Yes." Piper drew a long breath. "This doesn't come easy for me, but I came here to apologize." She glanced at the twins who, along with Grace, were busying themselves with a stack of comics. "You called on me, and I didn't show."

"You're talking about the night Alice McAleese showed up at my parents' house?"

"Yes. I should have been there for you. I wasn't, and I'm sorry."

Rose swallowed down her anger to speak in a calm voice. "Piper, that was two weeks ago. I haven't heard a peep from you since."

Piper's eyebrows shot up. "That's not true. I sent texts."

Rose said nothing. Yes, Piper had sent all of two texts in answer to Rose's many calls since that night. The first, delivered the day after the Irish encounter, had said: ***Sorry, was tied up.*** The second, which Rose had received six days later, and only after Rose had asked in a voicemail if Piper still had a treaty with the Order, had said: ***Yes***.

And that was it. Two weeks, two messages. Olivia had done her best to defend her mother, but she had no more clue why Piper had gone radio silence for all that time than Rose. The two of them didn't chat often since Olivia had become Rose's guest. Not that Rose could blame either of them for that. She certainly didn't speak daily with Valerie Satterfield, whom Piper had taken into custody as part of the prisoner exchange built into their peace agreement. Whenever Rose did speak with Valerie, they kept their conversations vague and never talked about Order business.

"Will you at least tell me what happened?" Rose asked.

"The night you called, I was in the middle of an important negotiation with a vampire named Louis Bancroft."

"Is negotiation a euphemism for 'battle to the death?'"

"Not at first, no," Piper said, punctuating each word with a dip of her chin. "But...yes, things went south. I wanted him in my coven queendom; he wanted me dead. We came to a compromise."

"You made him dead."

"There was no way I, or any of my kids, could have gotten to you in time. I needed everyone for that fight."

"Did we lose people?" asked Olivia, a look of dread on her face.

"Four wights. Your girl fought with us, Rose. Valerie is hell on wheels when she gets going. She took out three of Louis's minions on her own."

Rose shook her head. "We've discussed this, Piper. Why the hell are you taking on the other coven kingdoms right now? It's too soon. I thought after Felix, you'd slow down, maybe even listen to me and stop altogether until we can back you up. The Order isn't in any shape to go fighting all the enemies you're making."

"Making?" Piper's voice remained calm, but her face flushed pink. "I didn't make these vampires my enemies. They did. The instant they heard I was allying myself with a group of succubi, they announced open season on my family."

"You never told me that. Who is *they*?"

Piper shrugged. "I don't know them all. It's a network of coven kingdoms all woven together for one purpose, to kill my family."

Something about Piper's words rang false in Rose's head. She glanced at Olivia, who had gone preternaturally still, her face like marble. Grace, whom Rose could see from the corner of her eye, wasn't so practiced at hiding her emotions. Though the teenage vampire was supposedly chatting with the twins about their work, she was obviously following her mother's conversation. A look of worry passed across her pretty features, there and gone in a flash.

Rose kept these observations to herself—something to file away for later. Right now, in the middle of a comic convention, wasn't the time to call her vampiric ally out for lying. It didn't take discernment to realize that might be a bad idea.

"That's the sort of information you should share with us," Rose said. "If you're being attacked without provocation, I'll do everything in my power to help you, and I expect the same in return. The Irish didn't attack us at my parents' house, but Melody was with them, so things could have gone bad."

"I'm glad they didn't," Piper said. "And again, I'm sorry I wasn't there. That won't happen again."

Rose nodded. "Are you going to have many more bad negotiations going forward? Do we need to rethink how we help one another?"

"I shouldn't. Not for a while anyway. Felix and Louis were two of the oldest vampires on the east coast. The underlings who have been attacking me for the last several months got their marching orders from them. With our win over Louis, my family should be safe, at least for a while. I'll need to travel a bit more over the next few weeks, make sure their minions know I'm the boss now. Should be a cakewalk."

Again, the discordant twang of discernment sounded in Rose's head, Olivia froze in place, and Grace wrinkled her nose as if at a foul odor. If Piper wasn't outright lying, she was at least stretching the truth beyond its limits, and her daughters knew it. So did Rose, but she had no idea what to do with the information. More and more, it appeared as though Piper would forever remain the Order's sole ally.

If that was true, it meant Rose needed Piper more than the other way around. Piper was already eliminating her competition without any assistance.

Question was, what would that mean for the future of the Order and the world at large?

7

REUNITED

Rose got the call at 6 p.m. sharp. She and her team waited at an upscale convention center in Kennesaw, Georgia, a suburb of Atlanta, ahead of a campaign speech Gloria Torres would give in an hour.

Rose glanced at her phone. A blocked number. "Hello?"

"Ms. Carver?" said a feminine voice with a pronounced Nigerian accent. "My name is Ugo Ikande. I am Director Thandiwe Buhari's personal assistant. I'm calling on behalf of the director. She would like to set up a meeting to discuss an alliance with the People's Consortium."

Rose had been expecting this call. After her failed attempt at wooing Renni and Lee's Society friends to ally with the Order, Buhari's Consortium became more attractive, if only marginally so. She still didn't see how foreign succubi could benefit her people, and with the campaign ramping up, time was at a premium. Still, it paid to have a plan B.

"It's good to hear from you," Rose said as she climbed down from the SUV with Matt's help. The temperature was a blissful seventy degrees, and the humidity was low.

Matt lifted an eyebrow at her phone, and she whispered, "Buhari."

Matt nodded, slipped her free arm through his, and together they followed Tanner Watts toward the convention center entrance.

"Would you be available to meet with Director Burhari on Thursday at noon?"

"I'll be honest—what was your name?"

"Ugo, ma'am."

"Ugo, I simply don't have the time right now. Couldn't she call me herself? I'd be happy to discuss anything she wants on the phone or on a face chat."

"I'm afraid that wouldn't do, Ms. Carver. The director doesn't trust open phone lines, especially those attached to mobile networks. She is, however, excited to meet you face-to-face. It would take less than an hour if you like."

"I simply can't," Rose said as she stepped into the convention center behind Watts. "Please give her my apologies."

"Very good, I shall do that, ma'am." Ugo sounded disappointed. "Have a pleasant evening."

Turning down a potential ally left a bad taste in Rose's mouth. She wasn't exactly spoiled for choice at the moment, but that didn't change the facts. At best, joining Buhari's consortium would distract from her true aims. At worst, looking for help when her new allies could provide nothing due to simple distance might end up hurting the slinkers. Better to say no now rather than string anyone along, either the consortium or the Order.

"This place is nicer inside than out," Matt said.

Rose slipped her phone into her dress pocket. "Yeah, I'm impressed."

This building had once been a cotton mill owned by the now defunct Stevens Corporation. That company had rebranded itself in the late 90s, changed its name, and moved all production to Malaysia, leaving behind dozens of plants to decay over time.

At some point, a smart investor had bought this one and converted it into an upscale meeting place for corporations, multi-level marketing cults, and politicians. Now that Rose knew more about managing a political campaign, she wasn't certain which of the latter two best described their little enterprise.

Where the factory floor once contained sprawling pieces of industrial equipment, some of them two and three stories tall, it now offered all the amenities expected from middle managers tasked with hosting corporate parties and training events. One end of the space housed a bar, shuttered at the moment. The other sported the kind of stage Rose associated with old school rock concerts and traveling televangelists. Several hundred folding chairs fronted the stage, all empty save for a handful in the center.

Gloria Torres, dressed in a conservative pin-striped pants suit, stood on the floor below the stage, chatting with the people there. She stopped when she saw Rose and the others approaching.

"Ladies and gentlemen," Torres said as if she were speaking to a crowd of thousands rather than dozens. "I present to you the current leaders of the Order, Rose Carver and Matt Snow."

The crowd, most of whom probably knew nothing about either Rose or Matt, dutifully applauded. Rose smiled and found she wasn't forcing the expression. She wished she had thought of gathering as many slinkers as possible for a private chat with Torres before every rally, but that had been Matt's brainchild. It showed locals they could have a voice in Society and regular government, and it seemed to be working, at least in cities where they managed to find any slinkers. Their sort didn't advertise their whereabouts, but Matt had spent years wrangling them for his father. Using those skills for good, he could usually coax at least a handful to turn up in exchange for a few bucks or some free food.

"How is everyone this evening?" Rose asked.

The crowd made a collective sound of contentment. They wore a range of clothes from dirty and careworn to fresh off the rack. Their hygiene ran much the same gamut. One or two smelled ripe, and not just with body odor, but the eye-watering scent of heavy alcohol or drugs. Others looked like professionals here for a business meeting. Rose had noticed more and more of this type at rallies and other events in the last several months. Without Society stepping on their throats every time they dared use their gifts, some were finding success in the world, and they wore it well.

"Has Gloria answered all your questions?" Rose let her gaze flit from person to person, inviting them to speak with a soft push of charm.

"I have a question." A young succubus raised her hand. "I like the idea of sending a slinker to represent us, but we're talking about the real American Senate here, right? That's what you're running for?"

"Yes," Torres said at once. "The real Senate, not just some nonexistent position in Society."

"Does that mean our votes actually count? Everyone in my family says all the races are rigged. Society decides who gets in and who doesn't. Is that a lie?"

"Your votes count," Matt said. "Society doesn't rig elections."

"That's good to hear," said the young woman, though she sounded doubtful.

"Unfortunately, that's because they have no need to rig elections," Matt went on. "If they don't like someone in Congress, they nullify that person's position either by charming them or simply outvoting them in a bloc. That's why they don't mind humans winning seats in either the House or Senate. They're easy to control and can't possibly offer any challenge to our kind."

"But she can?" A wizened incubus in the second row pointed at Torres. "Won't a slinker be a threat to the elitists' power?"

"Definitely," Matt said.

"Then they'll just kill her." The old incubus threw his hands in the air.

"Not if we can make agreements with the elites," Rose said. "Even as we speak, the Order is pushing to build alliances with members of Society willing to hear our case."

Several people moaned; others laughed outright and shook their heads.

"Might as well try signing a treaty with some ISIS fighters while you're at it," said a grizzled man in a trucker hat. "In fact, I'd bet you'd do better with them."

"I'm not going to lie," Torres held up both hands as if to show she carried no weapons. "We don't have a magic pill that will make Society recognize us. But we do have numbers. I'd wager there are more slinkers in Georgia than there are elites in Washington. In fact, I guarantee it. You vote me in, you'll be sending them a message, one that will resonate. Sure, they'll still be able to stymie my votes, but every time they do, they'll be forced to remember me, and how a band of slinkers put me in office. If there's one thing people with power fear, it's the loss of power. You vote me in, the first slinker ever to win a seat, you'll show them we have power to match theirs."

Matt, his lips turned up in a half grin, nodded his approval. "Exactly."

"I still say they'll kill you," said the old man down front. "You'll have a convenient accident or simply disappear one day, never to return."

"That might have happened five years ago," Rose said, doing her best to keep her voice cheerful despite the guy's dire predictions about her friend. "Or even a year ago. But we're too big for that now, too organized. I know many of you have never heard of the Order. It's not like we can take out ads on the internet, but we have thousands of members now, and we're growing every day. Gloria will never be alone while in office. She'll have Order bodyguards surrounding her everywhere she goes. Society has already seen what we can accomplish when we band together. They know better than to try pushing us around."

Some of the slinkers must have heard about the fear factory. They were nodding along with Rose's points. Others looked thoughtful, though she could tell she hadn't yet convinced them all.

Tanner Watts, who had taken up a position at the back of the auditorium, waved a hand, signaling that the event would soon begin.

Matt wrapped up their talk with the slinkers by admonishing them to support Gloria in November. He and Rose joined Tanner while Gloria headed backstage for a touch up on her hair and makeup and a chance to rehearse her speech.

Rose admired Torres for taking on this role. She hadn't wanted it.

She didn't like making speeches unless they involved sending recruits on ruck marches or storming enemy hard points on the battlefield. But something had changed over the last weeks and months of her campaign. Where early on she faltered or stumbled over her words during rally talks, her delivery had improved over time such that her speeches no longer sounded canned. She spoke from the heart and people listened.

"I think she can do it," Rose said as she, Matt, and Tanner climbed a set of stairs to a small viewing area cut off from the main hall. It was set up like box seats in a stadium with comfortable luxury chairs, one-way mirrored glass with a view of the stage, and a stocked fridge.

"She will," Matt said confidently.

Tanner pulled a walkie-talkie from his pocket. "We're all set up here. Open the floodgates."

Despite the enclosed space, Rose heard the sound of people pouring into the auditorium below. Succubus guides dressed in security vests directed them to the stands. The turnout wasn't as large as Rose hoped, especially considering the amount of money the campaign shelled out for internet and satellite radio ad spots, but it was decent. Torres's centrist platform avoided views from either the extreme left or right, which attracted a fair share of human voters in the current polarized climate. Planting dozens of Order ops meant to charm the crowd in her favor didn't hurt either.

"Do you believe that stuff we told the slinkers?" Rose asked after the announcer had taken the stage and was on the verge of introducing Torres.

"Which part?" Matt took a sip of non-alcoholic beer. Rose didn't see how he drank it; she couldn't stand the stuff.

"How we'll find a way to make the elites pay attention once Gloria's in office. I can't help thinking about that old man insisting they'd kill her."

"Maybe you haven't noticed, but senators are rarely assassinated."

"But they are silenced. I can't think of anything more infuriating than watching her try to make changes in Society—in America for that matter—only to have them ignore her, and us, completely."

Matt took a long draw from his bottle, collecting his thoughts. "To answer your question, yes, I believe what I said. There's no question Society will attempt to neutralize us."

"You mean neuter us."

"For sure. But we'll fight. They'll pay attention because we'll give them no choice. There are too many of us to do otherwise."

Someone knocked three times on the skybox door.

Tanner frowned, his gaze on Rose and Matt. "I told Myra to call if she needed anything."

Rose drew hearing, smell, and discernment. She expected to catch a whiff of cologne or perfume from whoever stood on the other side of the door. A pungent odor, one she never expected to encounter again, filled her nose instead. She stood up.

Matt followed her lead. "What is it?"

"Open the door." Rose drew speed, strength, and dexterity, causing her breath and heart rate to speed up simultaneously. "We've got an uninvited guest."

Tanner opened it to reveal a young Hispanic vampire named Rubio.

Matt tensed and shoved his luxury seat aside with drawn-bolstered strength that sent it screeching across the floor into the wall, clearing the path between him and the vampire.

"Hello, Rose Carver," Rubio said, moving only his lips. He stood supernaturally still, like a creature made of obsidian. Not even Matt's sudden move had goaded the vampire into flinching or showing the least bit of reaction. He wore an expensive-looking dark blue suit with a sport coat and no tie, his collar open at the throat. His black hair stood up in a rakish spike.

"What are you doing here, Rubio?" It took Rose a moment to master her instinct to fight. She had no particular beef with this vampire besides his creepy nature. Her quarrel had been with Rubio's father, Clemente, whom she had killed back in Mexico. Had Rubio tracked her down for revenge?

Slowly, Rubio tucked his chin against his chest so he peeked at her through his brows, his dark eyes glinting in the overhead lights. "I didn't come here to fight. I came to give you a ride."

"A what?" Rose glanced at Matt, who kept his gaze fixed on the vampire. "A ride to where?"

"Someone important would like to speak with you. He has asked me to act as intermediary. Will you come?"

"Who?"

Had the Irish sent someone new to harass her? Far as Rose knew, Alice McAleese was their leader, or at least their representative in the States. Perhaps she had sent one of her bodyguards to have a chat? Did the Irish use vampires that way? Rose had no clue.

"I cannot say. Not here." Rubio still hadn't moved.

"You know what? No. I'm not going anywhere with you. I don't give a damn who sent you to fetch me. Go tell your boss that."

Without a warning even Rose's amped-up senses could detect, Rubio swept into the skybox like a rush of wind. One moment, he stood in the hall, Tanner between him and Rose, and the next, he took up a position with his forehead pressed against the glass, his gaze on the crowd below.

Rose and Matt jumped back in unified surprise. His face flushed, likely as much from embarrassment as sudden anger, Matt threw a punch at the vampire's jaw.

Rubio caught it with one hand, never lifting his head from the glass, but otherwise remained still.

Slowly, sheepishly, Matt withdrew his fist and stood staring at it as if he had never seen it before. Between the two of them, Rose was faster. She possessed a much deeper draw on speed and far more votaries, but Matt was no slouch. He could move many times faster than any human, and with more precision than most succubi, yet Rubio thwarted him like an adult play boxing with a child.

Tanner, who had little speed to draw from, marched toward Rubio, fists curled. "He's fast, but he can't stand up to all three of us."

"Actually," Rose put a hand on Tanner's chest, "from what we just saw, I have a feeling he might. You been making a lot of blood ties lately there, Rubio?"

"You're going to come with me," Rubio said, ignoring her question. "You'll want to in about ten seconds."

"Why is that?"

Before Matt finished speaking, Rubio pointed at the crowd. As if by his direction, no fewer than fifty faces turned to gaze at the skybox, pallid faces, ageless faces, each baring a double row of sharpened fangs. They held that pose for three seconds before turning, en masse, back to the stage, Torres and the rest of the crowd none the wiser.

A cold shiver raced through Rose's body.

Tanner's radio squawked as four voices tried to speak at once, asking if anyone else had seen what just happened and what they should do about the vampire infestation in their midst.

"You're bluffing," Matt said, his voice quiet but serious. "Those are humans down there. You massacre them, you'll expose vampire kind. And even if you can somehow cover it up, the old coven kings will rip you to shreds."

"What coven kings?" Rubio whispered. "Your friend, Piper Ross, has put the fear of *Dios* into their sour hearts, those she hasn't killed outright. They no longer come to America. How do you think I have gathered so many votaries? There is no one to stop me."

Rose and Matt shared a glance. They knew Piper had been attacking other covens, but had she really taken out enough of the old guard to frighten off what remained?

"Then why hasn't she stopped you?" Rose asked, at once curious and fearful of the answer.

Slowly, Rubio turned to face her, as expressionless as a cadaver. "Because I have a friend."

He pulled a phone from his pocket and held it up so they could see the screen. An image appeared that set Rose back on her heels and left Matt staring open-mouthed.

Jason Kraft, disgraced former senator and leader of the Indrawn Breath, the rebel faction responsible for taking over Society and plunging the United States into an ill-advised and, thankfully, short-lived invasion of Mexico, stared out at the world with a knowing smile.

"Matthew, Rose, if you're watching this, it means Rubio has tracked you down. I'm sending this message because I think it's time the three of us sat down for a chat. Neither of you will want to do that, of course, but perhaps this will change your mind: Barbara Griffith is dead. I have my suspicions as to the culprit, though I doubt you'll like my conjecture. Either way, the results are the same. Society's about to plunge back into turmoil, and I honestly don't know how to stop it."

8

BETTER THE DEVIL

Rose felt the charm the instant she exited the convention center. Succubi in the vicinity were attempting to control her. The feeling was distinct from vampire charm. It put her in mind of a boa constrictor coiling around her head and squeezing until her brain ached, whereas the vampire charm felt more like rats gnawing at her defenses. They weren't strong enough to control her—few succubi were these days—but they might wear her down given time.

Matt felt it too. He scrunched up his nose and scanned the parking lot, though the area looked empty.

"You have succubi working with you?" Rose asked.

"Some." Rubio glided down the convention center steps like a shadow, arms pinned to his sides.

"More than some," Matt said. "This is concentrated charm I'm experiencing. Either you've got a dozen, or the ones you've got all have more votaries than the norm."

"You better not have harmed my sentries." Tanner withdrew his radio. "Stevens, Myra, do you hear me?"

"Five by five," said Gregory Stevens, one of Tanner's deputies on guard for the night.

"I read you," Myra said. "Who's the man in front of you? And why are you all leaving? I thought you planned to stay till the end."

Rose couldn't spot them, but they obviously had eyes on her and the others. She wanted to swipe the radio from Tanner and demand to know how the sentries had let dozens of vampires slip into the rally, but she had a feeling she knew the answer. Stevens' next call confirmed her suspicion.

"Myra, who are you talking about?" Stevens sounded confused. "I only see Tanner, Rose, and Matt. Is there someone else nearby?"

"Directly in front of them." Myra spoke in slow, deliberate words, as if fighting to convince herself of what she was seeing.

Rubio paid no attention to Tanner's walkie-talkie. The vampire didn't seem to care whether some faceless Order ops caught sight of him, and that worried Rose. He crossed the sidewalk into the main parking lot without haste. Hunched forward slightly, he kept his arms plastered to his sides, fists bunched, chin tucked. He led them to an outsized SUV-style limousine parked in the second row, opened the rearmost door and stepped back. The car was empty.

"Where's my father?" Matt asked.

Rubio remained silent, though his eyes flicked up to gaze at Matt for a second, before sliding back to the ground.

"Do you need us down there?" Myra sounded drugged, the same as Stevens, her words slurred, but she was fighting the charm well enough to see the truth.

Four figures materialized out of the night. Rose got the impression they had been hiding between parked cars all this time, but she never detected them. Two were vampires. They must have been Rubio's people, because they moved like him or, rather, didn't move. The female's platinum blond hair shone in the light cast by overhead lamps. Besides her scuttling feet, it was the most lively thing about her. Same went for the short male vampire at her side, a dark-haired man dressed in jeans and sneakers—utterly mundane except for the double row of sharpened teeth glinting between his parted lips.

Though she could feel their charm sawing away at her mental defenses, Rose was still taken aback when she recognized the other two figures as succubi. Beautiful to the point of unreality and dressed in expensive designer clothes, they looked like a couple of fashion models who had gotten lost from a photoshoot. Rose didn't know them but she knew their type: elitists born to wealth, station, and privilege. Their charm, even combined, did little, but the feeling of condescension they exuded, even without uttering a word, made her want to grind her teeth.

The taller of the succubi, a redhead with a perfect pixie-style haircut, nodded at Rose. "They said you were strong, but I never imagined you'd be able to withstand all of us combined, and you've got enough to spare for your boyfriend and the tank here. Respect."

"Who's they?" Rose tried to stare the woman down—she had been told her gaze could be intense when she got pissed—but it slid off Pixie Cut like criticism off a sleazy politician.

"I know people who know people who fought you in Mexico."

"Breathers?" Rose shrugged one shoulder. "Not many of them lived."

"Believe me, I don't envy them." Pixie Cut waved a hand at the SUV. "None of us are here to fight. We're your escorts."

"But if we don't go with you, your vampire friends kill everyone inside?" Matt stood with his feet spread apart, his hands dangling in a nonchalant manner that meant he was ready to fight.

"I'd prefer we never find out. Please, get in the truck."

Seeing no other choice—she certainly wasn't going to take on that many vampires at once with a meager security detail at her back—Rose climbed inside. Matt hesitated a moment longer before following her.

Tanner started to climb in but, moving with preternatural speed, Rubio got in front of him to place a hand on the big incubus's chest. "Not you."

Tanner looked at Rose and Matt. He had the worst sort of expression on his face—none at all. He possessed no fear whatsoever of either succubi or vampires, not even Rubio. At a word, he would go on the attack without question or hesitation.

"Stay here." Rose cocked her head to indicate the convention center. "Keep Torres safe."

"I don't like this." Tanner backed off, his jaw set, his muscles tensed beneath his security vest.

"We're not going to harm them, big guy." Pixie Cut made a point of brushing close to Tanner as she slid into the SUV, making eyes at him once inside.

All in a rush, the male vampire swarmed into the seat next to her and assumed a statue-like stillness, his dark gaze focused exclusively on Rose. He continued plying her with charm. Fortunately, though she had lost some votaries since the *Drawn* graphic novel deviated from her real life, she retained the majority of the die-hard fans who first bought into the mystique of Rose Carver, succubus. The charm she borrowed from them amounted to a mere trickle from each individual, but its accumulated strength turned the vampire's single-minded attack into little more than an irritant at the edge of her consciousness.

They drove, Rubio at the wheel, for ten silent minutes. Rose wanted to engage the succubus woman—the vampire gave her the creeps, she wanted no part of him—but she got the feeling neither of them would volunteer any information anyway.

A wrought-iron fence topped with sharpened spikes longer than Rose's hands soon appeared outside the limo to the east. It unfurled next to them for several minutes before Rubio slowed to turn.

"Talk about deja vu," Matt said as a gate opened before them, and they started down a narrow, tree-enshrouded drive.

"Mexico all over again," Rose agreed. The first time she met vampires in the flesh had been in a walled *hacienda* in Mexico.

Another five minutes brought them to a house plucked out of Victorian England. Floodlights shone upon its stone face, picking out dozens of windows precisely formed from terracotta brickwork in sharp relief. A large front porch, also made of stone and inlaid with intricate designs, gave onto the mansion's wide doorway, which stood open, silhouetting a slim figure waiting there.

Rose nodded to herself in relief. Despite the fact she had killed

Clemente, Rubio's sire, and a real bastard who had once murdered an innocent child in front of Rose, she had harbored serious concerns that he might have somehow survived. Unlike in the movies, though, real vampires were living creatures. Their hearts beat, their blood flowed, and when you killed one, they didn't come back.

"Matthew and Ms. Carver, greetings," said the man on the porch the instant they climbed from the limo. "Ms. Carver, my name is Donald Selway. Welcome to Oakmoore Manor."

Matt stopped short as if he had run into an invisible tree, his gaze nailed to Selway, who stared back with cool calmness.

"What's the matter?" Rose inspected their vampire and succubus escorts, half expecting an attack, but they hadn't moved.

"Where's my father, Don?" Matt nearly growled.

"This guy works for Kraft?" Rose asked.

"Don's his personal man. He practically raised me."

Selway, whom Rose pegged as an incubus on sight, wore a fine tuxedo matched with a short coat and embroidered blue vest. The faintest smile stretched his lips, there and gone in an instant, before he stepped back, opening the way for his guests to enter. "Mr. Kraft is inside. He is eager to speak with both of you."

Rose knew better than to refuse. She and Matt could probably fight their way out of this situation—though from what she had seen of the new and supercharged Rubio, he could pose a problem—but what then? Torres was still speaking to a crowd liberally doused with bloodsuckers. What exactly would set them off? Rose had no idea but harming one of these people seemed like a sure bet.

Together, she and Matt strode into the house. Rubio and Pixie Cut followed, leaving the others behind. Selway led them through a grand entranceway and receiving room—the latter looked big enough to host a skate park—and along a hall wide enough for two people to navigate side-by-side without rubbing shoulders. It was, by orders of magnitude, the finest home Rose had ever visited.

"It's good to see you, Matt," Selway said, his heels clicking on the polished parquet floor.

"I don't have any ill will toward you, Don. You were always good to me growing up. Disciplined, but fair. Unfortunately, you work for a monster."

Selway made a faint noise of disapproval in his throat but said nothing.

Not for the first time, Rose wondered at Matt's upbringing and the way he hid it. They had been dating seriously for over a year now, and he never mentioned Selway. He sometimes referred to servants caring for him while his parents went off pursuing opposite goals, but those had been faceless entities he skirted around on the rare occasions she cajoled him into talking about his childhood. Here stood a man who must have comprised a large part of that period in Matt's life, and yet he seemed underwhelmed on remaking his acquaintance.

Growing up a slinker, Rose always thought herself disadvantaged compared to children in rich, powerful families, but at least she had her mother and father, strange as they were, to care for her. Matt had a man in fancy dress who raised him by proxy for his disinterested parents. It broke her heart to think of it.

Selway pushed through a large, mahogany door inlaid with a pastoral carving of cattlemen driving stock across a river. It opened onto a cozy study with several plush chairs and a couple of leather couches surrounded on all sides by bookshelves. Ensconced in a chair facing the door sat Jason Kraft.

"Dad." Matt said the word without a molecule of emotion, but Rose imagined she saw waves of red wafting off him like heat. Here sat his father, the man responsible, whether indirectly or not, for his mother's death. Any moment now, she expected Matt to launch himself across the room to end his father's life.

If he did, Rose wouldn't stop him.

"Selway bet me you'd show. I thought, even with the video, you'd rather fight and lose people than allow someone to strongarm you. That's fifty dollars I owe you, old friend."

Selway bowed at the neck in acknowledgment before leaving the room, leaving Pixie Cut and Rubio behind.

"I guess that shows how little you know us," Matt said. "But then, how could you? You don't know the meaning of the word loyalty."

Kraft's back tensed, and his smile morphed into the sort of straight-lined frown worn by military commanders, nurses, and football coaches in the heat of their respective trades. He started to say something but clamped his mouth shut and drew in a breath through his nose.

Dressed in a sport coat and slacks—who the hell wore that kind of ensemble relaxing at home?—the middle-aged incubus with his graying, unruly hair and salt-and-pepper beard looked weary but dangerous. Dark circles colored the tan skin beneath his eyes, and he no longer filled out his clothes the way he had when last Rose had seen him on the news.

Though she had never met the man, Rose knew Kraft's reputation for irresistible charm. A Sing, meaning he could draw no more than a single trait at one time from his votaries, he nevertheless possessed the capacity to overwhelm most anyone who dared stand against his will. To hear Matt tell it, his father's career stood on a mountain of borrowed charm and shrewd political maneuvering. Skills he had more than willingly used on his wife and son in the past.

Oddly enough, Rose felt no charm emanating from Kraft now. Rubio and Pixie Cut, yes. Though they had ratcheted down the attack from the limo to a subtle probing, their attentions lingered, swarming about her, enticing her to accept whatever Kraft might say. But from Kraft himself, nothing. For some reason, the wily politician wanted Rose's and Matt's unvarnished attention.

"I deserve that." Kraft relaxed, easing back in his chair. "I suppose from your vantage point, I've never been loyal to anyone but myself."

"You're damned right." Matt remained ready to pounce, his muscles quivering with pent up energy, but a hint of doubt flavored his voice. His father's docility put him off his stride.

Rose placed a consoling hand on her lover's shoulder. A moment ago, she would have joined him in fighting this man, but Kraft's demeanor intrigued her.

"How do you know Barbara Griffith is dead?" She had watched a news stream minutes before leaving for the rally in case one of the top poll makers released a campaign update. There hadn't been any mention of a prominent politician's death in Washington.

"I still have connections in Society." Kraft's sly smile returned. "I might be on the outs with everyone you speak to, but not with everyone I speak to."

"Let me guess," Matt said, "you're going to enlighten us as to who killed her?"

"As I said in the message I sent you: I have my suspicions."

"And why wouldn't we assume you did it? It's a move straight out of your playbook. Off the competition at every opportunity."

Kraft shook his head. "I wouldn't have anything to gain by killing Barbara except more enemies. Besides, you may find this hard to believe, but she was one of my oldest and dearest friends. As for regaining my foothold in Society leadership, I couldn't care less at the moment. The two of you, and that vampire firebrand you've aligned yourselves with, made that an impossibility. I couldn't host a dinner party in DC right now, let alone take the reins of power."

"Thank God." Matt pointed a finger at Kraft. "But it's not enough. You belong in a prison cell for the rest of your unnatural life for what you did...for killing my mother."

Kraft nodded slowly, a look of genuine anguish stealing over his features. "The raid on Camp Den was ill-planned and ill-played. I never meant for it to go that far. David Lord had strict orders to capture you, your mother, all the leaders within your little cabal. Your mother and I had our disagreements, but I never would have harmed her, not like that. She died because I trusted David Lord."

"What about the fear factory?" Rose held Kraft's gaze. "Was that all David Lord? Was it just a mistake that cost my parents' their sanity?"

"No. Not a mistake. A stopgap," Kraft said, his tone full of resignation. "I was only doing what would have happened eventually. Do you think that was the first of its kind? Children, please. Those sorts of places have been around as long as there have been succubi to use them. They're as old as whorehouses. A thousand years ago, there were champions whose prowess in battle relied primarily on the number of votaries they could maintain in the throes of ecstatic fear. Probably fifty thousand years ago, it was the same for all I know."

Matt was shaking his head. "No one knew how to steal courage except a small number sworn to the secret. Those champions you're touting were used only in dire need."

"Is that what your mother told you about the fear draw?" Kraft looked amused despite his pain. "Leave it to Robin to idealize into triviality something as nuanced as our entire way of life. The secret wasn't kept hidden because Society needed heroes every now and again. The rich saw to it no one beneath landed status could know it back in medieval days. They wanted to keep it to themselves. So, when someone beneath their station happened upon the secret, they killed them. That's how your people came about, Rose. The slinkers are simply an ancient outcropping of powerful, educated succubi culling the peasant crop."

"In other words, nothing's changed," Rose said. "They did it, you did it, and whoever comes to power now will likely do the same unless we stop them."

Kraft leaned to one side to address Rubio and Pixie Cut. "I'm the worst criminal this world has ever seen. Move over Pol Pot, Hitler, here comes Jason Kraft, Satan among succubi."

"Are you going to defend the fear factory? Is that your plan?" Matt's face had gone ruddy with his anger. "Our kind has done this throughout history, and that somehow makes it right?"

"Our people have done it throughout history, and I saw no way to stop it, so I centralized it. What do you think is more likely to draw human attention, ten thousand fear factories, or one? You have no idea what it was like before the Indrawn Breath seized control of Society. Every rich, privileged succubus in the country had his or her own warren of woes. Some claimed they stocked them with criminals, and maybe that was true, but it didn't change the fact that the practice was widespread. As the times changed, cameras became ubiquitous and the internet made it possible for humans to communicate what they saw or heard instantly. I knew something had to be done."

"So, you consolidated." Rose could hear blood rushing in her ears, though her nose and lips felt cold. Why in the name of God did she understand the logic here? She didn't want to understand. She wanted to hate Kraft, and she did, but she could also see where his story was going, and it turned her stomach.

"It was the main reason I created the Indrawn Breath in the first place. No one would listen to my warnings. I told them we couldn't keep ourselves hidden with fear votaries left to individuals. I took charge in order to shut down the private factories—"

"—and set up one to service all," Rose said, awestruck in the most horrific way possible. Try as she might, she couldn't seem to marry her old image of Kraft as a power-hungry tyrant bent on dominating the world, with the reasoned monster sitting before her now. Both disgusted her, but at least this new one possessed grounds, albeit distasteful ones, for the things he had done.

"You two did more to spread fear factories throughout America when you exposed that one than anything I could have managed. Now, instead of fear drawing from a small, collective group under constant guard from outside forces, succubi all over the country have gone back to their old ways of kidnapping people off the streets, financial and political rivals, and poor human vagrants. We are more exposed than we've ever been."

"And you did this, why?" Matt asked.

"You think I didn't see people like Alice McAleese coming? Europe has been vying to throw its yoke over us since the revolution. Granted, I never thought it would be the Irish who managed to usurp their masters and sweep across the continent, but I knew we had grown too cozy here in the New World a century ago. We've had it all our own way for too long, and we haven't prepared for an outside force to come calling. I was making those preparations when you ended my career in Congress and Society."

"No, you're lying." Matt shook his head. "You don't care about any of that. You want to be the one in charge. You want lesser succubi like the slinkers to bow before you and to make humans your chattel."

"I never said chattel." Kraft sounded reproachful. "Yes, I want us to reveal ourselves to the humans, eventually. I can't see how that won't happen one way or another, no matter what we want as a people. Instead of letting it happen blindly, I say we make ready, and when the time is right, we show them who we are. If they accept without rancor, so be it. The world will go on as it always has. If they turn on us in some fashion, our preparations will have put us in a place to master them."

"I don't believe any of this," Matt said. "You're making excuses for your crimes, trying to blame them on everyone but yourself. No one's making fear factories in their poolhouses and basements. Only a handful of people even know how to steal courage from their votaries."

Kraft chuckled. "You had a campaign fundraising dinner in DC a couple of weeks ago, the night you had to bail out Piper Ross when she bit off more than she could swallow attacking Felix Maer. I guarantee you, every American succubus at that rally either owns a fear factory outright or else borrows from friends. What you're saying might have been true five hundred years ago, but today nearly every succubus family of any worth has one, and they're using them liberally."

Rose eyed the vampire standing by the door. Rubio hadn't twitched a muscle or even batted an eyelash since arriving. "What's in all this for you? Wasn't it Kraft who sent the Army to attack your people in Mexico?"

"That was then," Rubio said with all the lip movement of a master ventriloquist. "Now we have a deal."

"What deal?"

"I help Kraft, I get Piper."

"Hell no." Rose spun to face the vampire, instantly drawing speed, strength, and healing.

"Calm yourself, Ms. Carver." Kraft sounded like a school principal dressing down a kid in his charge. "I understand your feelings. You've made a pact with the so-called Vampire Queen, but I wonder if she would be as quick to defend you if your roles were reversed."

"Of course, she would."

"Seems unlikely to me since she's done nothing but lie since the day you swore allegiance to one another."

"What would you know about it, hidden away here in your mansion? You're a liar."

"Where was Piper the night Alice and your sister paid you a visit?"

Rose swallowed. "We discussed it. She was indisposed."

"And you accepted that answer."

"We're friends," Matt said. "That's what you do when friends tell you something; you believe them."

"Then perhaps it's time you reconsidered her side of that friendship." Kraft clearly savored the words flowing between his glossy white teeth. "Piper knew you called for her. She ignored that call because she has a peace treaty with a vampire named Vincent Stillman. Your parents' former home, the one you so quickly moved them from after Alice's visit, happens to lie within Stillman's territory. Rather than break her treaty with Stillman, one she entered into less than a week before the incident in question, she broke yours."

The room fell silent. Rose didn't want to believe Piper would place her treaty with a fellow vampire ahead of the one she had made with the Order, but deep inside, she accepted the possibility. That could explain Grace's and Olivia's reactions at the con when Piper swore she hadn't gotten Rose's calls for help.

Worse, discernment told Rose that, true or not, Kraft believed what he was saying. He wasn't lying, though she held out hope Kraft's informant was mistaken.

"Even if all that's true, what do you want from us?" Rose asked.

"Simple. Remedy the mistake you've made in allying yourself with a pariah like Piper Ross and throw your lot in with me."

Matt reared back as if his father had slapped him. "Why would we ever do that?"

"Because, in the long run, we want mostly the same things. Right now, you want your girl, Torres, in Congress to speak for the slinkers. I want someone there to help me save Society from an outside takeover. You don't have a chance in hell of getting her elected, and even if she somehow wins a seat, she'll have no voice. Let me backchannel for her, and I guarantee she'll not only win the seat, but she'll also win the nation."

"And throw our alliance with Piper in the garbage?" Rose demanded. "I'll admit she let us down before, and maybe she does have a pact with this Stillman you mentioned, but that doesn't change the fact that she aided us when we needed her in the past."

"We know something about loyalty and how to maintain it." Matt started to turn away, but his father's next words froze him in his tracks.

"What if Piper killed Barbara Griffith?"

"You'll say anything to break our alliance, won't you?" Matt asked. "You disgust me."

"Facts are facts. They don't care about your disgust or your loyalty." Kraft folded his arms, his eyes riveted on his son. "Who has more to gain than Piper by fomenting chaos in Washington?"

"Alice McAleese," Rose said without hesitation. "She's the one trying to overthrow Society."

"Yes, by wooing its top members, not killing them. Why sabotage all the goodwill she's earned by assassinating the very woman who could have given her what she desires most, legitimacy and a voice at the seat of power? Piper, on the other hand, has a world of freedom to gain by shattering Society. She's already devastated her most powerful vampiric enemies. What's her next logical target besides Society?"

Rose shook her head emphatically. "She wouldn't do that. As you say, she isn't killing succubi; she's fighting a war against her own kind."

Kraft's smile could have turned back global warming as he sat forward, hands on his desk. "But Rose, dear, don't you realize? We are her kind."

9

RHAPSODY

It was past 2 a.m. before Torres's rally broke up and Rose could assemble the thirty team members they had brought to run it. Tanner's security team swept the convention center three times to ensure none of Jason Kraft's people remained. Even then, he went around barking orders, scolding himself and his team for their failure to detect the vampires earlier in the day. It had gotten so bad, Rose and Matt had been forced to have a quiet word with Tanner. Few succubi in the world could have seen through the charm screen spun by Kraft's infiltrators. It wasn't his or his sentries' faults they had been taken unawares.

With everyone crowded near the stage, Rose and Matt recounted their meeting with Kraft. They glossed over Kraft's accusations against Piper, how she had possibly been the one who executed Barbara Griffith. The gathered succubi had murmured about Kraft's offer to help Torres win her seat, but Olivia appeared hung up on a different part of the tale.

"Rubio?" Olivia's brows shot up. "We're talking the old school, Mexican cartel vampire Rubio? Clemente's son?"

"That's the one." Matt leaned back against the stage, elbows up, next to Rose. "Seriously, the last person I ever expected to see cozying up to my father. I hadn't seen him since he was holed up in that basement in Mexico surrounded by American soldiers."

"And all that thanks to Kraft," Rose said.

It was common knowledge in succubus circles, even outside the Beltway, that Kraft orchestrated America's invasion of Mexico, which had soured the US's reputation internationally. Worse, it failed to stop either the drug trade or illegal immigration across the southern border. The unsuspecting human public blamed Kraft as well, but only as a minor player following former President Judy Hershel-Smith's orders. The all too human Hershel-Smith had suffered full impeachment by the House and removal from office for high crimes by the Senate, while Kraft disappeared underground and evaded justice.

"Mother had some clashes with Clemente and Rubio about twenty years ago when they tried opening a corridor for drugs into our territory." Olivia draped an arm over the folding chair next to her in an unconsciously languid repose that drew quite a bit of male attention from the incubi in the auditorium and somehow complimented her light southern drawl. "They were tough, not just because they knew how to fight, but they had numbers. Most of my kind are loners. The few who know how to organize—"

"Like your mother," Matt quipped.

Olivia smiled, showing her human teeth. "Like my mother, they're the ones who gain power. Clemente wasn't all that old, maybe two hundred, I guess, but he had amassed a following that caught attention from the ancient vampires down in South America. He remained loyal and did their bidding whenever they called on him, so they let him live. In fact, some of them trusted him with their business matters. I guess he taught Rubio everything he knew."

"And now Rubio works for Kraft." Tanner sounded bitter. "I guess strange bedfellows and all that, but it's damned scary if you ask me."

Several people nodded or spoke their agreement.

"What chance is there you'll make a deal with him?" Olivia asked the question without a hint of emotion, but Rose knew her well enough after all these months to recognize the vampire's anxiety.

"Zero," Matt said.

"Not zero." Rose glanced at his incredulous expression before turning back to the equally astonished crowd. "We're not in the best of positions right now. We've pinned our hopes on this campaign, and you all know it's not going so well."

Torres nodded slowly. "She's right. We can get people excited, assuming they show up to these rallies, but only by charming them, and that wears off within hours. Polling shows I've got less than ten percent of the vote in the state, and that's mostly in the east. Atlanta numbers are far worse. Georgians don't want a transplanted Texan female Democrat representing them in Washington."

"It's early days yet." Myra Hanks turned in her seat to face Torres. "You're the underdog trying to unseat an incumbent. That kind of thing takes time."

"Too much time. We've only got six months left."

Alfred David Saxby, the incumbent senator Torres aimed to unseat, was a clueless human easily, and often, manipulated by his succubus peers. More than once, at cocktail parties and fundraisers, Washington elites had intimated they had no inclination and certainly no intention of exchanging him for a slinker like Torres. His malleability made him too valuable.

Matt stood up from his slouch, his eyes intense, flitting from Torres to Rose and back again. "You two are seriously talking about siding with my father, the man who set up the fear factory? The man who imprisoned and tortured innocent people, including your own family, Rose? This is insanity."

"This is politics." Torres looked no more pleased by the prospect than Rose felt. "You do what you must to get your foot in the door. Reform doesn't happen if no one ever knows you're there."

"I'm not saying I want to join him necessarily." Rose let her gaze travel from face to face in the crowd as she spoke until she reached Matt. "But I'm not going to shut the door on the idea. At some point, we have to admit we're fumbling around in the dark when it comes to succubus politics."

"And real politics." Torres's otherwise exquisite features sagged into a glum expression, like a businesswoman at the end of a harrowing day realizing she has accomplished nothing.

"Our people need a win."

"At any price?" Matt stared at Rose as if he had never met her.

"No, but at some price." Rose could feel the crowd's eyes on her, on them. She and Matt rarely argued; they were too busy managing the campaign and a growing enterprise that required all their time and energy. Several in the room, Tanner Watts in particular, became visibly uncomfortable. Rose understood their discomfort, but better that than keeping secrets from them. Though she and Matt couldn't afford to share every detail of how the Order functioned, they had agreed at the beginning to disseminate what they could. After a year spent hunting down the fear factory, she had come to despise secrets, especially the institutional sort.

Matt turned his attention to Olivia. "What about Piper? How do you think she'll react to the news if we ally ourselves with Rubio? How's that going to look to her?"

"She won't like it one bit," Olivia said. "But Mother's practical, she'll be willing to listen if we explain the need, and I think she'll come around. She knows this election is important for us all."

Matt lifted his eyebrows at Rose. She took his meaning without a moment's reflection. *We should tell Olivia everything, don't you think?* Matt didn't possess mental telepathy. That wasn't a thing amongst succubus kind so far as Rose knew. But she heard the question in her head all the same.

"Olivia," Rose said, steeling herself for what she was about to say. "Kraft told us something more—something we need to discuss." Rose's insides felt like jelly. Though Olivia's time with the Order had begun as a hostage exchange, she and Rose had grown close over the last several months. Rose treasured Olivia's friendship, but she hadn't realized how much until this moment when her next words might well destroy it.

Olivia's beautiful features took on an inquisitive expression. "Say it. I'm a big girl."

"Kraft told us Barbara Griffith is dead and that he thinks your mother did it."

The crowd erupted in chatter, people talking over one another to lament the death and debate its cause. Matt lifted his hands for quiet, and they settled, though some continued whispered conversations in the back.

"No." Olivia scrunched her pretty nose and shook her head. "Mother wouldn't play you false like that. Not to mention, we've got a vested interest in stabilizing Society, so you can join it. Killing Barbara makes no sense."

"Unless she thought she could get away with it, and that Barbara's death would open a way for us to get ahead." Matt frowned as he spoke, but there was a measure of certitude in his voice. "She might have thought she was doing us a favor."

"Liv," Rose met Olivia's gaze. "Is there any chance you knew about this?"

Day-to-day, or more correctly, night-to-night, Olivia presented a human face to the world and, more importantly perhaps, her succubus captors: the gorgeous, demure, and somehow shy visage of a woman in her mid-twenties, fully matured into the ripe beauty of womanhood. Not once in Rose's presence had she let slip the vampire beneath that outer facade.

Until now.

All color drained instantly from Olivia's face so her already pale skin blanched to a near iridescent white found nowhere in nature. Her green eyes shone like polished jade, whether from some preternatural cause or by simple contrast to her pallid skin, Rose had no idea. A vein high and to the right side of her forehead pulsed with the rapid beating of her heart as the double set of sharpened fangs, otherwise hidden beneath her gums, slid partially from their fleshy sheaths.

Almost as quickly as Olivia's face had changed, it returned to normal. Almost normal. Her sharpened teeth receded, her eyes dulled back to their natural green, and the veins in her face submerged like ships succumbing to the ocean's embrace. Only her color remained off. Some of the natural pigment flowed back into her cheeks, nose, and hairline, but not all. She remained far paler than she had been.

It all happened so quickly, Rose, dumbfounded, failed to react. She drew nothing from her votaries, though her heart sped up, and the tiny hairs at the nape of her neck came to attention. It occurred to her after the moment passed that Olivia might have been preparing to attack. The realization chilled Rose to her core. She didn't want to believe Olivia capable of harming her. She simply wouldn't do that. Whatever Rose had witnessed a moment before, it had been involuntary—a vampire's autonomic reaction to a mental blow, no more in Olivia's control than was the exchange of oxygen in her lungs.

Was it, though? A niggling worry deep in Rose's brain, one she fought hard to bury, kept whispering at her. She felt sure the news of Barbara's death and Kraft's accusation came as a shock to Olivia. Drawing discernment nearly confirmed that to Rose. But discernment hinted at something more. She got the feeling Olivia believed Piper not just capable of executing a high-level leader within Society but perhaps even disposed to it. It wasn't like Piper kept Olivia abreast of her plans. Who knew what sorts of machinations her mother busied herself with these days? Olivia's doubt about her vampiric mother might have amounted to nothing more than a fleeting concern, but fleeting or not, it was there.

"Mother told me nothing," Olivia said, enunciating each word with care. She leaned forward, her expression going suddenly soft, her eyes sparkling with unexpected tears. "I wouldn't do that to you, Rose. I would think you knew that by now."

Rose's discernment confirmed Olivia's sincerity. Whatever Piper might have done, she hadn't shared it with her daughter.

"I believe you, and I'm sorry, I had to ask the question." Rose held her friend's gaze, hoping she still had that friend.

At length, Olivia sat back, sniffed, and wiped at her eyes. "I understand. Really, I do. I just don't want you to think so little of me."

"It won't happen again."

Olivia fished a tissue from the clutch at her feet and used it to dab at her eyes. It came away pink with her tears. "See that it doesn't, you brat. You made me cry."

"I'm sorry," Rose said and let a smile touch her lips. "But since I've got you emotionally vulnerable, I might as well ask a favor."

"What favor?" Olivia looked wary.

"Can you set up a meeting with Piper? I think we should clear the air—no reason to hesitate."

Watching Rose closely, Olivia nodded. "I'll do my best. She's been too busy to return my calls lately, but I think she'll answer if I make her understand it's urgent."

"It is."

10

OUTSIDE LOOKING IN

Rose and Matt huddled around a cheap, three-legged hotel table where she placed her phone on speaker mode. The time on the screen read 10:10 p.m.

Matt looked exhausted. They had been apart most of the day, separated by the demands of running three campaign rallies in three different cities around Atlanta. Rose had seen him once or twice during the frenzy of each meeting, and again when they road-tripped from site to site, but she hadn't noticed his gaunt coloring or the deep circles under his eyes until now—badges of fatigue they shared in common. The work was running them ragged.

The phone rang three times before someone picked up on the other end.

"Hello, Rose." Emily Walsh sounded as tired as Rose felt.

"I'm sorry to call so late," Rose said. "We haven't stopped moving until now. It's been a long day."

"I know that feeling. Sometimes life on the trail can really suck. Mom and Dad said to expect your call. So, what's up?"

"We're curious how things are going in D.C. after all the trouble." Though Rose doubted anyone could listen in on her phone—her friend, Moss, had tinkered with it and pronounced it proofed against eavesdropping—she chose to keep her words circumspect. Better to err on the side of caution than mention Society outright.

"The word chaotic comes to mind," Emily said with a wry tone. "No one knows how to proceed. Sheila's told her staff to hunker down and keep quiet. We're going to let the big dogs fight it out until a replacement steps forward to take the reins."

The twenty-four-hour news cycle had already run its course on the Barbara Griffith story. To an agency, even in international news, they had reported her death as resulting from natural causes—a heart attack. Sad, but hardly newsworthy. Whoever Society elites paid to keep the media charmed had done their jobs. That had concerned Rose in the first hours after Barbara's death. With Society in turmoil—its presumptive leader killed—she worried no one would coordinate the narrative, and some eager reporter would manage to ferret out the truth. Instead, the talking heads on the streaming services mentioned the late senator's heart attack once every hour for a day before dropping it in favor of the next sensational horror story to move the popular attention meter.

"Who are the big dogs?" Matt asked. "Anyone prominent making a legit bid for leadership?"

"A few, but it's all a lot of yelling and chest thumping at the moment. It's too early to tell who's winning."

"Some billionaire, of course." Rose didn't even try to hide the bitterness in her voice.

"No doubt."

"What about Sheila?" Matt leaned toward the phone as if that would emphasize his suggestion to Emily. "Can't she make a bid for leadership?"

"No way," Emily said, her voice flat. "She's a junior senator and way too young. The old guard would slap her down hard if she even made a squeak right now."

At sixty-three years old, Sheila Isaacson, Emily's boss and a senator out of Ohio, hardly counted as young in Rose's book. Considering that most succubi lived well into their two hundreds, however, Rose took Emily's point. Some of Society's leaders had held their positions for a century or more, often taking a decade or two off to reinvent themselves, their offices held by human dupes, before returning to prominence. In fact, holding office personally had only come into vogue in the last fifty years. Before that, most succubi in government used human proxies, whom they would exchange every so often, to retain their power and prestige.

"You know the Order would back her if she changed her mind." Rose couldn't hide the eagerness in her voice. "If she steps up, we'll fight for her. We have the numbers."

"I know you have numbers," Emily sounded cautious, like a friend unwilling to offend and yet compelled to speak her mind. "I don't know that you can motivate them. Slinkers, and forgive me for saying this, aren't the sort to march in lockstep."

"But that's what they did when we took down the fear factory," Matt countered.

"Once. That's not enough to prove your merit to Sheila, not with her life in the balance."

"We get that." Rose shrugged at Matt, who shook his head in frustration. "But our people are better organized than you think."

"And committed," Matt said.

"Doesn't matter. They aren't proven, and, frankly, they aren't respected in Washington. No one's going to take a chance on them, especially not..." Emily's words petered out.

"With us allied to a vampire," Rose said.

"Yeah. That. And one who's proving herself a real nuisance. You know Piper took out that night club in Baltimore?"

Rose lifted her eyebrows and shared a look with Matt, who frowned and uttered a whispered curse. Two nights ago, unknown gunmen had terrorized a club in the city, killing over a dozen people. Police arrested a suspect, but witnesses had reported more than one shooter.

Rose curbed her impulse to smack the table. A few weeks ago, she would have blamed her sudden anger and frustration on the unfairness Society elites showed Piper and other vampires, affording them zero trust or respect. She wouldn't have believed such an allegation.

Considering Piper's antics of late, however, Rose conceded that Emily's statement might well bear out.

"We had no idea," Rose said, managing somehow to keep her voice even.

"The club was a known vampire hangout. I think she killed the main coven leader and a handful of his cronies, whichever ones wouldn't join her. We tried keeping it out of the news, but that obviously failed, so the powers-that-be are spinning the narrative to look like a lone gunman. Honestly, it was nearly a fiasco. You've got to get her reined in. Society's too disorganized to effectively cover up these sorts of gaffes."

"You're certain it was Piper?" Matt asked, though he sounded resigned to the expected answer.

"No question. Cameras caught her and eight of her daughters in the bar and on the sidewalk before, during, and after the fight. Or maybe I should call it a battle. It was an all-out turf war. Three of the victims were human, by the way. Caught in the crossfire."

Rose sat up straight, her breath caught. "What's Society going to do?"

"Nothing, probably. I heard a few senators and congressmen talk about it in passing today, but things are too insane right now for them to pay much attention. Some rogue member might be daring enough to send a crony after her, but I doubt it. Truth to tell, I think most of them are afraid of her. She's stitched together the biggest coven kingdom I've ever seen in the States. She replaces every reigning vamp she kills with one of her daughters. Those who bow to her swear to serve. Guys, she's seriously frightening, and I don't think too many of our kind are paying enough attention to her."

"We knew she had taken on a few of the old establishment vamps," Matt said. "But you're making it sound like she's taking over the nation."

"Seems that way to me, but what do I know about vampire networks? I have no idea how many there are in the country or where they're based. Someone must have been paying attention to that sort of thing before now—slapping vampires down when they got too uppity—but whoever that might have been, they've stopped. We're all too busy arguing over who gets to lead."

Rose never questioned the rightness of destroying the fear factory; she would do it again tomorrow and a thousand nights thereafter. However, the aftermath, especially over the last month or two, often kept her up at night. Only now, with time and understanding of how succubus Society functioned, did she see the ramifications of what she and the Order had wrought. Though she refused to carry sole blame for the outcome—Society's dysfunctional organization and corrupt leadership predated her by centuries—she couldn't deny her actions directly resulted in the turmoil her kind now faced. While the elites bickered, the world changed. She worried those changes might bring calamity.

"We've arranged a face-to-face with Piper in the next few days," Rose said. "We'll discuss what she's planning."

"You'd better do more than discuss," Emily spoke in a low, insistent voice. "Everything she's doing is playing right into Irish hands."

Rose perked up. "What about the Irish? Are they up to something?"

"Alice McAleese was on the Hill today."

Matt cocked an eyebrow. "Speaking before Congress?"

"No. She doesn't even pretend she's here on some official Irish government business. She's organizing a closed-door meeting with as many elites as she can gather. Some of them aren't even US officials—actors and sports stars have been flying in to speak with her. I think a lot of them are lending her support. They're leaning on the DC crowd to hear her out, and it's working."

"What the hell does she want?" Rose asked.

"Control. She's not saying that outright, of course, but everyone knows what the Irish do when they see a power vacuum."

"What are her chances, you think?" Matt asked.

"Better than they were a few weeks ago. Sheila doesn't like her, or the Irish overall, one bit. We've heard some horror stories out of Europe and West Asia, how the Irish strip locals of all their assets and leave them penniless if they step out of line, but everyone's saying those are lies. I guess a lot of folks up here believe that, because all indicators point to her getting a meeting in the next couple of days. She's been using Piper and the rise of a vampire threat to make that happen."

"Okay, but what is she offering in return?" Matt looked incredulous. "That American Society be run from afar? I can't imagine anyone in Congress is taking that seriously. They all want autonomy."

"No, they all want stability. You're not here to see how disorganized things have gotten. Two days ago, the president informed her Secretary of State she's being manipulated by mind control and that no one in the White House is to be trusted. Luckily, he called in her physician, who happens to be a succubus. She charmed them both to forget, so everything worked out, but can you imagine the President and her cabinet members walking around thinking for themselves? Someone really dropped the ball, and it could have been a debacle."

Rose disagreed with manipulating America's elected leaders, but she understood the necessity. Society long ago enmeshed itself with the U.S. Government so that the one became indistinguishable from the other. She could imagine no force on Earth powerful or delicate enough to untwine them. And though she hated the corruption endemic in both bodies, she knew Society's governance, repugnant or not, served to protect succubuskind from discovery by the world at large. In Rose's estimation, charming human politicians fell into the category of a necessary evil, one she reviled and yet accepted as part of the world outside her control.

"Is Sheila going to this meeting with the Irish?" Matt asked.

"She's not planning on it, but if the pressure mounts, she'll have to. And I don't imagine this will be Alice's only run at Congress in the coming weeks, maybe even months. She can't charm them into siding with her—there's too many of them, and most are far too powerful—but I'm already hearing people on the Hill repeat her rhetoric. I honestly think Alice has a shot at a takeover. Some people see it as the best way to avoid a meltdown."

"Maybe up there, but the slinkers will never follow her."

"Maybe not, but does that even matter in the long run?"

Rose shook her head, her jaw tight. "We'll make it matter."

11

ALIAS ALLY

It took three days to nail Piper down for the proposed meeting. Even then, Rose had been unable to speak with her directly, relying instead on Olivia as her intermediary, passing text messages to her mother. They settled on meeting in South Carolina, not too far from Piper's secluded home. Rose had let the vampire choose the spot, something she was beginning to regret.

They drove along South Carolina State Road 152, locally called High Shoals Road, on the outskirts of a town named Anderson. Night had fallen several hours before, bringing with it a pantheon of constellations ruled over by a full moon that lit the surrounding forest with a pale light. The lonely two-lane put Rose in mind of old horror movies where the unsuspecting couple picks up a hitchhiking ghost or blunders into a town lost in time. To make things even gloomier, the day had been hot for April with scattered showers in the afternoon, which resulted in clinging fog swirling at ankle height.

"She did this on purpose," Olivia said from the backseat of their van. The vampire shook her head in Rose's rearview mirror. "She wants to creep you out."

"It's working on me." Watts sat next to Olivia in the back, watching the shadowed trees on either side of the van pass by.

"I don't know," Matt said, "it's sort of pretty out here, and it's not like Piper could meet us during the day. She probably picked a spot where we don't have to worry about humans bumbling into us by accident."

"It doesn't have to be one or the other," Olivia said dryly. "I know Mother. She's always working more than one angle. Bringing you out into the middle of the woods on a full moon night isn't something she does by accident. And this fog. If I didn't know better, I'd say she rented a machine to whip it up."

Rose's phone, mounted on the dash, informed her she had reached her destination. She slowed the van to a crawl, searching both sides of the road for a cross street.

"There's supposed to be a turnoff here?" Matt twisted around to look at Olivia.

She shrugged. "Honest to God, I've never been here before."

"Didn't you live here for like the last forty years?" Tanner asked.

"Yeah, near here, but I didn't spend my time in the woods. I'm a city vampire."

Tanner laughed. "Anderson, some city."

Rose pulled the van onto the wide, grass-covered shoulder near the red icon on her phone. She saw nothing outside beyond darkened trees and a bridge a hundred feet ahead.

"Shall we?" Matt opened his door and slid out, leaving the others to follow.

The temperature had dropped to around fifty after midnight, chilly for Rose, who preferred summer heat. She slipped into her leather jacket and drew warmth from her votaries to fight the chill. To that, she added drawn sight and awareness. The sight did nothing to alleviate the darkness, but it sharpened her vision so she could more readily pick out shapes in the moonlight.

Crickets, frogs, and other nighttime creatures sang a raucous chorus that filled the surrounding area with their chaotic chirrups, croaks, and warbles. There had been a time, before her training at Camp Den, when Rose would have hated being surrounded by so much nature; now it soothed her. Though Olivia had a point about the creep factor.

"Should I text her?" Olivia withdrew her phone.

"No need," said a feminine voice from within the tree line to their right.

Everyone jumped, including Tanner, who looked embarrassed by his own reaction.

"Grace?" Olivia called.

A shadow emerged from the forest, growing more distinct as it neared, taking on the alluring curves of a young woman. Grace's blond hair appeared silver in the spill of moonlight.

"It's me, and wow, did I make you all jump." Grace sounded delighted with herself.

"Ha-ha." Olivia gave her sister a hug. "Where's mother?"

"On the bridge." Grace went about hugging or high-fiving each succubus depending on their mutual level of acquaintance.

Rose, who got a hug from the young vampire, peered at the bridge. Even with drawn sight, she could make out no figures standing there. "Where?"

"Not that bridge. Crybaby Bridge. C'mon, follow me." Moving with the agile quickness of a doe, Grace darted into the forest, her moon-silver hair bouncing behind her like a thick ribbon.

Rose was forced to draw speed and dexterity to keep Grace in sight. The others must have done the same, otherwise the speedy Grace would have left them behind. She led them through the underbrush to an open path wide enough to accommodate four people walking shoulder to shoulder. A thick carpet of grass covered the ground, but the way obviously saw enough use to prevent trees from growing up. The path curved out of sight to the east, lost in a wall of trees and hanging vines. To the west, it opened above a shallow stream almost wide enough to be called a river, and an ancient, rusted bridge.

"Do I want to ask why they call this Crybaby Bridge?" Tanner lifted one eyebrow at Grace.

"There's a legend that a lady drowned her baby up here way back in like the twentieth century. Well, that or her baby fell off the bridge. Either way, they say if you come out here at night, you can sometimes hear a baby crying down by the water. My sister, Katy, swears she saw the mother walking out here one time dressed all in white."

"Katy's a liar," Olivia said.

"Yeah, I know, but it's a good story." Grace gestured up the lane. "Look, there's the mother now."

Piper stood alone at the center of the bridge bathed in moonlight, her otherwise black hair gleaming. She wore loose jeans and a short, low cut yellow top despite the chill night air. Fog, lifting up in columns like gray fingers from the river below, swirled about her. Olivia was right; Piper had definitely chosen this spot on purpose.

"Stop doing that to me." Tanner playfully swatted Grace's shoulder, and the young vampire laughed.

Despite appearances, discernment, bolstered by a rank stench, told Rose there were wights nearby, even though she saw none of the semi-intelligent creatures on the bridge or along the tree line. Piper had brought backup. Neither of them fully trusted the other.

Maybe that was for the best.

"Hello, Rose." Piper spoke with a deep southern drawl that put emphasis on her Rs.

"Piper." Rose stepped onto the bridge's cracked and weather-worn asphalt with wary caution. She didn't want to fear Piper, but even drawing calm couldn't entirely quell her sense of anxiety. Things had changed between them in ways she didn't yet understand.

"It's good to see you, honey." Piper closed the distance between them, her arms outstretched, and enfolded Rose in a tight hug. "I'm sorry I've been so hard to reach lately. Things have been pure chaos these past few weeks."

Rose endured the hug. It felt genuine enough, the sort of familial expression two good friends would share, but she couldn't shake the tension it induced in her. Piper must have noticed. She withdrew and favored Rose with a questioning grin.

"I get the feeling we're not meeting at my house because you all have something on your mind." Piper gave Matt a nod of acknowledgment before turning back to Rose.

"Someone killed Barbara Griffith," Rose said.

"I heard."

"Was it you?" Rose saw no reason to exchange pleasantries for five minutes before getting around to the question she wanted answered. Better to rip that bandage off right away.

"No. Why would I?" Piper met Rose's eye without flinching, though Rose expected nothing less. She had fought next to Piper when they took the fear factory. While the diminutive vampire appeared harmless, Rose knew a beast lived inside her, one more cunning than Rose realized.

"Got any idea who did?" Matt asked.

Piper shook her head. "Why would any vampire attack Society? Death wishes are one thing, but that's like poking a sleeping giant. It'd give them an excuse to exterminate as many of us as they want."

"Back at the con in Kentucky, you said you would kill Barbara to get her out of my way." Rose drew all the discernment she could handle in anticipation of Piper's next words. She wished she could have brought Myra on this trip but had decided against it since that would have put almost the entirety of the Order's leadership team within Piper's grasp.

"That was a joke, girl." Piper looked offended. "I don't go around executing succubi—I don't go around executing anybody."

"Except other vampires." Rose's discernment brought her nothing, but observation told her she had struck a tender spot when one corner of Piper's mouth curled up in what might have been a grin but verged more on a sneer. "You got us to help you overthrow Felix when we weren't ready, and you've moved on to take out many more like him since. How many other vamps have you killed?"

Piper remained silent for a long moment, fog curling about her legs like loving spirits come to pay homage to their queen. Rose couldn't see her eyes for the darkness, yet she could feel Piper's gaze boring into her.

"You're right," Piper said at last. "I didn't stop at Felix. Taking him out was a stepping stone to seizing more territory up north, mostly because his offspring and peers moved against me after that. Me and mine were fighting for our lives most of the last three weeks."

"Why didn't you tell us that?" Matt asked.

"Because you all made it crystal clear I wasn't to go adventuring outside my territory. I couldn't expect any help from you, so I didn't bother asking for it."

"But you did," Rose said. "Go adventuring, as you put it, outside South Carolina. From what we've heard, you've been fighting your own kind up and down the east coast."

Piper glanced at Olivia before turning her attention back to Rose. "Those others of my 'own kind' didn't give me any choice, did they? They threatened friends of mine. In fact, in one case, they killed a vampire I had known for fifty years. He died because he knew me. I can't let that sort of thing stand. I took out the vamps who did it."

"And set up your daughters to control their former territory," Matt said in a flat tone. "Did you think Society would ignore that sort of thing?"

"What would you do if someone killed your good friend and threatened to do the same to your family, Matthew? You're an incubus. It's easy for you. If you didn't go after them yourself, and probably get away with it, you could at least plead for help from Society. Someone might even assist you. A human could call the authorities and get the bastards locked up for life. Vampires don't have either luxury. I can't turn a vampire in for murder. In the first place, no human would be able to capture them, and even if they did, Society would charm them free and then execute me for revealing our kind to the world. If I sought justice from Society directly, the elites would laugh me into chains. There's no justice for my kind except the justice we create. That's the hard truth."

Rose couldn't deny Piper's logic. She had spent more than an entire human lifespan under the thumb of both Society and her fellow vampires. It made sense she would rail against both once she gained the power to do so.

"If it wasn't Piper, that leaves the Irish." Rose turned to Matt, who nodded.

"You mean Alice McAleese." Piper nearly growled the succubus's name.

"You've had dealings with her?" Rose asked.

"She's tried to kill me on three separate occasions. I might not like how my family's treated here in the States, but at least no one's trying to exterminate us—not like Europe. The Irish have been systematically murdering vampires there for the last ten years. They make a sport of it like fox hunting."

"I didn't know," Rose said in a small voice. She supposed she shouldn't feel surprised. No one in Society particularly liked vampires. They tolerated them, sure, but they also kept them politically and, often, financially weak. It made sense the Irish, who seemed to her like an extreme instance of their American counterparts, would take such an ideology to the next, horrific level.

"If you want to know who killed Barbara Griffith, I'd start there." Piper folded her arms, nodding as if deep in thought. "I'm sure you know the Irish are worming their way into your Society."

"It's not my Society," Rose said. "But I take your point, and, yeah, we've heard."

"What better way to sow distrust in your leaders than to take out Griffith?" Piper asked. "Now, Alice has every succubus with the least bit of power vying for leadership. That sort of destabilization leads to panic. Who can the succubi trust when everyone is backstabbing everyone else?"

"Alice and the Irish," Matt said, nodding. "We might hear some odd rumors coming out of Europe and the Near East, but at least things are stable there."

"Exactly." Piper put her hands on her hips. "Who's passing those rumors anyway? Alice's opposition. They're just a bunch of backward succubi holding onto tradition—crusty old politicians clutching at their power base, afraid of new ideas."

"And the Irish's way of dealing with vampires only strengthens their argument," Rose said in sad wonder.

"Exactly." Piper gazed down at a spillway filled with rushing water below them. The full moon shone in its wavering surface. "I know I've broken our treaty a couple of times, and I'm sorry for that, but I swear I've had good reasons. If there comes a time when you have to choose between your family or our agreement, I hope you choose family. I'll understand. I'll forgive."

"If I had known that was the problem, I would have done the same." Rose joined Piper at the bridge's guardrail, its rusted steel cold under her palms. "But you didn't tell us that. You went radio silence. If we're going to make this alliance work, we have to communicate."

"You're right. I'll do better. I've never had to consult with anyone about anything before. From now on, I won't make a move without letting you know how and why."

"And we'll do the same," Rose said.

Piper turned to lean her back against the rail, focusing on Matt, Grace, Olivia, and Tanner. "So now that our fence is mended, what are we going to do about the Irish? All this time, you've been concerned about shortening my leash and I've been focusing on beating back my own kind to save my neck, Alice has been twisting Society to her will. Sooner or later, she's going to own it outright if we don't do something to stop her."

Rose nodded in the dark, her face set in a chiseled expression of resolve. "I couldn't agree more. She's been working to split us apart; I say it's past time we send her packing."

12

SOUGHT AND FORGOTTEN

The offices of Run Time Error, one of many companies owned by the Order, wouldn't have impressed executives from the likes of Microsoft or Google. The five-story tower with the company's blue and orange logo plastered on top looked shabby next to the buildings surrounding it in Atlanta's skyline. But that didn't fool Rose.

Run Time Error, which started life as a computer programming advice website, had expanded tremendously since its inception five years ago, transforming from a two-person operation to a sixty-employee enterprise with a software repository and database backup facilities housed on-site. Much sought after for consulting, they had recently expanded their teleconferencing software to include 3-D imaging with connections to offices around the planet. Much of that growth took place in the last four months after the company hired a young programming phenom named Randall Moss.

A bank of ten turnstiles neatly split the building's main entrance in half, with a security desk on one end and a steel wall on the other. The guards behind the desk eyed Rose and Matt in askance until the couple clicked their ID badges against a reader and the turnstiles' spinning arms let them pass. Rose and Matt, through the Order, owned one hundred percent of Run Time Error. The guards might have been surprised to learn Rose's and Matt's badges, which they received in the mail that morning, gave them access to every room in the building.

"Not exactly cutting edge, is it?" Matt whispered. "I expected something out of a techno-thriller movie."

"It's like every elementary school I ever attended," Rose agreed. Her heels made an annoying click on the shiny, gray epoxy floor. She wished she had worn sneakers like Matt.

"Elevator's this way." Matt pointed to a sign affixed to the wall.

"Shouldn't we wait on Moss? He was supposed to meet us."

"Maybe he got hung up."

They rounded the corner as the elevator dinged and Moss stepped out. Rose, who hadn't seen the young incubus in months, stifled a shocked intake of breath. The man standing before her looked more like Moss's father than the slim, energetic hacker she had trained with at Camp Den. His lank hair hung in clumps to his shoulders. An unkempt beard, patchy yet as long as Rose's hand from wrist to fingertips, sat on his chest like an overgrown spider. He wore wrinkled jeans with an equally wrinkled Schlock Mercenary t-shirt and a pair of brown Oxford shoes so worn the seams had busted in several places.

"Hi, guys."

"Hey, Moss." Schooling her face against her instant repulsion—Moss smelled like a cosplayer on day three of a hot con—Rose gave him a hug. He grew stiff, perhaps taken aback by the contact, but didn't resist.

Matt, obviously the brains in their couple, settled for a handshake.

"It's good to see you both." Moss pressed the elevator's up button without meeting their eyes. "You were pretty mysterious on the phone. What's up?"

"We need to track someone without them realizing it," Matt said. "Probably by cell phone, but however you do it is fine with us."

The elevator doors slid open, and Moss stepped inside. Rose

cringed inwardly at getting cooped up with his stench, but she had been in worse positions.

"Tracking people's easy," Moss said. "Who's the target?"

"A succubus named Alice McAleese."

Run Time Error's development lab—Rose read the name off a placard at the entrance—put the building's outdated facade to shame with its cutting-edge design and modern technology. Housed on the eastern side of the fourth and fifth floor, the lab sprawled across three sections of the edifice. Computer stations run by technicians, some standing, others reclining in gaming chairs, dotted the space.

People nodded at Moss as he led Rose and Matt to the lab's sole office. A curtained window next to its door read *Randall Moss, President—Research and Development*. Moss ushered them inside and shut the door.

Unlike the man himself, Moss's office was tidy. Five screens aligned in a gentle curve stood atop his pressed wood desk. Behind one monitor, facing away from Moss, stood a framed picture of Leslie Phelps, his old flame and Rose's best friend. Leslie, dressed in tac gear and cradling her beloved M40 sniper rifle, smiled at the camera, her gleaming eyes so full of life and eagerness it nearly split Rose's heart in two.

"This from the day we graduated?" Rose picked up the frame, her eyes going misty.

Moss nodded without looking at her or the portrait.

"I miss her too," Rose said and placed the image back on the desk. Moss clearly had no desire to reminisce.

His seat creaked under his weight when he sat. "So, who is Alice McAleese?"

Together, Rose and Matt explained what they had feared to discuss on the phone. Filling in forgotten parts for one another, they brought

Moss up to speed on the Irish, the crisis within Society, and Torres's bid for election—all of which seemed new to him.

Sometimes, Rose forgot what it was like to be a regular succubus living a day-to-day life entirely removed from Society, the Order, and vampire treaties. For a moment, she felt jealous in the extreme toward Moss, stench and all.

"You got the phone she called you on?" Moss lifted an inquisitive eyebrow.

Rose unlocked it and handed it over. "Want me to navigate you to her number?"

"Nah." Moss poked and brushed the screen several times before he grunted.

"That a good sound or bad?" Matt asked.

"Give me a sec." Moss hooked a cord to the phone and started typing on one of the three keyboards at his station. He did this in silence for a few minutes before he grunted again. "She called you from a throwaway phone."

Matt whispered a curse. "That means we're out of luck?"

"No." Moss spun the screen around on its stand. It showed a high-def image of a large, balding man with a star-shaped scar on his check standing at a counter inside a kiosk. "Either of you recognize that guy?"

Rose nodded. "He's one of Alice's guards. I don't know his name, but he was there the night she paid me a visit at my parents' house."

"He bought the burner phone with a corporate charge card that belongs to a shell company. I've traced it back to the main corporation, which is called Seana Enterprises. Where do you think they're based?"

"Ireland," Matt said with a laugh. "I'd lay money on it."

"And you'd win, too." Moss spun the screen back to face him.

"Does that do us any good, though?" Rose could feel Moss's excitement through his natural-born charm, something that had been missing only a minute before, but that didn't guarantee he had solved their problem. Programming always excited him.

"It does, because your Alice McAleese sits on the board of Seana

Enterprises. In fact, according to the documents of incorporation, she's the majority stockholder." Moss clicked the mouse a few times, typed something, and grinned. "Gotcha."

"You found her phone?"

Moss nodded as his grin spread into a smile. "It amazes me how little people think about their cybersecurity. Living in this age, and with all the horror stories you hear of assholes stealing identities, you'd think they'd hire competent professionals to protect their data. Your Alice went to all the trouble of having Scar Cheeks purchase her tosser phone with an obscure credit card, then put her real phone number on her corporate website. That wouldn't be enough to track her under normal circumstances, but let's face it, I'm damned extraordinary."

He turned the screen around to face them. It showed a map of Manhattan with a red tack stuck into it. "She holds a lease on that place, and her phone is there now."

"Moss," Rose said, her eyes wide. "You're not extraordinary, you're scary, and I love it."

"Is there a way for you to dump this information to our phones when we need it?" Matt pointed at the screen.

"I can do better than that. I'll write an app dedicated to following her. Shouldn't take more than a couple of days. I'll want to test it a bit before I give it to you."

"Perfect," Rose said.

"Do you mind me asking what you plan to do to her? You going to ice her?" Moss had never been squeamish when it came to tactical work, and from the look on his face, Rose didn't think he had become so anytime recently. He was genuinely curious.

She shook her head. "Not if I can help it. We're just going to send her a message: get the hell out of the States and don't come back."

"And if she doesn't take the hint?"

"I'll hammer it home."

13

INTIMIDATION

Better than his word, Moss delivered the tracking app less than a day after their meeting. Not only did it work as promised, but it also provided a pattern-of-life function built to track Alice's movements, detail repeated actions, and subsequently deliver a prediction of future travel choices. From it, and a bit more snooping on the internet, Rose's team determined Alice maintained two residences: the one in Manhattan and a second in DC—the two major spheres of influence within Society. Using both gave her access to the billionaire succubi on Wall Street and the political types in the capital.

It took another week for Rose and Matt to lay out a plan, gather their people, and coordinate an attack with Piper and her daughters. Alice spent most of her time on Capitol Hill these days, wooing senators, congressional representatives, and judges to her side by day and sleeping at her DC condo by night. According to Moss's app, which took into account her phone history since her arrival in the United States several months earlier, she would maintain this pattern for another month before switching back to her Manhattan apartment. Given her habitual movements, she tended to return home early on Sunday nights, when Congress conducted no business. Most Sundays

—and this one in mid-April was no exception—Alice spent most of her time schmoozing with elite succubus families at their homes or meeting them at upscale restaurants. Afterward, she would return home for a challenging workout in her home gym, perhaps a movie, and then bed by 10 p.m. to get an early start on Monday.

Rose's crew hit the condo in the middle of Alice's workout.

"Cameras are down, front door is unlocked," Moss said over the main comm channel from his office in Atlanta. "I've deactivated the alarm system and blocked all outgoing calls from the local cell area. Can't maintain this too long, though. People are going to take notice right away."

"Roger," Matt said. "We're inbound."

Situated in a residential area outside the main hub of capital traffic, Alice's brick condo stood amongst hundreds of its kind—the sort of overpriced luxury space favored by high-power, mid-level executives too focused on their climb up the corporate or government ladder to spend time at home. The sun had set more than an hour ago, leaving the streets and sidewalks empty save for a lone driver puttering east along the separated lanes in front of the building. Later, in a police statement, he would swear he saw nothing, even though twelve people dressed like SWAT members entered the condo at that exact moment.

Rose pushed through the entrance on point, her blacked-out subgun pressed hard to one shoulder, muzzle down. Her combat boots made almost no sound on the plush carpets as she jogged toward the front desk and a wide-eyed man dressed in a sport coat and tie. She glanced at his name tag.

"Hi, Rick. How are you tonight?"

Rick shut his mouth, his eyes suddenly glistening, and smiled as Rose's charm washed over him like steam. "I'm great, ma'am. How can I help you?"

"By forgetting you ever saw my friends or me." Rose checked behind. All eleven succubi had assumed tactical positions inside the condo's entrance. No one on the street seemed to have taken particular notice of the group thanks to their cloud of combined charm.

"Okay," Rick said, staring right through Rose and the others.

Matt motioned toward the elevators, and five of the crew peeled off to follow him that way. Rose led the remaining five to the building's wide, carpeted stairwell to begin the climb toward the seventh floor. Her team all possessed a draw on speed, strength, and endurance, including Olivia, who had refused to separate from Rose. Negotiating a full-speed run up six flights of stairs presented nothing more than an excellent warm-up for them. Rose took pride in the fact they beat Matt's team to the top. She would rib him about that later.

They congregated outside Alice's section of the building, maintaining an onslaught of charm to keep neighbors on the floor from getting nosy. A bright white security door made of steel barred Alice's unit. It reminded Rose of a smaller version of the doors you saw on bank vaults.

Tanner Watts gave Rose a questioning look, and she nodded.

Though not much bigger than the average incubi at 5'8", Tanner possessed a deep draw on strength matched only by his ability to heal. Those two factors made him an ideal entry man since he could mend any damage he caused himself when he drew strength and kicked the door with the power of a five-ton hammer.

Forged in steel or not, the door's frame bent with an earsplitting screech before the hinges failed, sending the door hurtling backward. Moving with drawn speed, Tanner rushed into the apartment fast enough to catch the ricocheting door with his shoulder and thereby keep it from bouncing back on those who followed him inside.

Rose sped inside on Tanner's heels. After hours poring over the condo's blueprints, she knew exactly where to go. The foyer, wide enough to admit two people abreast, opened at an angle on the dining room, which gave way to the unit's living area. Trusting the team at her back, Rose passed through the kitchen in a rush of wind to crouch behind a leather sofa, her subgun aimed directly at Alice McAleese's forehead.

Dressed in yoga pants and a sports bra, Alice looked less than prepared for armed intruders. As planned, Rose had caught her in the middle of her nightly exercise regimen. A fitness video blared from the flat screen affixed to the wall, the host encouraging those at home to squeeze out one more rep. Alice, a seventy-five-pound dumbbell in hand, blanched at Rose, her gaze momentarily flitting beyond her to the rest of the team.

Melody stood next to Alice, similarly dressed and covered in a sheen of sweat. She narrowed her green eyes at her sister. Her glare could have put a linebacker off his game.

A couple of Alice's men, the guys she referred to as lads, stumbled out of the master bedroom, but were headed off by Matt and Tanner, who held them at gunpoint.

Alice, who had schooled her expression from her initial shock, grinned with one corner of her mouth. "Rose Carver. I take it you want to chat; otherwise, you would have already pulled that trigger."

"Put the weight on the floor and back away," Rose said. "Both of you."

Casually, Alice placed the dumbbell on the carpet without a sound and motioned Melody to do the same. The younger woman gave her a peevish frown but followed suit, and the two of them backed off.

"Do you have any other guards in the building?" Rose asked.

"What do you want, Rose?" Alice's accent sounded deeper than the first time they had spoken. And while she showed no fear, she did appear angry, which was almost as good.

"Tell me if there are other guards in the building. Where are they?"

Before Alice could answer, the sound of shuffling feet came from an outside patio, followed by a glass door sliding open near Alice. A tall incubus with a star-shaped scar on his cheek, bald and florid, tripped into the room, encouraged by a kick from Piper. The petite vampire looked like a finch harrowing an eagle, but Rose had seen her in action and knew the strength she possessed. Four of her daughters swept into the room behind Piper, their hair pinned back to protect their vision, followed by six wights of varying genders. Valerie Satterfield, one of Rose's good friends and treaty hostage to Piper, followed behind the wights with Piper's son, Preston, bringing up the rear.

"Got the jump on you, did they, Figgin?" Alice asked the man with the star-shaped scar.

"Sorry, Alice. They came up the wall all quiet-like. Never knew they was there til they had the drop on me."

"Ah, well, can't go poking the mote in yer eye when I've a pole in my own." Alice turned back to face Rose. "That's the lot. You got 'em all, Rosey. Now what?"

"Now you slither back to Ireland, and you never set foot on U.S. soil again." Rose maintained her crouch, her gun still trained on the Irish leader. Part of her wanted to pull the trigger. So many problems would melt away if Alice McAleese disappeared. Of course, killing her would create a whole new set of complications. Rose doubted the Irish would forgive her for killing their leader. They would retaliate, and if they couldn't reach Rose, they would likely attack regular members of the Order who lacked the sort of security detail she enjoyed.

No. Better to stick with the plan.

Figgin, who had taken a spot between Alice and Melody with his hands raised, laughed and rolled his eyes. "This one's not the full shilling, is she?"

"She's yet to be schooled s'all." Alice's upper lips curled into a cross between a smile and a snarl. "You know, Rose, when I first arrived on your shores, I thought you'd give me trouble, especially after all the things I'd heard about your vaunted Order. Melody here swore I'd have you pounding on my front door inside a week. But then, when nothing happened, I thought all the rumors were false—you had no steel in yer spine. But now, look at you. Here, in my house, throwing shapes like a pissed bloke trying to impress his friends."

Rose had no clue what half that meant, but she got the gist. Alice wasn't afraid of her, and she wasn't going to take intimidation lying down. Time to up the ante.

"You're taking advantage of people in crisis." Rose stood, making sure she kept her gun trained. "You've killed enough people, no one would fault me for shooting you in the head, but I don't want war with the Irish. I want you out. Still, if executing you is the only way to bring peace to American Society, I'd do it ten times a day for the next hundred years."

Figgin's already red cheeks flushed nearly purple as Rose spoke. His meaty fists clenched at his sides, and his shoulders bunching under his coat. "Try it, girlie."

"The only things I've killed since coming here are vermin or—" here Alice met Piper's eyes. "—or as you'd call them, vampires. Your country's infested with them if you didn't know."

"You didn't kill Barbara Griffith?"

Alice laughed. "Kill her? Jesus, Mary, and Joseph, I was trying to win that fat bitch's support. I needed her endorsement. Would have had it too, except someone killed her before she decided to give it. Want to know who? Look no further than the beasts standing behind me."

Rose glanced at Piper. The vampire's expression remained calm, unaffected.

"What? You expect her to break down and confess?" Piper asked. "She killed Griffith to make way for her own ascendancy. She's not going to admit it."

"Right now, I don't care," Rose lied. "I'm giving you a chance to leave. Don't pack, don't call anyone, gather your people—and that includes Melody—get on a plane, and go."

Alice, wholly unimpressed by Rose's threat, started to speak but was cut off when one of Piper's daughters, Tamika, swarmed forward like a fleeting shadow to smack Alice's unprotected head with an elbow. The blow made a THUNK like the report of a small-caliber rifle. Alice, caught unawares, pitched forward, ass over elbows into the couch.

Figgin spun like a distributor on a twentieth-century hot rod and punched Tamika in the face. She hurtled backward into and through the glass patio door, sending shards in every direction.

A fraction of a second later, Melody scooped up her discarded fifty-pound dumbbell and flung it at Rose, who had to dive away to avoid having her skull caved in by hurtling iron. The weight struck Barry Holmes, a longtime member of the Order, in the right knee. The joint buckled and, from the sound, the surrounding bones shattered. Barry screamed and inadvertently fired a burst of five rounds from his subgun into the ceiling.

By the time Rose regained her footing, Piper's wights had split into two groups, three climbing around Figgin like enraged chimps and the remaining three going after Melody. Though Rose thought all her familial love for her sister had long ago evaporated, something inside her cringed at seeing the pale monsters clawing and snapping at Melody's throat. Part of Rose wanted to shoot them, and she might have done it if Melody hadn't caught the nearest wight by the chin, planted her bare feet its hip, and ripped the beast's head from its shoulders trailed by a length of spine.

Everyone froze in place.

Rose had seen some horrific sights during her time fighting for the Order, but nothing like this. Blood and viscera flew in all directions, splattering the floor, the couch, the other wights. A stench like rotten meat filled the room. It made Rose want to gag as she stared in stunned silence. Even the other wights, creatures whom Rose had seen shrug off bullet wounds like bug bites, appeared momentarily dumbfounded. They shuffled back from their fallen comrade and the lithe young woman who had neutralized him, their mouths hanging open.

Piper, her face a rictus of anger, was the first to react. Hands spread wide like claws, she rocketed toward Melody with a scream that shook loose what little glass remained in the patio door. Sharpened fangs bared, she closed to within a foot of Melody before a spinning dumbbell, moving as if fired from a rifle, smashed into her face. Seventy-five pounds, being an appreciable percentage of Piper's weight, sent the vampire flying after her daughter Tamika, her face a bloody pulp.

Alice, back on her feet and moving fast enough to make the wind snap around her limbs, vaulted the couch. She landed in the middle of the Order ops, who, despite their experience, appeared caught by surprise. Tanner squeezed off a burst of rounds at Alice but missed wide, succeeding only in killing her flat screen. Alice repaid him with a supersonic Muay Thai kick to his right leg. He gasped and would have collapsed had she not taken him by his harness and spun him like a mini-tornado into Thomas Black, who, in turn, stumbled into Matt.

The entire process of neutralizing Rose's team took perhaps one second and resulted in freeing Alice's other two goons to act. Like workmen plying a trade, the lads set about inflicting as much damage and pain as possible to the eleven armed ops in their path. It was like watching a movie sped up four times. A couple of people, including Matt, attempted to use their subguns, but were thwarted each time by Alice or her people.

Drawing speed, Rose hurled herself at Alice. Despite her size compared to the lads, she dealt out the most damage, making her the prime target. Rose shoved the barrel of her gun into the woman's unprotected back and squeezed the trigger, only to scream in surprise when Alice spun away and Rose found herself blasting Sarah Hensley's Kevlar vest. Sarah grunted and shuffled back but looked whole. No blood seeped around the new deformations in her armor, thank God.

Rose abandoned the subgun due to the confines of the fight, letting it swing from her harness, and spun to catch Alice a blow with her fist. She punched nothing but air. The Irish succubus had not only weaved under Rose's punch, she likewise avoided a kick aimed at her by Sarah, and a slash from a knife-wielding Nathan Moore. Alice turned her dodge into a fluid attack by punching Nathan in the throat where his armor didn't protect him and then kicking Sarah into the kitchen table.

It took all Rose's dexterity to avoid tripping over a choking Nathan as he fell, clutching his throat with both hands. Awkwardly, she side-stepped him, intending to land a kick on Alice that would send her into one of her lads. By the time Rose's foot left the floor, Alice had already closed the distance between them, her face as stoic as a monk's. She smashed her elbow into Rose's nose like a crowbar, sending a jolt of pain so sharp through Rose's head, she nearly blacked out.

Only drawn healing coupled with dexterity kept Rose on her feet. Baring her teeth, she went after Alice again, drawing all the speed her votaries could provide.

It wasn't enough.

Alice slipped Rose's punches and kicks like an adult playing with a six-year-old. All the while, her expression remained fixed, a look Rose knew well from experience. Alice was drawing fear and, by the way she moved, a lot of it. No matter how Rose struggled, no matter what depths of drawn abilities she plumbed, she could not match the Irish woman's physicality.

Alice McAleese was playing with her.

Fear seized Rose's mind. She felt it coming, knew its source, and yet could do nothing to stop it. Her legs turned to jelly, her stomach tightened, and her hands shook. Tears sprung to her eyes as she scuttled away from Alice, struggling in vain to lift her gun, but her arms felt too weak.

Alice pursued Rose slowly, as unconcerned about the armed Order ops surrounding her as a lioness encircled by baby chicks. They wore expressions of utter fear, their eyes glistening, their jaws sprung open like haunted caves. Even Matt, who had time and again proven himself against charmed mind control, shrank under Alice's fear-induced onslaught. He cowered on his knees before Alice's lads, his hands spread palm down on the floor.

Rose glanced across the room, hoping to find help from that quarter. What she saw dashed whatever hope remained in her heart.

Of the four daughters who accompanied Piper on this death mission, two remained along with Preston and Satterfield. Piper, Tamika, and the wights had fled. While the vampires appeared unaffected by Alice and her crews' fear draw, and they were getting some blows in against their opponents, the fight was by no means going their way. Melody, moving with more speed and power than Rose had ever witnessed in her little sister, wielded a splintered chair leg like a club. She caught one of the daughters a resounding blow on the side of her head that left the vampire visibly dazed and followed it up with a punch that sent her flying. Neither she nor Figgin showed any signs of vampire bites, which might have slowed or even incapacitated them with its venom. They were clearly adept at avoiding such attacks, instead forcing the vampires to fight with fists, elbows, and knees—a realm where the succubi clearly dominated.

Satterfield, cowering on the floor in a pile of broken glass, played no role in the battle. Chest heaving, eyes and nose glistening with wetness, she looked up at Rose and shot her a pleading gaze. Please make this stop. Somehow, make it stop.

But Rose couldn't make it stop. She had no power, not even those drawn from her votaries. She belonged, mind and body, to Alice McAleese.

A titanic, banshee wail reverberated through the building with such force, Rose had to clamp her hands over her ears. Even then, the sound penetrated to her brain like a knife plunged through her skull. She reeled back, adding her scream to the sound, too overwhelmed to realize what was happening until a racing shadow crashed into Alice and a large knife bloomed from her chest.

Piper pulled the knife free and plunged it into Alice's breast a second time. She followed that blow up by sinking her fangs into Alice's throat.

Blood flew.

Rose, the fear that had seized her shattered by Piper's scream, watched dumbfounded as Alice's two nearest lads scrambled to aid her. Piper spun away before they could lay hands on her, so they settled for dragging Alice's limp form down the adjacent hall and into a bedroom. Melody and Figgin broke off their fight with Piper's daughters to join their fellows in protecting Alice.

Tamika, who looked battered but whole, aided her mother in standing between the Irish and the Order ops as the former retreated and the latter regrouped.

In the next instant, Rose found herself moving and speaking as much by instinct and rote drill as by conscious thought. She drew voice as she socked her subgun to her shoulder. "Retreat! Everyone out!"

"What?" Piper glared at Rose, her bloodied fangs shining.

"We're getting out of here while we can." Rose motioned for her team to back toward the exit, barrels out.

"We have them. Help me finish this."

"And expose my people to the fear draw again?" Rose shook her head. "To hell with that. We're retreating while we can."

14

OPEN ARMS AND COLD SHOULDERS

They chose to hide out in a motel on the outskirts of Manhattan called The Haskills Motorlodge. The place had probably been something to see back in 1960 with its ridiculous Art Deco awning set at an impossible angle over the drive-thru and the pendent chandelier hanging in the foyer. Much of the awning had given way to rust, and the chandelier's faceted crystals appeared yellowed with age, but the maids kept the rooms clean, and the place was off the beaten path, so they rented four rooms and settled in for the night.

Too keyed up to sleep, Rose sat on one of the room's queen-sized beds, chatting quietly with Olivia while Matt tried to catch some shuteye next to her. She had never mastered the technique of sleeping whenever possible like him. Given five minutes and a means of getting at least marginally horizontal, Matt would sleep, no problem.

"Is Piper answering your messages?" Rose gave up texting the vampire an hour ago for lack of response.

Olivia glanced at her phone. "Nope. She was pissed when we left her at the condo. We should give her some time."

Though Piper had escorted Rose's team from the building, she had split off from them the instant they reached the street. Her children followed after her into the shadows. Satterfield lingered for a moment as if she might stick with Rose before waving goodbye and running after her vampire hosts.

"She can be pissed all she likes. I stand by my call."

Olivia shrugged one shoulder, and though it obviously pained her, she nodded. "I think it was the right one. We were getting mauled in there. You all got sidelined by the fear draw, and I simply couldn't hang with Alice's goons. They were too fast, too strong."

"Don't feel bad, neither could I."

"I saw that. Looked like Alice was faster than you."

"Yeah, she was." Rose appreciated Olivia's brutal honesty. It was one of the reasons the two of them had grown close, but that didn't make it sting any less.

"I didn't think that was possible."

"Problem is, I was starting to think that way myself. It's been so long since I came up against someone faster than me, I forgot what it feels like."

"Feels like shit," Olivia quipped.

Rose chuckled quietly so as not to wake Matt.

"Well, I forgot what it was like to fight succubi using the fear draw." Olivia shivered for effect. "Reminds me of fighting David Lord."

"Only, it was like five of him. Melody drew fear, too. Makes me wonder who they're using for votaries."

"You're thinking there's a new fear factory somewhere?"

Rose shrugged. "If what Kraft told us is true, there might be hundreds of private ones all over the place, maybe thousands."

Someone knocked on the door, and Matt sat up, blond hair disheveled.

"Who's that?" he demanded, though Rose could tell he wasn't fully awake.

"Piper," said a voice from outside.

Matt rolled out of bed, pulled on a pair of jeans, and opened the door bare-chested. Piper and Grace stood there. The younger vampire made an appreciative "ooh" sound. Piper whacked her lightly on the belly, though she glanced once at Matt's muscled physique before returning her gaze to his face. "We need to talk."

Matt stepped aside to let them enter and shut the door behind them. He made a point of pulling on a t-shirt before joining the group.

Piper wore an expression Rose couldn't read—not precisely angry, but cold like the uncaring depths of winter. She didn't sit on the bed but stood at the edge, staring down at Rose, her lips fastened tight about her teeth as if to hold back her words.

"I think I know what you're going to say." Rose sat up straight to gain some height. She considered standing but decided that might not be the best course of action when facing a pissed-off vampire who could take it as a threat.

"You might be surprised," Piper said.

"Oh?"

"Mama thinks you were right," Grace drawled. "She told me all about the fight with the Irish and how they used the fear draw on y'all, only it didn't work on her or my sisters. She said you fought hard, but there's nothing anybody can do when they get their courage stolen. Mama—"

"Grace." Piper held up a hand to stop the girl's babble. "I swear the girl does go on, but she's right. I came here to apologize. I can't tell you how angry I am with myself. I shouldn't have pushed you to go after Alice after your people were nearly slaughtered. I don't know what a fear draw feels like, but I've seen it used twice now, and it doesn't look pleasant."

"Imagine hell and multiply that by at least ten," Matt said. "Then you're getting close."

"I should have realized your people couldn't recover from that sort of thing in a few seconds. I'm lucky you didn't run out of that building screaming. It would have served me right if you had. I attacked when I should have waited, and we all nearly paid the price for that mistake."

Rose nodded, pleasantly surprised and relieved by Piper's apology. It sure as hell beat arguing, but it didn't change some of the questions swirling around in her mind. Some things about the situation made no sense. "Why did you attack her, anyway?"

Piper blew air between her human teeth and shook her head. "She accused me of killing Barbara Griffith. I should have shrugged that off, but I let her goad me. It was a childish thing to do."

Discernment confirmed Piper's words for Rose. She spoke the truth.

Except.

Grace, who had been standing patiently to her mother's right, watching the conversation avidly, dropped her gaze to the floor when Piper spoke Barbara Griffith's name. A long strand of blond hair fell across Grace's eyes, and she absently pushed it behind an ear, but did not look up.

Piper lied. She did it so convincingly, Rose's votary-boosted discernment couldn't see through the deception, but her youngest daughter lacked Piper's many years of practice. Grace had been a vampire for a mere two years, and at twenty, she wasn't even old for a human. Not only did Rose detect the lie through Grace, she saw clearly that the girl detested it.

With an effort, Rose schooled her expression against her shock. Piper *had* killed Barbara Griffith. For what reason, Rose couldn't fathom. Perhaps to open a way for the Order to establish dominance within Society? That might make sense if Piper were immensely stupid or ignorant of how Society functioned. Infighting over succession wouldn't somehow make Society's elites more open to slinkers taking charge. And since everyone knew the Order had allied with Piper, should her actions come to light, blame for Barbara Griffith's death would fall on both sides equally. That would spell the end of their alliance, and possibly even their lives. Rose could well imagine Society elites using Griffith's murder to excuse hunting her and all her people down for execution.

Piper was no fool. She wouldn't take that sort of chance without good reason and forwarding the Order's bid for acceptance didn't fit that criterion. Rose could think of only one other goal that might entice Piper to kill Griffith—a simple aim that frightened Rose to her core. Piper wanted to destabilize Society for her own reasons, ones that didn't involve the Order whatsoever.

"Sun will be up in a couple of hours," Piper said as Rose's attention returned to the present. "We're going to get some sleep and then head home. Do you want to travel at night so we can coordinate protecting one another, and Olivia can stay with you? I wouldn't put it past Alice to track us on the road. She's not going to let this attack go unpunished."

Drawing more discernment and adding mental acuity to it, Rose tried to think fast what to say and how to act to prevent Piper from suspecting her inner thoughts. She shook her head slowly. "I'm not too worried about that. You bit her. That should keep her down for a while. Maybe, if we're lucky, she won't wake for a few days. She can't draw healing while she's unconscious, so her body has to deal with your venom the way a human would."

"I doubt it will be days before she wakes. My venom's weak. That's why I have so many children; it doesn't kill humans the way most vampire's venom does. A succubus like Alice might sleep a day, but she'll rouse soon enough, and when she does, she's going to be pissed, which means we all need to take extra precautions against reprisals. She'll seek revenge on us sooner or later, and with her temper, I think it will be sooner."

"All the more reason to split up." Rose turned to Matt, pleading for him to agree without showing it on her face. "In fact, I think we should rent a couple more vehicles and split up our teams. They can travel back in twos and threes."

"Definitely." Matt lifted his eyebrows at her but otherwise hid his curiosity.

"You're probably right." Piper took Grace's hand. "We'll be in touch. If you have any sort of trouble, call me. I'll make myself available, I promise."

"Same here." Rose stood and gave Piper and Grace each a hug, thankful for her draw on calm to keep her heart rate low. She followed them to the door and shut it after they left. Rose stood there for a long, silent moment, collecting her thoughts, wondering if she should include Olivia in what she wanted to say next, or save it and speak to Matt in private later. Olivia spared her the decision.

"Mother just lied to you," she said, her voice flat. "I think she killed Barbara Griffith."

Surprised, Rose watched Matt to gauge his reaction.

He nodded and stood up from the chintzy motel chair. "I suspected as much, but I wasn't getting that vibe from Piper. She lied through my discernment like it was nothing. I didn't know for sure until I saw how Grace reacted."

"You saw that too?" Rose plopped onto the bed with a relieved sigh.

"You thought you were the only one?" Matt asked, one corner of his mouth turned up in a half-grin.

"I was working up the nerve to tell you. I figured you'd say I had gone insane."

"The insane one is Mother." Olivia, whose skin usually ran pale, grew whiter still as the blood drained from her face. She threw off the covers to pace the room in her stocking feet. "What could she be thinking?"

"She's thinking about the future," Matt said. He leaned back on the TV stand, arms folded. He started to say more, shut his mouth, and began again. "Olivia, you've been living with us for months now. I like you, and I know Rose does as well. Sometimes, I forget why you're here. We're friends, but we aren't family."

Olivia stopped near the motel's dirty window. Wan light from a digital sign above the nearby highway washed over her, white on white, so she took on the appearance of a ghost. "You don't trust me."

"That's not exactly—" Matt began.

"You shouldn't." Olivia turned to them, her expression pained. "I wouldn't trust me in your place. I'm your treaty hostage, and the daughter of a vampire who killed your peoples' leader then lied about it to your face."

Rose crossed the room to take Olivia's hands. "We trust you. What Piper did, that's on her."

"But you can't know I'm not a part of it." Pinkish tears glistened in Olivia's dark eyes. "I might be playing you right now. How do you know I won't inform Mother about your suspicions?"

"Because you voiced them first." Rose squeezed her friend's hands. "They're your suspicions too, and I can tell they're tearing you up inside."

"At some point, we have to trust," Matt said. "My discernment tells me you're being honest."

"The same discernment that didn't work on Mother?"

"I don't know Piper. I know you."

Olivia began to sob, and Rose enfolded her in a hug. The vampire's blood tears would probably stain Rose's sleeping shirt, but that didn't matter.

"What happens if my mother has gone out of her head?"

"She's not out of her head." Matt put a hand on Olivia's shoulder.

Olivia lifted her chin to stare at him. "You said that before, but what else explains killing Griffith? It makes no sense. It puts us all in danger."

"Not if Piper gains enough power to threaten Society."

Rose nodded. "Exactly. She's not thinking about the Order gaining favor in Society and then eventually helping vampires in turn. She's planning her own takeover."

Olivia reared back as if Rose had struck her in the face, her expression morphing from shock, to introspection, to eventual realization in the space of five seconds. "Oh, God. Killing Griffith fomented chaos in Society."

"Enough to give her the time she needs to grow her coven queendom." Matt shook his head in disgust. "I really think she's planning to destroy Society."

"I didn't know any of this, I swear," Olivia whispered.

"We know you didn't," Rose said.

"We have to stop her." Olivia wiped at her damp eyes with a motel tissue. "I might not like Society, or how it treats my kind, but it's stable. If Mother destroys it, the entire government will crumble. That's not the sort of thing you can hide from humans no matter how much charm you have."

"You get we're talking about fighting Piper?" Rose almost said, "killing Piper," but reined herself in at the last second.

"Yes, and I'm not going to lie and say I like the idea. She's the only mother I've ever known. Whatever human parents I once had, those memories are faded. But she can't do this. She's putting millions at risk."

Rose nodded, filled with pride at her friend's resolve despite the pain it caused her. "So, we stop her. Question is, how?"

"We could try warning Society?" Matt said.

"And have the elites declare open hunting season on vampires?" Olivia asked.

"Slinkers too, probably," Rose added. "No. Society can't protect itself. Their bigotry makes them vulnerable."

"I'm not siding with my dad." Matt looked Rose in the eye, his lips turned down. "If that's what you're thinking."

He knew her too well.

"He has loyal succubi and Rubio's vampires on his side. We could do worse."

"No. We couldn't."

"What about the Africans?" Olivia asked, cutting in before Rose got a chance to clap back.

"Couldn't hurt to talk with them," Matt said. "They claim they've kept the Irish out of their territory for more than a decade. Must mean they know how to fight."

Rose shrugged reluctantly and at last nodded. "I'll give them a call."

"Good." Matt dusted off his hands as if that settled everything.

"But first, I'm calling the twins." Rose crossed to retrieve her phone. "I've got a story idea for them. If they like it, maybe I can win back some votaries."

15

FANGS OUT

Thandiwe Buhari asked Rose to meet her at the Thomas Brady Prescott library on Franklin Street in Richmond, Virginia. The location choice puzzled Rose until she entered the building. At 6 p.m., the library was nearly deserted. A handful of college students sat clustered around a table nearest the research stacks, chatting quietly or else jacked into tablets and phones. Otherwise, Rose saw no one besides two librarians behind a desk at the front.

A slim, muscular man dressed in a tan suit tailored for his physique stood when Rose, Matt, and Tanner entered the building. Rose was accustomed to meeting handsome incubi; their attractiveness, whether engineered by Providence or nature, served to make them more alluring to women—and men too when it came to that—but this particular incubus took her breath away. His broad chest and narrow waist gave him the look of an avid swimmer. That coupled with unblemished caramel skin, expressive brown eyes, and an infectious smile left Rose momentarily frozen in place.

"Rose Carver?" he asked, his voice low, his accent light but distinctly similar to Thandiwe's. His brown eyes turned golden when he grinned.

Rose swallowed and nodded.

"My name is Chibueze. Director Buhari asked me to escort you to the meeting."

A strong cloud of charm surrounded Chibueze. For a moment, Rose thought he might be trying to influence her thoughts, but no, the man simply exuded charm as a natural consequence of his existence. It billowed around him like steam rising from an underwater lava jet.

"Lead the way," Rose said, resolutely NOT staring at his strong jaw, chiseled shoulders, and taut backside. To her dismay, even his calves showed through his dress pants to good effect when he walked.

Matt shook his head when he caught her staring but then shrugged and whispered, "Can't say I blame you. He is pretty."

Rose took his arm. "But he's not you, love."

They followed Chibueze along a wide hall framed in stone and hung about with paintings by local artists. Some of them weren't half bad.

Tanner sidled up to Rose as they passed the last painting. "How much do we trust this Consortium?"

"I don't know yet," Rose admitted.

"I haven't seen any obvious plants watching or following us." Tanner glanced over his shoulder. "That means either they trust us, or they're better at concealment than I guessed."

"I think they're showing a little faith in us," Matt said. "They want the Order to side with them, and they're not willing to threaten that by pissing us off on day one."

"Could be," Tanner allowed, his gaze roving about the library's main hall. "Or maybe they suck at security."

"Not if they've been holding their own against the Irish." Rose knew Tanner loathed working personal security. He would rather manage the team outside, keeping watch for incoming threats, than babysit Rose and Matt, but she hadn't given him a choice. After the disastrous fight with Alice and learning Piper had played the Order false, she wanted someone she could trust, someone strong, at this meeting. She knew next to nothing about the Consortium. This entire setup could be an elaborate trap.

They passed through a doorway and descended two flights of stairs to an area set aside for meeting rooms. Chibueze ushered them into the largest of these. The placard next to the door read *The Cardinal Room* and bore an image of the red and black bird.

Rose stuttered to a stop just inside the door as an audience of more than two hundred twisted in their seats to stare at the new arrivals. Matt and Tanner likewise froze, their eyes wide.

Thandiwe Buhari stood behind a lectern atop a small dais at the front. She wore an African-style gown of emerald and gold matched with a traditional *gele* headdress that flared back and above her like the crest of some untamed and exotic creature. Thandiwe smiled, and Rose knew at once her expression stemmed as much from her guests' sudden discomfort as from pleasure at their arrival. The woman knew how to put on a show.

"Here they are now, my friends. This is Rose Carver, Matthew Snow, and forgive me if I mistake your name, young man, Tanner—"

"Watts, ma'am."

The crowd clapped politely as Chibueze herded the three of them to the dais. Two chairs had already been placed there, and he added a third to accommodate Tanner before taking a seat in the front row.

Rose, her heart pounding, drew calm to soothe her nerves. She had expected to meet perhaps five or six representatives from the Consortium, members willing to provide a rousing endorsement of the coalition's many benefits, not a room filled with people. Had Thandiwe brought the entire Consortium to impress her? If so, it was working. These sorts of numbers made joining more attractive, though she cautioned herself to avoid appearing too eager. She would need some convincing before committing the Order to anything, and she knew Matt felt the same.

After the tepid applause petered out, Thandiwe turned back to the crowd and cleared her throat. "Ladies and gentlemen, I know many of you dislike the idea of accepting the Order into our ranks. I admit, their application for membership wants in some respects, but I believe they would make a fine addition to our esteemed alliance. That is why I've invited their leaders here to argue their case before you."

Rose's eyes went wide. She turned a questioning expression on Matt and Tanner, who appeared equally stunned by Thandiwe's words. She raised a hand.

"Yes?" Thandiwe nodded at Rose.

"Argue our case? We're not convinced we should join at all. We came here to make that decision."

"Good." A man in the second row dressed in a fine brown suit shot to his feet. "I say you keep that decision forever."

"The chair has not recognized you, Sammy Wolf." Thandiwe struck the lectern with the flat of her hand.

"Thandiwe," Sammy said, stretching the director's name out in a plaintive moan. "You promised us a discussion, and now you tell me to be silent?"

"We'll have a discussion, but we'll do it by the rules. You want to speak, you raise your hand, same as ever. You understand me?"

"Okay, okay." Sammy held up one hand, the other across his breast. "But we are eager to speak."

"Show that eagerness with respect."

Cowed, Sammy resumed his seat. A woman two rows back from him stood, her hand raised.

"One moment, Nahla." Thandiwe turned to Rose. "Everyone gathered here represents one of our coalition groups. I will announce them for you before I let them ask questions."

"We didn't come here—" Rose began, but Matt cut her off.

"Thank you, Madam Director. We'll do our best to field whatever questions your members put forth, but first, may we have a moment chat before the meeting starts in earnest?"

Some in the crowd voiced their displeasure at the delay, but Thandiwe called them to order.

"Of course, you may. Take all the time you need."

"I promise we won't be long." Matt took Rose by the hand and led her to one side of the dais opposite Thandiwe's microphone. Tanner came along, and the three of them huddled with their heads together.

"What the hell is this?" Rose tried to whisper, though her voice came out louder than she intended. She felt the way she always did right before a firefight: spine stiff, muscles tensed for battle, her body filled with borrowed strength and speed she hadn't meant to draw.

"It's a test," Matt spoke in the clear, calm voice he used whenever Rose overreacted to a situation.

Sometimes that worked, and sometimes it pissed her right the hell off. At the moment, she couldn't decide which would prevail.

"They're testing us to see if we're good enough to join their little club?" Rose wrinkled her nose at the insult. "We have over two thousand members."

"Yes, they're testing us," Matt allowed. "But it's more than that. They want to know who we are. Are we snobs, only willing to ally with them because we're in need, or are we humble enough to appreciate what they have to offer?"

"We know they have numbers," Tanner said.

"I'll admit this is a fair-sized group, but—" Rose began.

Tanner shook his head. "Didn't you hear what the director said? Each person here is a representative for one of their member groups. This isn't the Consortium; it's like their ruling body."

Rose let her gaze wander across the waiting crowd a second time, her estimation of the Consortium's benefits realigning as her gaze roved across the many faces. Even if each one represented just a hundred other succubi, they would number more than two thousand, a conservative estimate considering Thandiwe had said the Consortium boasted members from many different countries.

"Exactly," Matt said, watching her expression. "I think we've been looking at the question of joining the Consortium completely backwards. If what Thandiwe said is true, they're the ones with something to offer."

The truthfulness of his words echoed in Rose's ears. After their failed attack on Alice, and with Piper going increasingly rogue, the Order needed allies it could trust. More than that, it needed allies with the strength to defend it against a rising tide of shadowy, indistinct enemies.

As it turned out, Matt's calm voice had worked. It usually did.

"Okay," Rose said. "Let's make our case."

"Are you prepared to go on?" Thandiwe asked as the three of them resumed their seats.

"May I ask a question first?" Rose broadcast her voice with a minor draw so people in the back of the room could hear.

"Of course. We encourage it, always."

"Does this body represent all members of your Consortium?"

Thandiwe nodded. "We are missing only two at the moment: the representatives from Chad and Grenada."

"And each member here represents more in their respective countries?"

"Thousands."

Rose watched Thandiwe watching her. She struggled to keep her face placid but knew she failed when a self-satisfied grin curved Thandiwe's lips. Humility weighed so much in that instant, Rose feared it might crush her. She felt duped, and Thandiwe's smug reaction wasn't helping. Rose wanted to storm from the room in a huff, or maybe draw speed and blow the door off its hinges on her way out.

She did neither.

Running belonged to her old self, her slinker self, the woman who dashed off at the first hint of difficulty or strife. Rose had buried that identity in the fear factory, exchanged it for a life of duty to others of her kind. She wouldn't go back now if a legion of fear-fueled succubi stood before her. So what if joining the Consortium meant smothering her pride and enduring Thandiwe's condescension? Rose's pride stood on the proverbial house of sand. Yes, she ran the Order, but truth told, they weren't a large operation, and though many of their members took their oaths of fealty seriously, an equal number did not. Slinkers had heart; they just couldn't always find it when needed.

And as for Thandiwe's smug attitude? Hadn't she earned it? She knew all along what the Consortium had to offer Rose and her little band of misfits. Rose hadn't even bothered to listen. Instead, she prejudiced herself to the Africans, ignoring their entreaties until the Order's need became dire. From her perspective, Thandiwe probably felt justified since the foolish American succubi had finally come calling after repeated attempts at setting up a meeting. And why shouldn't she feel a measure of satisfaction? She had been right. Rose had been wrong. Humility might weigh a ton, but it wasn't a patch on hindsight.

Rose straightened in her chair, turned her gaze to the crowd, and drew a deep breath. "We're ready to chat when you are."

They fielded questions from the Consortium's leaders for the better part of two hours. To Rose's surprise and relief, few of them showed Sammy Wolf's blatant distrust for the Order. Many, like Thandiwe, favored the idea of adding Americans to their group. They saw it as not only an opportunity to create close ties in the States, but a vehicle for enticing new members in the future. Many people knew of the Order's wins against the Indrawn Breath and Rose's personal exploits both on the battlefield and in daily life from the *Drawn* graphic novel. Adding her to their ranks could—probably would—woo reticent prospects. That idea seemed to warm the crowd to the Order's cause. Even Sammy nodded when Thandiwe pointed it out.

The subject of vampires, however, presented a stumbling block for the entire assembly.

"They are not like us," the representative from the Republic of Palau said. The thin woman wore a violet business suit and a small hat that accentuated her short hair. "They aren't meant to congregate. They cannot be trusted."

"Do you hear how prejudiced that sounds?" Part of Rose shrank from defending the Order's ties to Piper and her growing coven queendom as she called it. Despite Rose's suspicions, and the doubts of her most trusted friends, including Piper's own daughter, Piper might not have killed Barbara Griffith. Rose had no proof to the contrary, and Piper vehemently denied the allegation when confronted. They could all be mistaken.

Could.

Rose glanced at Matt, who nodded his agreement—she was going the right direction.

"A white American woman telling a room full of Black folk they're prejudiced?" Sammy waved his arms up and down at the ceiling. "That's one for the record books."

"I didn't—" Rose began, but Thandiwe cut her off.

She smacked the lectern with a resounding blow. "No more outbursts, Sammy, or I'll have you hauled out of here."

Sammy bowed his head, lips pursed in a conciliatory fashion.

With the crowd silent, Thandiwe turned to Rose and the others. "I understand your treaty with Piper helped you overcome the Indrawn Breath and destroy the fear factory."

"Yes, it did," Rose said, grateful for the defense.

"But I'm afraid I must agree with most of our members. Vampires are loyal to two things: their sires and themselves. We have seen it many times in all of our countries. Wherever the vampire is allowed to flourish, the nation suffers. They are a blight on the Earth. Their votary chains are too easily built and span family ties, giving them many lines of power for every one person they bite. Only their inability to easily reproduce has kept them from long ago usurping succubus rule the world over."

A large woman on the third row dressed in a pink and lavender skirt mated with a navy blue shirt stood, hand raised until Director Thandiwe acknowledged her. "That isn't so with Piper Ross. From what I've heard, she has many children. No one knows the exact number, but I've heard ten or even fifteen."

"This in a world where two created in one century is considered a miracle," Thandiwe added.

The crowd broke into scattered conversations, some heated, some loud, all urgent.

Rose needed to do something if the Order had any chance of retaining the Consortium's dwindling favor. She stood, both hands raised, and said in a booming voice, "We will not break a treaty we signed in good faith."

Everyone quieted, all eyes on Rose. Some appeared shocked, others impressed, but no one looked away.

"When my people—when I—had no one to aid us, when we

thought our last hope had died in Mexico, Piper Ross extended a hand of friendship. No succubus came to assist a group of poor slinkers whose families had been kidnapped and tortured. A vampire did that. I'll admit, things haven't always been perfect between our two groups, but we honor our promises. And isn't that worth something to you? What sort of members do you want in the Consortium? Ones who break their deals on a whim, or when a mishap befalls them, or when some more enticing deal comes along? I call that false faith. I wouldn't respect it, and I hope you agree that's a bad way to run a coalition."

Silence hung in the room as the stunned audience watched Rose minutely, probably wondering if her tirade had fully abated or if the mouthy American would start up again. Satisfied she had at least spoken the truth even if it ruined her chances of gaining the Consortium for a partner, Rose plopped back into her seat to wait. She had no idea what to expect.

"Good job," Matt whispered. "Even if we lose this chance, at least they'll know we stand by our principles."

"Thank you, Rose, for that impassioned address," Thandiwe said without a hint of irony or condescension in her tone. "I respect your loyalty. It is a rare thing these days. However, you must understand, should we covenant with you, our agreement will include the Order and the Consortium alone. We will make no treaties with Piper Ross or any vampire."

Rose wanted to argue, but she knew better. Matt was right. The Order needed this deal. If Piper had ulterior plans that included usurping American Society, they would need strong allies to combat her.

"We understand and fully agree," Rose said, glancing at Matt, who nodded again.

"Very good." Thandiwe motioned at Chibueze, and he hurriedly wheeled a flat-screen onto the dais. "We shall now take a vote for including the Order in our ranks."

"You're voting now?" Rose stared from the crowd to the director and back again.

"Of course."

"Doesn't anyone want to deliberate?"

"We just did, girl. Now we vote." Thandiwe held up her cell phone for the audience like a piece of courtroom evidence. "You'll see Chibueze has updated the voting app. You may now simply click the star-shaped icon to vote yes, or the—" Thandiwe stared at her phone in consternation for a moment and rolled her eyes. "Or the poop emoji for no."

The people laughed, no one louder than Chibueze, and set about tapping at their phones.

Thandiwe switched on the TV, which showed a real-time representation of the vote count in the form of a simple bar graph. The two columns stood almost equal, with about twenty percent of the final tally counted.

Rose squeezed Matt's hand. "I came in here on the fence about joining, and now I'm scared to death they won't let us. Am I being charmed out of my senses and I don't know it?"

"No. This is what getting your worldview turned upside down feels like. I'd laugh at you if I wasn't experiencing the same thing. We need this."

16

MANIPULATION

Rose looked over the crowd from a corner of the mobile stage and whistled under her breath. A sea of faces stared back, at least twelve hundred according to her team's initial count, with more people trickling in as the band warmed up. The smell of freshly cooked hot dogs and bratwurst made her mouth water, reminding her she hadn't eaten all day. There had been too much to do, too many last-minute details to hammer out for a rally of this size.

Three weeks of advertising, acquiring permits, and spending cash like water had culminated in transforming part of Atlanta's Centennial Olympic Park into a nighttime festival. Granted, the bulk of people in the crowd probably showed up to flout the open container law and drink a beer unmolested by the Atlanta PD—one of those permits Rose had acquired—but if all went to plan, they'd leave here convinced to vote for Gloria Torres.

"I told you an open-air venue was a good idea." Chuck Folsom, senior senator out of Arkansas, spoke with an even deeper southern drawl than Torres. "You make these things fun—an event folks enjoy—and the humans turn up in droves."

"They turned up because you're here," Rose said.

"I don't draw these kinds of crowds by myself." Torres shook her head, her eyes sparkling with delight.

Unlike most politicians, Chuck Folsom enjoyed an unheard-of approval rating in Congress, especially in the deep south, mostly owing to bills he wrote dealing with poverty and job protections. Whereas other succubus senators relied on charm to woo constituents in person, which would inevitably wear off, Folsom earned legitimate respect for his work, and he genuinely seemed to care about people, even humans.

Rose attributed Folsom's empathy to his upbringing. Folsom's father became a prominent banker in the 1890s, defying the ruling class in that business by innovating bank services. Because his father played the game well, the family managed to avoid the elite's wrath and slowly insinuated themselves into Society. Though Folsom benefited from this move, he never forgot his youth as a second-class citizen slinker in the early 1900s. Thus, when Thandiwe Buhari, whom Folsom had known for the better part of a century, and to whom he owed several large favors, asked him to back Gloria Torres's bid for a Senate seat out of Georgia, he contacted Rose and Matt immediately with a strategy.

Folsom, dressed in a dark suit with an American flag pinned on the left lapel, made a sound between a grunt and a laugh. "They didn't come for me; they came for the hot dogs. Free food's an attractive lure in the south, especially anything highly processed and stuffed with trans-fat."

The band on stage, some regionally famous group Rose didn't know, started in on a new song. If you could call it a song.

"I thought these guys sang country," Rose said to Veronica Briggs, a succubus stage manager on her crew.

Veronica covered the mic in front of her lips. "They are, ma'am. They do country rap."

"That's a thing?" Torres lifted her eyebrows.

"It's a big thing." Veronica gestured toward the crowd. "Look at them."

Veronica was right. Cell phones flashed as people either snapped pictures or simply held them up in tribute. Most folks were dancing, and many of them sang along with the lead. Rose had to admit, the man could belt out a tune.

"That guy one of us?" she asked.

Veronica shook her head. "I don't think so. Then again, he could be and just doesn't know it. You know how that goes."

"What's the band called?" Folsom asked, his gaze on the crowd, his expression calculating.

"Cypress Spring."

"I might have to use them on my reelection tour."

Prevailing wisdom preached against using live bands at campaign rallies. Audiences tended to get disappointed when politicians showed up to speak about tax plans when all the crowd wanted was more music. That logic held true for human rallies, but succubi could rely on charm to keep the crowd's interest high. Rose could feel that charm brimming over the stage from the dozens of plants she and Folsom employed for that purpose. She let it wash over her, sparking her own enthusiasm like a glass of potent wine. It brought a smile to her face and warmed her inside like good food and wholesome happiness.

Cypress Spring wound to a close, and the crowd roared. Matt, MC for the night, strode onto the stage from the opposite wing, cheering them as they exited. He looked sexy, dressed in a casual sport coat, no tie, his blond hair stylishly disheveled. Rose held a sneaking suspicion he had quietly changed up his wardrobe after their induction into the Consortium. Chibueze probably influenced that decision.

"Ladies and gentlemen, thank you for coming out to rally for Gloria Torres tonight." Matt's words carried across the greenway boosted by powerful speakers, inciting another cheer from those gathered. "Together, we're taking her message to Washington. No more corrupt career politicians in office, term limits for Congress, and sensible economic plans to get America back to work!"

That brought another cheer, and Folsom grinned. "He's not half bad. Matt ever think of running?"

Rose shook her head. "Not with his father's legacy hanging over his head."

"Oh," Folsom grimaced at his *faux pas*. "Sometimes I forget he's Kraft's son."

"It's my honor and privilege to introduce one of Ms. Torres's most influential backers and one of America's true patriots, Senator Chuck Folsom."

"Wish me luck." Folsom tipped a nonexistent hat to the ladies and marched onto the stage like a general going to address his soldiers. He shook Matt's hand, and the two of them exchanged words drowned out by the roaring crowd, before taking his place at the podium.

"How'd I do?" Matt asked the instant he joined Rose. He always struck her as cool, calm, and in charge. Seeing him nervous tugged at her heartstrings.

"Spectacular." She gave him a quick kiss.

"You were perfect," Torres said.

"Thanks."

Something in Matt's tone, the way he held himself, set off alarm bells in Rose's head. This went beyond mere nerves from addressing a crowd. He caught her staring at him sidelong and shook his head minutely, and she turned her attention back to Folsom. Whatever weighed on Matt's mind, he didn't want to say in front of Torres. That, more than anything, put Rose on her guard. They rarely kept secrets from Torres since she would, hopefully, be the one representing the Order in Society by next year.

Neither Veronica nor Torres noticed Matt's odd behavior. They were too busy listening to Folsom, who had launched into a towering speech about America's slipping greatness and how citizens might stem the tide. His words, combined with charm from every succubus in the area, roused the people to a controlled frenzy that saw them cheering uproariously between his every statement.

"Damn, he's good."

"And he's here for you, girl." Rose hugged Torres, careful not to smear her makeup or muss her perfectly coiffed hair as Folsom led up to introduce her.

Torres stiffened when Folsom called her name but plastered on a smile and walked toward the podium with confidence. Folsom shook her hand and exited the opposite direction. He had a flight to catch back to Washington.

"This thing has to go right." Matt slid his arm around Rose's waist, his gaze on Torres, who had begun her speech. "We need her to win."

"Have you heard something I haven't?" Rose kept her voice low so Veronica wouldn't overhear.

Matt nodded, his face grim. He glanced at Veronica before turning back to Rose. "Let's get some air."

He led Rose down the back steps to a narrow alleyway created by the stage's two-story backdrop on one side and Torres's prep trailer on the other. He handed her a Bluetooth earphone and called up a video on his cell. "I got this about twenty minutes ago."

The screen showed a close-up image of Jason Kraft, his brows drawn down, his lips pursed into a frown. His usually tame hair stood up in a rooster tail on the back of his head as if he had moments before been asleep.

Rose tapped the play icon.

"Matthew," Kraft said, his voice grave. "I know you don't want to hear from me. That's fine. But I think you should know what your pet vampire has been up to. She executed one of Alice McAleese's top lieutenants, an incubus named Barney Dolan, in the middle of Manhattan about an hour ago, and she wasn't quiet about it. She used seven of her full-blood daughters and an untold number of wights for the job. They didn't even try to conceal themselves. Footage of the entire fight is already on the internet. You know the state of Society right now. Whoever should have been policing for leaks missed this one completely. A couple of local news agencies even got in on the action, and their reporting is getting picked up by the international press. I had my assistant place a link at the end of this message. I suggest you watch it."

With trepidation, Rose tapped the new link, which switched the screen to a video in progress.

"Ladies and gentlemen," said a voice-over as the video cued up.

"What you're about to see is actual footage of a fight captured this evening near Radio City Music Hall. Nothing in this video has been digitally enhanced or altered. It was inadvertently captured by a drone pilot filming aerial shots of the city and delivered directly to our producer."

The digital recording showed a nighttime street, heavy traffic moving slowly along three lanes. At first, nothing happened, but then a figure, running faster than humanly possible, shot from the bottom of the screen along a sidewalk, dodging between people like a flitting shadow. Two more shadows trailed the first, traversing the screen so fast the camera momentarily lost all three. It reoriented in time to catch the first shadow slide to a stop in front of a brightly lit store with a green awning. As the shadow slowed, it resolved into a man, his features indistinct from this vantage, who clotheslined the next shadow, a woman dressed in a black running suit.

The perspective switched to a street view obviously captured on a witness's phone. It picked up where the last had left off, the woman in black hurtling backward. Bystanders screamed and scurried in every direction as the third blur entered the frame. It too resolved into the shape of a woman, this one likewise dressed in black. Rose immediately recognized Tamika even from behind. The curvaceous vampire ducked under her flying sister to tackle the man at the knees. She sank her fangs into his thigh as he fell, blood gushing from the wound to paint the sidewalk.

A different man appeared at the top of the screen before Tamika and her victim had stopped sliding along the sidewalk. Rose recognized him as well—Alice's lad with the star-shaped scar, the one she called Figgin. Moving with preternatural speed, he kicked Tamika squarely in the head, flinging her away from his fallen comrade. His victory was short-lived, however, because a swarm of wights scrambled into view with Piper at the fore. The bleached white killers surged toward Figgin, howling inhuman screams. He just had time to throw the fallen man over one shoulder and run, though Rose doubted he made it far. Even Tamika, her lips bloody, managed to gain her feet and rejoin the chase in less than two seconds.

There was more footage, but Rose switched it off. She had seen enough. "I guess since we couldn't kill Alice, Piper decided to go after her people."

"And to hell with informing us about it." Matt slid his arms around Rose. His embrace reminded her of what stability felt like.

"She can't lie about this one." Rose pressed her cheek into the hollow of Matt's shoulder. "Unless she wants us to believe someone in Society doctored the footage."

"I doubt she'll lie about it. She'll be proud. Oh, that reminds me. My dad sent a follow-up message." Matt opened the screen again.

Kraft's dour face reappeared. "You probably wonder if your supposed ally has gone insane, letting the world see her like that. I wondered that myself until Rubio suggested something I hadn't considered. Piper is far too clever to pull a stunt like this without reason, and anger alone wouldn't have been enough to motivate her. Even with Society weakened, she knows they'll come after her for this. But if her ploy works, they won't be able to touch her. She's already becoming something of a folk hero for vampires all across the States. They view her as a rebel against succubus tyranny. What she did tonight, not just killing Alice's man, but letting herself get filmed doing it, will cement her status in their minds. She already has less powerful vampires flocking to her banner, wanting to join her coven kingdom. After tonight, some of the old guard might well do the same. She spit in Alice McAleese's eye, a woman who scares most of the elites in Society. The vampires will love that.

"Matthew, it's time you and Rose joined us. I know you're smart enough to see what's happening here. Piper's building an army, one to rival us in every capacity. Rubio hates that idea every bit as much as I do. We're determined to stop her, and we'd like the Order to help."

"He's right, you know," Rose said, handing Matt his phone. "She wouldn't have taken on Alice again without using us. We barely escaped last time. She's up to something."

"We don't know that," Matt said. "Piper didn't take on Alice, she took on one of her people, and she won. Maybe she did it for us, for the treaty, and maybe she did it for other reasons. We can't know for sure until we speak with her."

"Are you forgetting about Barbara?" Rose pulled back from him, shaking her head.

"No, but again, we have no proof Piper killed her, only conjecture. She denied it, and my discernment said she wasn't lying, so did yours, for that matter. I don't want to trash our agreement until we know for sure what she's doing and why."

"She's continually breaking our deal, that's what she's doing." Rose folded her arms. "And how are we going to talk when she won't answer our calls?" Despite Piper's promises to remain in touch with Rose and Matt, they hadn't spoken in nearly a month, not since their disastrous attack on Alice.

Matt shrugged. "I don't know. I'm as frustrated as you. I'll admit, ignoring our messages is a dick move on her part."

Rose started to answer when her own phone rang. She switched on the video conference feature and smiled when she saw Olivia. "What's up, *chica?*"

Olivia grimaced, showing flat human teeth. "We've got a problem. I think you and Matt should come to the concessions stand."

"What problem?"

Olivia panned her phone to reveal three people standing behind her: her sister Grace, her only brother, Preston, and Valerie Satterfield.

17

SIGHT UNSEEN

Rose and Matt were forced to circle around the crowd. Even on the fringes, the press of people slowed their progress. The pall of charm hanging in the air kept the onlookers enthralled, but it also turned them into a wall of nodding, cheering obstacles when all Rose wanted was a clear path to the concessions stand. She resisted the urge to draw strength and barrel through them like a mini-bulldozer, but only by dint of utmost self-control.

"Rose." Matt took her hand and squeezed.

"What?" But she knew his meaning before the question left her mouth. It had been months since she first drew courage from her votaries during the battle for the fear factory. Doing so had filled her with power, more than regular drawing ever could, but it had likewise robbed her of emotion. As the draw increased, her caring for the world around her fell away at an equal rate. Since then, whenever strong emotions threatened to overwhelm her, she had the tendency to draw courage, or as the elites referred to it, draw fear. She never did it on purpose. It was like a bad habit she found herself returning to without conscious thought, a comfort that gave her power and dulled her worries.

She hated it.

"You're right," Rose said, squeezing back as they hiked through a copse of trees on the eastern side of the park. "Sorry."

"You have every right to be worried," Matt said. "I certainly am. Just don't let it overwhelm you."

At the outset of their treaty with Piper, Rose and Matt—mostly Matt—agreed to a hostage exchange. Olivia came to live with them while Satterfield took residence with Piper and her children. Satterfield's presence here without Piper could mean only one thing: Satterfield had fled. Based on the written agreement they all signed, that act alone nullified the treaty. Satterfield knew that. Rose could think of no one more conscientious or loyal than Valerie Satterfield except perhaps their deceased commander, Gunny Lipe. She would never endanger the Order without a damned good reason. That was what worried Rose the most.

They found Satterfield and the vampires huddled together near the main concessions stand apart from the few humans buying beer and funnel cakes.

"Rose!" Grace wrapped her in a tight hug. "We've got a lot to tell you."

"Not here," Olivia said, pulling at her little sister's shoulder to separate them.

Grace gave Olivia a withering glance. "Of course, not here. I'm not stupid, Liv."

Satterfield, her expression worried, gave Rose a tentative hug and drew back to meet her eyes. "I'm so sorry. I had to come."

"We know that." Rose pulled her friend into a second embrace. "Let's go somewhere we can talk. We've got a hotel."

Satterfield shook her head against Rose's shoulder. "Better not. She's been keeping tabs on you. Both of you."

Rose stiffened. "Seriously?"

"It's true." Preston, the only man Piper had ever successfully converted from human to vampire, moved to stand beside Satterfield and took her hand, an exchange that didn't pass Rose's notice. "She's got humans trailing you. Seven of them we know about, possibly more."

"Like private detectives?" Matt surreptitiously scanned the crowd.

"Yeah," Preston drawled. "The sort the Church of Scientology hires."

"Are they watching now?" Rose asked.

"I'm sure some are." Preston threw a questioning look at Satterfield, and she nodded. "We found a few skulking around here. I bit two. They'll be too sleepy to cause any harm for the next day and a half."

"And I charmed three more into heading back to their hotels for the night," Satterfield said. "It won't last, of course, but we'll be gone before they come back. Come with us. We've rented a van; we can talk there."

Rose turned to the stage where Torres had replaced Folsom. The would-be senator's voice rang clear across the park's greenway, echoing off nearby buildings. "Is she safe? Maybe we should stay until the event is over."

"Tanner and Myra will see to her," Matt said. "I think we should go. The sooner we know what's happened, the better."

Reluctantly, Rose nodded. They followed the others along a brick walkway out of the park and crossed the nearest street to a Waffle House where Preston had parked their van. They climbed in without speaking. Preston took the wheel and they headed for Atlanta's main perimeter highway, I-285. No one spoke until he had merged into the nighttime traffic.

"Mama killed Barbara Griffith," Grace said in a flat tone that nonetheless carried a hint of buried emotion. "Did you know that?"

Matt winced and shook his head.

"We suspected," Rose said. "But she denied it, and we wanted to believe her."

"I knew it the second she lied about it," Olivia countered.

"You saw it happen?" Matt twisted around to focus on Grace, who rested her head on Olivia's shoulder.

The young vampire nodded. "I was there. Mama broke into Griffith's house. There were ten of us in all. We out-charmed her guards and—" Grace broke off.

"She ordered us to kill them." Preston finished for her. "They were all succubi. We got the jump on them."

"Were you there, Val?" Rose asked.

Satterfield shook her head. "I didn't know any of this until two days ago. Piper kept me in the dark."

"Mother swore us to secrecy." Preston shook his head as he spoke, his voice bitter. "You don't know what it's like when your sire gives you an order. It's not charm exactly, but there's this compulsion behind her every word. I don't know how to explain it better than that."

"Even if you don't agree, you do what they say," Grace said. "Otherwise, you feel sick, depressed. You can't think for wanting to confess."

"We call it a poisoned tie," Olivia said.

"You're feeling that now?" Rose looked in wonder at Preston and Grace. They had countermanded their instincts to come here. Every moment must have been torture.

"It comes in waves," Preston said. "I think it's worse whenever we're in Mother's thoughts. We're tied to her by blood, same as we're tied to our votaries. Valerie tells me your kind sometimes feel things your votaries feel?"

"Spillover," Matt confirmed. "It's rare for us. Only people with huge votary counts get it."

"Like me," Rose said. With fans of the *Drawn* graphic novel spanning the globe, the number of people Rose could draw from was immense. That meant she enjoyed an incredible depth and breadth when it came to borrowing traits, but it also made her vulnerable to the emotional bonds forged between her and her votaries. Usually, that counted for little besides engendering feelings of happiness and heroism in her. The fans thought of her as a superhero, and those warm emotions made her want to become one. Once in a great while, however, such as during a hurricane, earthquake, or other natural disaster, enough of her votaries became fearful, angry, or nervous to affect Rose. When that happened, her borrowed anxiety became a liability. Spillover made the fear draw at once particularly nasty and alluring since the fear she engendered worked like a feedback loop. The more she drew courage away from her votaries, the more fearful they became and, thus, the more susceptible to that draw, all with the added bonus that Rose couldn't feel the growing fear, only the courage.

"Multiply that by about a thousand," Grace said. "Mama's busy a lot of the time right now—out fighting the Irish mostly—so she isn't thinking about us all the time, but don't I know it when she does."

"We broke our word to her." Preston changed lanes to pull around a semi in his path. "We promised we wouldn't tell what she's doing to anyone outside the coven kingdom."

"Outside the family," Grace interjected.

"But we don't like what's happening." Preston met Rose's gaze in his rearview mirror. "I love my mother. I believe in fighting for our rights, but the way she's going about it...I can't be a part of that any longer."

Satterfield took Preston's free hand, and he nodded at her in grim appreciation.

"Is there anything you can do to alleviate that feeling?" Matt asked.

Everyone grew still, the sound of the van's engine and tires suddenly deafening. Rose shared a look of uncertainty with Matt.

"Did I say something wrong?"

"There's only one way to break a poison tie." Olivia sounded like a child, her voice high and toneless.

"How?" Rose asked, fearful of the answer.

"Sever it."

"No." Grace sat up straight, her eyes wide. "We talked about that. We're not going to kill Mama."

"What if she gives us no choice?" Preston asked.

Grace turned her gaze to the window, her long hair obscuring her profile. "I can make her listen to reason."

"Grace, honey, you already tried that," Satterfield said.

"You confronted her?" Matt asked.

"We both did." Preston sat quietly for a moment, seemingly lost in the past. When next he spoke, his voice came out gruff with emotion.

"Mother's been quietly executing old guard vampires for months now."

"Not always so quietly," Rose said.

Preston nodded. "The ones you've heard about, she did that on purpose. She's become a beacon to the unattached—vampires without covens of their own. Your kind have always made it hard for us to congregate. They let some of the old guard build covens, but even those were small. Most vampires have traditionally lived alone for fear of succubus intervention. Mama's changing all that, and the downtrodden are flocking to her."

"So, her coven kingdom isn't comprised solely of you and your siblings?" Matt asked.

"Nope," Grace said. "Mama's broken up the east coast into ten regions with one of my sisters at the head of each, but a lot of the vampires serving them aren't family."

"Family or not, they're loyal." Preston changed lanes to pass an SUV and immediately exited the highway, his attention bouncing from the road to his mirrors.

"They're the ones she's been using to move against Society," Satterfield said. "Most of those executions aren't making the news. We don't know if Society is suppressing them out of embarrassment or if the succubi she's killing aren't prominent enough to rate full coverage."

"I doubt Society's holding back coverage." Matt shook his head, his jaw tight. "It looks to me like they've become completely disorganized. That's why the report about Piper attacking Alice's goons went public."

Preston turned west at the top of the ramp onto a busy freeway. "Thankfully, most people figured that for a hoax." "I get why Piper's fighting Alice." Rose adjusted her seat belt to lean forward. "But you're saying she's been killing Society elites?"

Satterfield nodded, her expression grave. "Three in the last week."

"That we know of," Preston said.

"Her network is growing. None of us know how big it's gotten. She has people everywhere now, and she's constantly sending orders to one of the girls or another."

They passed a slew of fast-food restaurants, strip malls, and gas stations on the outskirts of a small town feeding off Atlanta like a remora. Less than a mile from the highway, the state road narrowed to two lanes with heavy forest on either side.

"Mama's gone a long way fast," Grace said. "Society is just now catching on to what she's been up to."

"She's been strategic about it." Preston gunned the engine to pass a pickup despite oncoming headlights in the opposing lane. "Every succubus she's killed contributed to the power struggle going on in Society. The more they focus on that, the less they notice what some vampires are up to."

Rose twisted in her seat to look out the back window. Another car whipped around the truck Preston had passed, its headlights illuminating the rear seats. "Is someone following us?"

"I wasn't sure till just now," Preston said. "They were discreet on the highway. There's two or three of them, and they kept switching out every few miles, making me think I was imagining things."

A second car passed the pickup to assume a position behind the first, which was rapidly gaining on the van. The lead driver flashed the high beams as if signaling Preston to pull over.

"Any idea who they are?" Matt asked.

Preston, his face bathed in white light from the mirrors, shook his head. "No, but I can tell you one thing, they ain't human."

18

BEYOND HER GRASP

Preston slowed the van to turn onto a narrow gravel lane marked with blue reflectors but no mailboxes. It looked like a fire road, which Rose took as a good sign. The last thing they needed right now was a neighborhood full of nosy humans. The two cars followed, staying close. Though the moon was full, little of its light penetrated the thick canopy, leaving the road essentially black outside the cars' headlights.

"What's the plan?" Matt asked.

"We're going to confront them?" Rose wished she had worn her Kimber pistol. The model 1911 would go a long way to easing her fear about two carloads of attackers overwhelming her side.

"I don't see any alternative." Preston continued several hundred feet before pulling to a stop. He threw the van in park and killed the engine.

"Is Piper back there?" Rose didn't know how she felt about the idea. She wanted to speak with Piper, find out what she was thinking, but she got the feeling whoever was in those cars didn't have talking in mind.

"No." Olivia stared through the back window, her face illuminated. "I'd feel her if so."

"We all would," Grace said.

Car doors opened behind them, and shadows appeared between the vehicles.

"That's our cue." Matt pressed the button to open the sliding door next to him, letting in the muted scents of exhaust and pine trees.

He climbed out, and Rose followed. Preston and Satterfield joined them, with Olivia and Grace in the rear. Two figures from the other cars sauntered forward. At first, Rose couldn't make out their faces for the bright light at their backs, but once they passed the rear edge of the van, the shadows gathered, and she recognized them both.

"Tamika." Preston said his sister's name without emphasis, but the feeling in it brought her up short.

The young woman next to Tamika, whom Rose had last seen the night Piper duped her into attacking Felix Dietrich, stopped a step behind her sister, her eyes twinkling despite the scant light. Stephanie appeared even younger than Grace, though Rose knew with vampires, as with succubi, someone's apparent age meant little.

"You aren't supposed to be here." Tamika stood with her feet under her hips, her knees ever so slightly bent—a stance Rose recognized from thousands of hours of training for hand-to-hand combat. Hopefully, that meant she had no intention of drawing the gun holstered at her hip.

"Mother sent you to pick us up?"

Tamika nodded slowly. She lifted a hand as if she might rest it on her pistol but let it flop back at her side. "She wants you home."

"I think you know, we aren't going," Preston said.

"Preston, get in the car." Tamika hooked a thumb over her shoulder. "You and Grace both."

"You know what Mother's been doing is wrong." Preston made no move to join her, and neither did Grace, though the younger vampire trembled.

"The blood pain can't be comfortable," Tamika said, not unkindly. "You're both feeling eaten up inside right now, I know. Come home. We'll work this out."

"She's killing succubi." Grace stepped past her brother to confront Tamika and Stephanie. "She promised Rose we wouldn't do that."

"That was before the Irish came and started killing our kind," Stephanie returned hotly. "She—"

Tamika placed a hand on her sister's shoulder to quell her outburst. "Preston, things are happening that you don't understand."

"Tell me."

"Tell all of us." Olivia stepped forward to stand next to Grace.

"It's not for your ears."

"Why? Because I'm living with Rose and Matt? There aren't supposed to be any secrets between them and Mother. That's our agreement, isn't it?"

"No," Tamika said, her voice flat. "Our agreement is to help one another when in need. That's it."

Rose couldn't fault that narrow interpretation of the Order's compact with Piper and her children. Neither had agreed to divulge secrets to the other. But they had vowed to keep one another apprised of information pertinent to their treaty. In her estimation, the need to kill succubi fell squarely into that category.

"No, that's not it," Rose said. "We agreed to complete nonaggression on your mother's part until after the Order won representation in Society."

Rose considered joining Olivia and Grace but thought better of it. This was a family affair. Wherever their disagreement coincided with Order interests, she would speak up; otherwise, she felt it better to remain as inconspicuous as possible.

"We haven't forgotten," Tamika said haughtily. She stared at Rose for a moment as if considering something. At last, she said, "I can't tell you all I know, Mother has her reasons for keeping quiet, but I will tell you that everything she's done has been for the good of the Order and our Coven Queendom."

"How is murdering succubi good for the Order?" Rose drew discernment, her gaze locked on Tamika's eyes.

"I didn't come here to discuss this with you. I came to collect my family."

"We're not going back," Grace said. "We don't like what Mama's doing; we don't like taking part in it."

"And what about me?" Satterfield still held Preston's hand.

"What about you?"

"You said you're here for your family. Is the treaty off? Am I supposed to go back to the Order now? And is Olivia going with you?"

Tamika paused a heartbeat too long for Rose's taste. Her gaze darted to Preston, to his hand holding Satterfield's, before she said in a gracious voice, "Of course, you come with us. But Mother wants to see Olivia for a couple of days—fill her in on everything that's going on."

Whatever gifts Tamika might have inherited from Piper when the latter changed her into a vampire, her mother's talent for deception wasn't one of them. Rose's discernment screamed like thunder trapped inside her skull. Matt glanced her way and shook his head minutely.

Preston let go of Satterfield's hand and squared his shoulders. "We're not going anywhere with you."

"No, we're not." Olivia's hands flexed at her sides.

"Don't do this." Tamika looked pained, her mouth set in a hard line. "We're family."

"Go home, tell Mother we're not coming," Preston said.

"You know I can't do that." Tamika motioned to the cars parked behind her, and the doors popped open. Four figures climbed out. Three were wights, their skin pale as the dappled moonlight through the trees. The fourth was a male vampire carrying an M16 nonchalantly across one shoulder.

"Who's that?" Preston asked.

"Does it matter?" Tamika slowly drew her pistol and held it at her side as the vampire and wights joined her. "We have firepower, and we have wights. Get in the cars."

Heat rushed through Rose's body as she drew speed, strength, and dexterity. She could tell by Matt's expression and the subtle change in his stance, he was doing the same. She'd give anything for a pistol, not to mention body armor, but she had left those in the trunk of her car back at Centennial Park.

"Preston," Satterfield said, "maybe we should go. I don't want to fight your sisters."

"You do that, and we're dead." Matt turned his gaze slightly to catch Preston's eye. "Look how many bodies Tamika brought with her. There aren't enough seats for all of you, not unless she was planning on taking our van."

"You're planning to kill them?" Olivia demanded.

"Mother's orders." Tamika flashed her fangs, white and menacing in the scant light. "What sort of daughter would I be if I didn't obey?"

Rose had seen succubi move fast. As a matter of fact, that particular trait ran strong in her, but nothing she had ever seen or done compared to Tamika raising her gun and shooting Matt. He must have sensed it coming, his discernment twigging him to the danger an instant before the vampire moved because he managed to dodge aside as the gun barked. Rather than enter his heart, a fatal shot even for an incubus, Tamika's first bullet ripped through the right side of his chest, and the second caught him in the shoulder. Matt cried out, twisting as he fell on the gravel road.

Without pause, Tamika reoriented her aim on Rose, or would have if Rose had obliged her by remaining still. She instead launched herself at Tamika with every ounce of speed she could draw. No easy feat since Preston and Satterfield, who hadn't moved, stood in her way. Apparently, they were too stunned to take action. While that suited Rose fine in one sense—they were, in effect, acting as a screen for her against their sister who looked to shoot her—Rose was forced to bat them aside as she arrowed between them like a missile homing in on its target. She would have struck that target, too, except a wight slammed into her before she could get her hands on Tamika or her weapon.

Teeth gnashing at her neck as they slid in the gravel, the wight, a male whose scent could have put her off eating for a decade, pulled her close, his fetid breath hot on her skin. Heart pounding in fear and borrowed stamina, Rose spun the insensate monster to the ground so that she sat atop it. The thing was strong, but she was stronger. While it clawed at her arms, digging bloody furrows from her elbows to the backs of her hands, Rose snatched a heart-shaped rock from the grassy verge between the road and the forest. Relying on her speed, she extricated her arm from the wight's clutches and brought the rock down with drawn-enhanced strength. The blow caved in the wight's forehead, and it fell still.

Tamika's pistol fired twice, followed by the staccato sound of a semi-automatic rifle. Rose spun away from her fallen enemy, her every sense sharpened by borrowed energy and towering fear.

To her short-lived surprise, she found Tamika lying on her back in the gravel, either shot or knocked unconscious. Satterfield had her gun, which she was using to pin down and distract the vampire with the rifle who had taken up a firing position behind the closest car. He appeared incapable of hitting Satterfield for fear of accidentally tagging one of the vampires or getting shot in the head. While a powerful vampire with a huge votary count might survive such a shot, he obviously had no intention of testing his luck.

Meanwhile, having healed his former injury, Matt joined Preston, Grace, and Olivia in neutralizing the remaining wights and Stephanie. Matt had retrieved a tire iron from the back of the van and proceeded to pummel both wights with bone-snapping force.

Seeing her side so ably disarmed and defeated, Stephanie dropped to her knees in the road, pale hands in the air. "Don't hurt me. I give up."

"Stay put!" Preston yelled. He turned to the rifle-toting vampire who was still taking potshots at Satterfield, though she remained elusive. "Stop firing. You're done."

"Shut up! I came here to do a mission for the queen, and—"

Rose cracked him in the back of the head with her already bloodied rock, and he fell like a trash bag full of toasters. She took his rifle and walked over to Tamika. The beautiful vampire was still breathing, though it looked like someone had smacked her across the forehead with a tire iron.

"Got your revenge, sweetie?"

Matt nodded, his face grim in the moonlight. "I didn't like having to do that, but she gave me no choice. She's too damned fast with a gun."

"I think we better get out of here before she wakes up," Olivia said. "Those wights we killed weren't Mother's. They were Tamika's. She's going to be royally pissed when she finds them dead."

"Will you go with us?" Grace asked, and everyone turned to her and Stephanie.

Stephanie shook her head. "No. I'm loyal. You should be, too. Mother's been good to us, you know."

Though it obviously pained her, Grace shook her head. "Good to us, bad for our kind. Killing succubi isn't going to fix what's wrong in the world. We need to find ways to work together."

"You need help getting them in the cars?" Preston asked.

"I'll manage." Stephanie started to say more but didn't. Instead, she hoisted Tamika easily over her shoulder. "You'd better hope Mother doesn't catch you now. You know that, right?"

"Go home, Stephanie," Preston said.

"I'm telling her what you did here."

"Good," Rose said. "Tell her something else too, something from me."

"What?"

"Next time she tries to kill me, she better not send one of her girls to do the job."

19

BELLWETHER

Rose stood on the balcony of a rented house overlooking a rolling private lawn surrounded by a brick fence with thick forest in every direction, none of which made her feel secure. The Order had taken the home on the outskirts of Atlanta on short notice in hopes neither Piper nor Alice would know where they had gone. Doubtful, but better the precaution than remaining in the open. She had canceled two of Torres's scheduled rallies for today and was entertaining the idea of postponing more. It wasn't like Torres's glad-handing was raising her polling numbers, and with the threat of both the Irish and vampires looming in the wings, the danger outweighed the benefits. The sun dropped below the tree line as she watched purple clouds gathering above it, their bottom edges glowing an incandescent red.

The sliding glass door behind Rose sighed open, and Matt joined her at the balcony rail. He looked haggard, his face wan, his hair disheveled from sleep. With Olivia's brother and sister staying with them, he and Rose had decided to follow their guest's nocturnal sleep pattern, as had much of their crew. Of course, the switch couldn't account for the sum total of Matt's appearance. He was worried, and it showed.

Rose slipped her arm through his. "Our guests awake?"

Matt's natural lopsided grin turned up one corner of his mouth. "Grace is up. She's just waiting for full dark before she comes up here to talk your ear off."

Rose chuckled. "I swear I must get half my votary power from that girl. If ever there was a super fan for *Drawn*, it's her."

"Can't say as I blame her." Matt hugged Rose's arm, pulling her closer to him. "I'm something of a fan myself."

"You better be." Rose grinned and kissed him, thankful for something familiar and altogether soothing in a world gone mad.

"If she gets too annoying, you can always tell Olivia. I'm sure she'd be happy to rein Grace in if need be."

Rose shook her head. "No, Grace is the best. She reminds me not all vampires are monsters."

"Or two-faced, conniving backstabbers willing to sell us out for power?"

"Or that." Rose turned her gaze back to the gathering twilight. The air here smelled sweet, like a fresh-mowed lawn with a hint of apples. "Honey, why are we doing this again?"

"This, as in running Torres for Senate?"

"This, as in all of it? The Senate bid, working to get Society to recognize slinkers, the whole bit. I wonder that sometimes, you know? With everything that's happening inside Society right now, it just seems like maybe we'd be better off going quiet—live our lives and keep our noses clean."

"Become slinkers?"

Rose shrugged her free shoulder. "Yeah, sort of. But slinkers with a stable income from the businesses we own. It's not like we'd have to move from town to town all the time searching for work."

"You really feel that way?"

"Sometimes, yes."

"And other times?" He watched her with a blank expression, no judgment, only frank interest in her answer. She appreciated that, the way she appreciated him. His openness epitomized their love.

"Other times, I know it would never last."

He nodded and turned to face the distant trees hidden in the gloom. "Like you say, it'd be nice for a while. We could pretend we're normal: get married, buy a home, have kids."

Rose would have kicked anyone who pointed out the sudden flush that touched her cheeks or the uptick in her heartbeat, but even in the growing dark, she couldn't hide them from herself. Matt had never spoken about marriage or starting a family, not out in the open like that. Neither of them had. Managing the Order kept them too busy for that sort of mundane planning. Had it ever crossed her mind? She'd be a liar to say it hadn't. And if there was anyone Rose Carver would ever consider marrying, it would be Matt Snow.

"I'd like that," she said, her voice husky, her throat tight.

"Me too. But what happens in five years? In ten? Eventually, someone is going to get the upper hand in Society."

"If Society still exists by then."

"Exactly. And what are the options? The Irish, who by all counts are choking the life out of Europe right now? How about Piper, who seems hellbent on ending succubus rule altogether and installing some sort of vampire court in its place? Where would slinkers rate in either system?"

"But if we were settled down, maybe even suppressing our powers—"

Matt turned to her, his eyes gleaming in the light reflected from the house. "Would you want that?"

"If it kept us safe..." She met his gaze. "If it kept our family safe, maybe it'd be worth it."

Matt shook his head. "Imagine if you and I had a little girl. Could you send her out into the world without knowing how to draw? That plan backfired for a lot of slinkers when the government people in suits showed up to collect them for the fear factory. A lot of them didn't even know they were succubi, and those who did had such weak command over their powers it did them no good."

"Like Leslie." Rose stared at the lawn, her vision subsumed by memories of her friend who had grown up unaware of her ability to draw. Though she had died at the hands of Rose's sister, she at least died fighting, aware of her true nature, her true potential.

"And a thousand more." Matt pulled his arm free and slid it across her shoulders. "We'll never know true freedom if we skulk away and hide. And even if we somehow escaped whatever tyranny other succubi or vampires brought down on the government, could you really enjoy your freedom knowing there were others of our kind out there suffering, even dying, because we did nothing?"

"No. I couldn't."

"I know." He hugged her tight and returned his gaze to the darkened lawn.

A handful of peaceful moments flowed by with nothing but the sound of crickets and frogs and other nighttime choristers filling the air before someone tapped on the glass door. Tanner stood on the other side, holding up Rose's phone. She had purposefully left it in the bedroom to avoid taking calls. She should have put it on silent.

"I'm sorry to bother you," Tanner said when Rose slid the door open. "It's Emily calling. She—I thought you'd want to take this one."

"Thank you, Tan." Rose took the phone. Tanner shut the door and retreated.

"Hi, Emily. How are you?" Rose walked back to the balcony to include Matt in the conversation.

"I've been better if I'm honest. Is this phone secure?"

Matt looked puzzled but nodded.

"Yes," Rose said. "We've got a guy."

"Good. Listen, Rose, I know my mom and dad want me to help you, and I've been happy to do it, but I'm afraid I have to bow out. Sheila's orders."

"Why? What's happened?"

"She doesn't feel comfortable helping an organization allied with Piper Ross. Surely, you've heard what Piper's been up to these last few weeks? Killing succubi in their homes. She's tried hiding her tracks, but Society owns the FBI; we know the truth. The senator can't be a party to that—she doesn't want her name spoken in the same breath as the Order."

From what Preston and the others had told Rose, it wouldn't take an FBI investigation to link Piper as the culprit behind several succubus killings. Society elites could congratulate themselves all they liked for their superior sleuthing skills, but Piper had meant them to know she committed those crimes. She desired their fear, and they gave it to her on a platter.

Not that Rose would say such a thing to Emily. Those words would only serve to paint the Order in a worse light.

"We're no longer allied with Piper. She broke our treaty doing those things." Rose lifted her gaze to meet Matt's. "As far as we're concerned, she's our enemy."

He nodded.

"I'm glad to hear that, seriously I am," Emily said. "But it doesn't change anything on our end. Shelia cannot get involved with helping the Order. Your name is poison in Washington right now, and not just because of the vampires. I don't know what you did to piss off Alice McAleese, but whatever it was, mission accomplished. Does she blame you for Piper killing her people?"

"I don't know." Rose wasn't about to mention the Order's failed assault on the Irish with Piper's assistance.

"Either way, Alice has been on the move in DC. I wouldn't have believed it two weeks ago, but she's managed to secure a huge number of supporters up here."

"Is she charming them?" Rose couldn't fathom anyone following Alice otherwise.

"No. They're joining her willingly. They see how powerful the Irish have become, how much control they exert in Europe and the Middle East, and they want that here. A lot of us are tired of all the infighting and jockeying for leadership. We want stability."

"And you see the Order as the force that took that away?"

"Not me, I still believe in your cause, but the majority of Congress see you as a rebel faction that will do nothing but cause more chaos if you're recognized in Society. They're far more favorable to Alice than the Order."

Rose shook her head, a feeling of bleak inevitability stealing over her. But what did she expect, to somehow overthrow thousands of years of tradition in a few months? Succubus Society around the world evolved its two factions, elites and slinkers, gradually. Its rulers possessed a vested interest in maintaining the status quo. If slinkers achieved parity with them, or even a lesser sort of disparity, they might threaten the elites' hold on power and wealth. To the ruling class in America, the Order looked like invaders—wild, untamed marauders come to steal their birthright. For them, recognizing the Order would be tantamount to inviting a thief you've caught in your den to stay the night.

"I get how Society might imagine we're a threat to them," Rose said.

"It's worse than that," Emily countered. "You've already proven you're more than a threat. You took out Jason Kraft. You and I both know he's a vicious tyrant who committed horrible crimes, but there are a lot of succubi in this town who quietly yearn for the old days when he ran Society. You ended that rule."

"And they hate us for it," Matt said.

"Right or not, it's the way most people feel." Emily sounded apologetic but frank.

"Alice offers them the same sort of feeling as Kraft," Rose said, nodding as the thoughts coalesced in her mind. "The Irish might put a boot on American Society's collective neck, but it's a familiar boot."

"And one most of them won't feel," Matt added. "It's not like Alice and her people will chase down elite succubi and murder them in the street."

"They have been, though," Rose said. "From everything Preston and the others told us, Alice has been killing elite succubi who get in her way."

"No one here believes that." Emily's tone carried a note of incredulity. "First off, it doesn't make sense. If Alice is looking to woo leaders on the hill, why murder any of them? If she's found out, American Society will turn on her, and that's the last thing she wants. Irish Society might be powerful, but they could never take over here by force, not while maintaining our secrecy from the humans. No, the

Irish want a bloodless coup, and they're well on their way to getting it. The murders your vampire friends have committed only forward that goal."

Rose wanted to disagree. It made perfect sense for Alice to knock off a few succubi who stood in her way, especially with Piper's crimes screening her actions. Pinning murders on a murderer sounded like the perfect alibi. When it came time to tally the body count, who would believe a vampire who had freely admitted to murdering droves of elite succubi when she claimed a handful weren't her kills?

In succubus Society? No one.

Rose got the feeling Emily wouldn't hear such logic. If the closest thing Rose had to a friend in Society plugged her ears to the truth, how much more so the rich and powerful elites who had nothing to gain from listening to theories that ran counter to their deeply held beliefs or interests?

"You understand this is it for us, Emily?" Rose asked.

"I don't believe that." Emily sounded apologetic, and though it was hard to tell through the phone, Rose trusted that she spoke from the heart. "The Order's cause isn't done. You just need to bide your time a little longer. Wait things out."

Rose shook her head though she knew Emily couldn't see her. Emily might believe that sort of vapid platitude—she didn't know life as a slinker—but Rose knew better. Nonetheless, arguing the point would only serve to drive a wedge between them. Emily had called to break up, and Rose knew nothing she could say would deter her.

"I understand," Rose said. "Tell Sheila thank you for everything. She backed us when no one else would. We'll remember that."

Matt looked a question at Rose, his head tilted to one side, his brows tight as if to ask why she had given up so easily.

She shrugged and shook her head.

"I will," Emily said. "Your time will come. My mom and dad believe in you, and so do I. Just wait; things will eventually change in Society. They always do."

Rose tapped the end call icon to cut the connection.

"What was that?" Matt sounded urgent. "You just gave up there at the end."

"We weren't going to convince her to keep helping, and it's not even Emily's call, it's Sheila's. Both of them obviously view the Order as a lost cause. Nothing I could say would change that."

"We're not giving up like she said." Matt placed his warm hands on Rose's shoulders, his expression grave. "The Order's worth saving, and I'm not about to see it disbanded over the Irish or Piper."

"I'm not giving up, hon, but I know a lost cause when I see it."

"So, what are you thinking? I know that expression. You're brooding; you've got a plan."

Rose nodded slowly, her thoughts racing as she drew mental acuity to bolster them. "We have nothing to offer Society, and like Emily said, they have every reason to distrust us. No one's going to believe we're no longer affiliated with Piper and fighting to convince them otherwise while Alice is busy souring our reputation is useless."

Matt shook his head as Rose spoke, his lips compressed into a line. "Please tell me you're not suggesting we go to my father and Rubio for help. We've got the Consortium. We can go to them. We can—"

Rose placed her hands over his on her shoulders. "Not Kraft. Alice."

Matt's eyes widened, and he straightened up as if he had heard sudden, unexpected thunder. "What about her?"

"Hear me out," Rose said. "We've lost our battle for recognition."

Matt started to speak, to argue, but Rose overrode him.

"Emily is right; we've got nothing Society wants. In fact, they positively don't want slinkers taking part in government. With Piper off the reservation, we've got no allies outside the Consortium, and let's be honest, they're powerful in their way, but they have no clout in American Society. They've allied with us because Thandiwe sees the Order as her means of getting a toehold in the States, but I wouldn't blame her if she reconsidered that decision now that we're on the outs with Sheila."

"Okay, granted, but we've got more to offer the Consortium than we do Alice. Maybe you recall we tracked her down and attacked her?

I don't think she's apt to forget that. And how's Thandiwe going to react if we make some sort of agreement with the Irish?"

"Alice is smart or she wouldn't have made the sort of inroads she has into American Society." Rose slid her arms around Matt and pressed her cheek to his shoulder. His skin felt warm through his shirt. "She knows we have a large network of slinkers. Yes, she can make our lives hell, but that's a two-way street. We could make her little coup insufferable, attack her at every turn only to fade back into the shadows."

"So what, we offer peace in exchange for some sort of recognition?"

"Yes. You heard Emily; Alice already has the elites sown up. They're falling in line with her a little more every day."

"And you want to fall in line with them." Matt spoke without heat, his expression earnest. Had he reacted otherwise, she might have dug in her heels, but his respect for her opinions gave her the latitude to examine them without bias.

It took Rose a moment to order her thoughts. She understood Matt's point of view. More than that, a large part of her agreed with him. The fighter in her yearned to rebel against the Irish, against Piper, against Society, while the pragmatist knew she would lose that battle.

"I want our people safe. I don't see another way to accomplish that besides playing ball with the winning side."

"And you don't see the Consortium as that side?"

"Do you?" Rose pulled back to look Matt in the eyes.

He met her gaze for a moment before shaking his head. "They haven't abandoned us yet, so that's something, but no, they're not as powerful as the Irish."

"Especially not once Alice takes over Society. She'll have all the might of the US Government at her disposal."

"So, that's our plan, humble ourselves before Alice and beg for peace? That's going to shatter our treaty with the Consortium."

"Maybe not. I think we can talk Thandiwe into siding with us. If Alice recognizes the Order as part of Society, Thandiwe might see that as her best means of keeping a finger in government here. She has to see America is going the way of Europe, and the Order isn't big enough or powerful enough to change that. The best we can do is carve out our own bit of autonomy. Because what's the alternative? A genocide on slinkers? A shadow war we're destined to eventually lose? Even if we don't lose, we'll spend generations living as insurgents in our own country. I don't want that for our people."

"When you're broke, a penny's better than nothing."

"Exactly."

Matt turned his gaze to the now star-filled sky. He stood that way for several seconds before nodding once decisively. "I don't like this plan, not one bit, but I can't think of anything better. It makes me feel powerless—like the Order itself is nothing but a hollowed-out shell."

"We're strong." Rose squeezed her arms around his middle to emphasize her words. "But we're young. We can't go it alone, not yet."

"I've spent my entire life watching Society's elites give slinkers and humans nothing but breadcrumbs from their tables. They always drop just enough wealth and prosperity to keep the masses from turning on them. That's what this feels like. We're picking up the crumbs when we should be taking a seat at the table."

"It won't be forever." Rose sank her check back to the familiar hollow beneath Matt's chin. She could hear his heart beating fast.

"Okay then, I'm with you." Matt leaned against Rose, his warm hands pressed to her back. "We stay this course until we can come up with something better. Let's set up a meeting with Alice and pray to God she's feeling charitable."

20

ARGUMENT FOR THE DEFENSE

It's working, isn't it?" Grace sat in a leather office chair opposite Rose and Matt in the basement of their rented house. The house's owner had converted it into an office complete with a table large enough to seat twelve and a video conferencing system built into one wall. It made for a convenient space to call Thandiwe Buhari.

"What's working?" Rose lifted her eyebrows. "The teleconference?"

"Not that. The new Drawn storyline—the one the boys call Sketched. It's getting you more votaries, isn't it? Olivia told me you were growing weaker the last little while, but you looked awesome when we fought Tamika."

"Grace!" Olivia smacked her younger sister's arm. "You don't go telling people what you've been told in confidence. And I never said she was growing weak."

"I said weaker." Grace cut her eyes at Olivia as if annoyed by the interruption. "And you never said not to tell Rose."

"It's fine," Rose said. "I'm not offended."

"It's just...I know it's taboo for a succubus to talk about her votary count." While Olivia meant her words for Rose, she stared at Grace to hammer home the point.

"I'm a slinker. I don't care about that sort of thing. It doesn't bother me. And yes, Grace, the new storyline is working. I lost quite a few votaries when Drawn diverged from my real life, it's nice getting some back."

"Don't get me wrong," Grace said, "but I'm not thrilled about the new line. I like the regular one's twenty-first century civil war stuff, and how a lot of humans know about vampires and succubi. Compared to all that, the new stuff is kind of..."

"Boring?" Rose grinned at the teenage vampire.

"I was going to say, 'tame.'"

"I can see that, but it's my real life at least, and according to the twins, it's selling well."

Though Rose had worried Luke and Brendan would find her idea for a new graphic novel based on her current life dull, as Grace obviously did, they had glommed onto the concept. Their fan base for *Drawn,* steeped in the idea of conspiracy theories in which powerful succubi ran the American government, must have agreed. They loved that Luke and Brendan had deviated from Rose's real life when it became nothing but strategy meetings for Torres's campaign and endless phone calls to secure rally venues or order catering for events. To keep sales flowing, the twins had been forced to invent a story that invigorated their core readers.

Rose had understood at the time, just as she did now, the need for that deviation. *Drawn* might have died otherwise. Unfortunately, the change cost her in votary count. How much, she couldn't say, but enough so she felt it whenever she taxed her powers as she had in the fight against Alice. She missed those votaries, but had she expected to keep them forever? Of course, her fame would eventually fade; that was its nature. She had accepted that reality, even come to terms with it as one might the slow decline of health with age.

But with Piper's defection, the Irish's encroachment on Society rule, and Rose's struggle to keep the Order not just relevant but safe, her life had once again become fodder for comic fans, enough to warrant an all-new graphic novel series: *Sketched.* She needed the votaries, and the new line provided them.

"I'm not saying I hate it." Grace held up a hand as if to stave off an attack.

"You shouldn't," Olivia said, her tone dry. "You're in it."

"As I should be. I'm a teenage vampire; who wouldn't want to read about that?" Grace flashed her fangs at Olivia, who rolled her eyes and shook her head. "I'm just saying it's all politicized and stuff where Drawn's got lots of you kicking ass the way you always have."

"A lot of people like political intrigue," Matt said. "That's my favorite type of novel to read."

Grace shrugged one shoulder. "To each their own, I guess. I think you'd get more votaries if you went after Alice again, or maybe took on some of the elite succubi in Society."

"Or fought Mother?" Preston, who sat on Rose's right with Satterfield next to him, leaned forward as if challenging Grace to refute him.

"No," Grace said, frowning. "You know I don't want that."

A punctuated buzz filled the air before anyone else could speak. It was accompanied by a phone icon's appearance on the blank wall across from them, cast there by an overhead projector.

Rose steeled herself, drawing calm mixed with wakefulness and discernment. She wanted every chance to make this call go well.

"Ready?" Tanner Watts held up the video conference system remote, one eyebrow raised at Rose.

She nodded, and he opened the call. Thandiwe Buhari's mahogany face appeared on the wall. For once, she wore no hat. Her black hair, straightened into wavy streamers, cascaded to her shoulders. She looked like a supermodel come to hawk the next big thing in cosmetics she would never need. Her eyes darted back and forth for a moment as she scanned the image on her side of the call, taking in all the people seated at the table. Though her expression changed little, Rose could tell Thandiwe noticed not all of them were succubi.

"Good evening, Thandiwe," Rose said. "It's good to see you."

"And you, Rose. I'm glad you arranged this call; I've been meaning to speak with you for some days now." She narrowed her eyes. "I see some of Piper's children have joined us."

Rose ignored the chilly tone in the other woman's voice at that pronouncement. She expected nothing less, given the Consortium's collective prejudice against vampires. The fact that Thandiwe recognized Preston and Grace as Piper's children, however, gave Rose pause. Thandiwe had seen Olivia in Rose's presence several times, but Rose had assumed this was a first meeting for the others. What did it mean that Thandiwe knew them on sight? Rose found that revelation troublesome, and from the look on Preston's face, so did he.

"I asked them here because I'd like their input into our discussion." The calmness Rose drew from her votaries kept her voice from warbling but did little to quell her worries. She long ago accepted that calm wasn't one of her best traits, whether her own natural variety or that she pulled from fans, but it at least took the edge off her nervousness.

Thandiwe's lips compressed into a flat line, but she nodded. "Very well."

"I'm certain you've heard our treaty with Piper Ross has unraveled," Rose said.

"From my own sources, yes," Thandiwe said. "Curiously, I didn't hear it from you, Rose. I would have expected you to share that sort of news with your allies in the Consortium."

Tanner stiffened in his chair, as did Myra seated next to him, but Rose maintained her composure. She had anticipated not only the veiled accusation but Thandiwe's subtly indignant tone.

"I'm sorry I didn't call you immediately," Rose said without missing a beat. "I'm sure you can appreciate how disorganized things have been around here the last few days. We had to suspend Gloria Torres's campaign, see to our people's safety and that of our guests, and generally try to prepare for unpredictable outcomes."

"Yes." Thandiwe dipped her chin in acknowledgment. "I understand your concerns."

"Then you also understand our situation." Rose stared into the camera mounted on the wall, her expression earnest, her voice as compelling as she could make it without overtly using charm against Thandiwe. "Our chance of gaining favor within Society at this point is, I think, nil. We're at odds with the Irish who, by all accounts, have convinced a large number of American Society elites to join their side. And Piper's rogue antics have estranged us to any others who might have considered allying with us."

"I agree." Thandiwe seemed to choose her next words carefully, her dark eyes roving over her audience. "Can you not convince Piper to stop her attacks on prominent vampires and succubi?"

Preston shook his head. "My mother has an agenda. She won't be convinced to change it for anyone. Believe me, I've tried. She'd rather break her treaty with the Order than adjust her plans."

Thandiwe's lips drew down at the corners, but she nodded. "That is unfortunate."

"And it brings us to the reason for this call," Rose said, mentally hardening her resolve in anticipation of her next words. "Thandiwe, I'm no politician. I'm a waitress who spent most of her life on the run from Society. I don't know the right way to say things besides saying them directly."

Thandiwe lifted an eyebrow. "In my estimation, that is the right way."

"Good. Then I'll say what's on my mind: I believe you might be reconsidering your treaty with the Order now that our chances of joining Society have dried up."

"No. The Consortium honors its promises. Who would we be otherwise? Our organizations made a pact. We will keep our end."

Rose and Matt shared a glance as she nodded and squeezed her hand under the table. They had planned this moment together. While Rose had remained cautiously optimistic about the Consortium's loyalty, Matt had voiced concerns. For once, she had been right, and from the expression on Matt's face, he was more than glad of it.

"Thank you," Rose said. "That means more to us than you know. We'd worried all our allies might abandon us."

"We are concerned, of course." Thandiwe held up one perfectly manicured finger. "There are some who question what contribution the Order can still make to our cause when you've been so compromised."

"We understand," Rose said. "In truth, we both know the Order can offer next to nothing the Consortium needs right now. That's why we'd like to discuss ways to increase our value. One way in particular."

"I'm listening." Thandiwe sat back in her office chair, her expression inscrutable.

Rose let her gaze drift from Matt to the others gathered around her, the people relying on her to keep them safe. Their confidence strengthened her resolve. "Because we see no way to stop the Irish takeover that's already happening in America, we believe our best chance at surviving the coming decades is to join them."

Thandiwe's eyes widened. and she drew in a breath as if slapped. "Tell me you're joking."

"We see no alternative," Matt said. "Alice has secured support in our government we could never hope to match, especially with our known ties to Piper's coven kingdom."

"The Irish are our enemy." Thandiwe leaned forward, her brows drawn together. "They are merciless. They've killed our people by the thousands in Europe and the near east."

"And they'll do the same here unless we do something about it," Rose said. "Tell me, Thandiwe, why did you ally the Consortium with us?"

"Because I saw in you a like-minded leader. You wanted independence, not enslavement, and you were willing to fight and die for it."

"You wanted a chance to influence American Society from the inside." Rose met the other woman's eyes, defying her to contradict her words.

"Of course, that was part of my motivation. I thought with the right help and encouragement, you could join Society."

"And bring the Consortium with us."

Grudgingly, Thandiwe nodded once. "Yes."

"I don't blame you," Rose said. "It's a practical plan, one I would have used had I been in your place. But it's not working. We, collectively, need a new plan, one with a chance of success."

"I take it you have come up with such a plan?"

Rose nodded. "We have almost nothing to offer the Irish. Alice has much of Society sewn up, they'll give her whatever she needs or even asks for, but they're the elite. Their kind were bound to fall in line behind some leader regardless. It's their way. But it's not the slinker way. We in the Order could make life a living hell for the Irish. We have a vast network of succubi adept at hiding amongst the regular human population. We could use that network to worry and harass the Irish for a century if we wanted. They might kill a few of us, but if modern terrorism has taught us anything, it's that there are always new volunteers willing to fight for the cause."

"That is your offer? To forego launching an insurgency against Society in exchange for some sort of official status?"

"It's a way in, Thandiwe," Rose said quietly. "We'll demand recognition for our people and a voice in how Society is governed."

"And where does the Consortium fit into this proposed deal?"

"If we negotiate a place for the Order, that spot will include the Consortium. You'll have your influence within Society, just not quite the way you had hoped."

"I don't like it," Thandiwe said. "How am I supposed to stomach making nice with the Irish in America when they are fighting a secret war against the Consortium in nearly every other nation?"

"We sue for peace," Matt said.

"Why would Alice McAleese ever accede to these demands? As you've said, she has your Society in her hip pocket. Yes, I see how your threat of guerilla warfare might give her pause, but in the end, I believe she will welcome the fight in exchange for the boon of controlling the American government."

"Not when we tell her every vampire in North America will side with us in the fight," Rose said.

"But you said your agreement with Piper is broken." Thandiwe looked perplexed.

"Does Alice know that?"

"She is well-informed. If I heard the news, I assume she has as well."

"We'll have three of her children with us to say otherwise."

Thandiwe opened her mouth to speak but hesitated. She tilted her head to one side, and her lips parted in a grin. "I see, but what if Alice has heard these children defected from their mother to your side?"

"We'll say Piper and we planted that rumor to obscure our true intentions—we did it to make Alice think us weak back when we believed we might defeat her," Rose said. "Now, we see our only chance at survival is to join her, and we're bringing Piper and the Consortium with us."

"So, you will tell Alice a half-truth? What happens when she discovers the lie?"

"We admit there was a breakdown in our alliance with Piper shortly after joining Alice's side," Rose said with a shrug.

"Or perhaps we stage one," Matt said.

"At some point, we'll have to deal with Mother." Preston turned his gaze from Thandiwe to his sisters. "She's out of control. I'd rather do that with the help of our combined forces than alone with just the Order. She's growing more powerful by the day."

"And you're certain Piper hasn't tricked you, Rose, by sending her children into your house?" Thandiwe asked. "What if all three turn against you?"

"I have my reasons to trust them." Rose met Satterfield's eyes, and the beautiful blonde nodded fervently.

Thandiwe sat silent for nearly ten seconds, her eyes unfocused, no doubt drawing discernment to analyze the Order's proposal. "What part would you have the Consortium play in all this?"

"We want you there for the negotiation," Matt said. "Not only because we'll need your input, but as backup if things go wrong."

"Wrong as in your previous attempt to kill Alice McAleese?" Thandiwe stared at them with a dry expression.

"Yes, exactly," Rose said, unabashed by the other woman's accusation. She leaned forward, elbows on the table. "It's a good opportunity, Thandiwe, probably the best any of us is going to get. We demand a place at the seat of power and then bide our time, waiting for the chance to oust the Irish when the time is right."

"Capitulate now, fight later?"

"Survive now; plan for later."

Thandiwe laughed. "Very well, you've convinced me. When do we meet?"

21

APPEASEMENT

They made arrangements to meet Alice in an abandoned playground on the outskirts of DC after nightfall. The location made sense to Rose. Who wanted humans, especially the police, to stumble upon a meeting between succubi and vampires? The time, however, puzzled her. Why would Alice McAleese, by all accounts a shrewd negotiator and tactician, afford Rose the opportunity to bring vampire allies along? She hadn't even argued the idea.

"You're quiet." Matt sat next to Rose in their rented van, scanning the darkened playground. Alice had agreed, without complaint, to let the Order's security detail inspect the meeting place ahead of time. Shadowy figures moved through the trees and overgrown brambles, flashlights scanning back and forth.

"Going over what I should say."

"Say what we practiced, and you'll be fine. Alice isn't stupid. She might be angry with us, but a leader like her knows a good deal when she hears it. She wants control in the States, not a hundred years of insurrection."

"Why did she choose to meet us at night, do you suppose?" Rose turned to watch Matt's profile.

He shrugged. "Probably the best time for her. She's busy wooing Society elites all day."

"But why give us an advantage? We could have Piper with us for all Alice knows."

"Maybe Alice heard we're on the outs with Piper, so she isn't worried about that."

Rose looked him in the eyes. "That doesn't make you nervous?"

"No." He drawled, favoring her with his lopsided grin. "I'm scared as hell."

Rose chuckled, heartened by his familiar humor. It did her good.

"It's going to be fine," Matt said. "I believe in your plan—I believe in you. We're doing the best thing for our people."

He leaned in and kissed her. The surprise of it mixed with fierce love did more to bolster Rose's resolve and belief in herself than any words ever could.

"Thank you," she said. "I needed that."

"I love you." Matt had said those words many times in the last several months, so often they had somewhat lost their meaning, but not this time. He pressed his forehead to hers. "When this is over, I want to have a real talk—about our future, about the future of the Order. It's been a while since we did that."

"Okay," she whispered. Rose knew he wasn't proposing a discussion about finances or how to reach new slinkers. He wanted to talk about the sorts of events that involved rings and white dresses. Her heart gave a little lurch in her chest at the thought, but she quelled it with a stiff draw on calm. She didn't have time for that sort of thing, not now, not with the entire Order on the line.

"I know," Matt said when he saw the look on her face. "Not now, but soon."

"Soon."

Car headlights momentarily lit the rental, and a large sedan pulled into the space beside them, its tires popping and crunching over broken asphalt long ago churned to gravel. Chibueze climbed out first on the passenger's side, followed immediately by Sam Wolf, who had been driving. The two of them scanned the area for a moment before Chibueze opened the rear door for Thandiwe.

"Here we go," Matt said quietly and opened his own door.

Rose followed him out to greet the newcomers. The air outside was refreshingly cool for late May, a welcome feeling considering the armor she wore underneath her clothes.

"Thank you for being here." Matt clasped Thandiwe's hand in both his own, his smile warm and genuine.

"We never leave a member of the Consortium to face danger alone," Thandiwe said as Rose took her turn shaking hands.

Four SUVs and a small bus had pulled in with Thandiwe's car and a steady stream of people dressed in black filed out of them and into the park.

"How many people were you able to bring?" Rose hoped the older succubus wouldn't take offense at the question, but at this point, her need to know outmatched her concern for etiquette. The Consortium director had been tacit with the details of how much support she could lend leading up to this meeting.

"Twenty," Thandiwe answered without pause. "I took the liberty of having my security chief report directly to your Tanner Watts."

Twenty. It was more than Rose had hoped and yet still seemed too few, even added to her own forty-three. She wanted insurance against Alice's forces should things devolve tonight. With enough bodies gathered on the Order's side, Alice would think twice about fighting. Worst case, should their peace talks break down, the two sides could simply walk away without anyone getting hurt. Or so Rose hoped.

"Where are we meeting?" Thandiwe asked. "Surely not in this broken-down car park."

"Alice didn't give us many details, only the address." Matt gestured toward a tree-lined expanse of grass that had once been a playground. "Do you think she meant for us to meet her there?"

"It's covered in dew," Rose said. "No thanks." Though she could see only a handful of their combined forces standing guard out there, she knew the rest wouldn't have gone far. Those positions gave an excellent view of the defunct lot. Still others, mostly Thandiwe's people, stood nearest the entrance, sub-automatic rifles strapped to their shoulders.

Rose wore a small body cam in a fanny pack across her midriff, its forward-facing lens tilted to capture everything in front of her. Though Brendan and Luke tried to insist she employ several drones to follow her interactions with Alice, Rose had forced them to settle for the pack alone. She doubted Alice would look favorably on having the contraptions buzzing overhead. Rose wasn't about to risk this meeting even for the sake of her votaries.

Strident voices caught the group's attention, and they all turned in the direction of the park. To Rose's surprise—and that of her forces judging by their reactions—more than a dozen shadowed figures had appeared in the park without warning. The plug in her right ear buzzed with excited, angry voices exclaiming their shock at the sudden intrusion.

"Enough!" Tanner Watts' voice cut through the chatter. "Observe radio discipline. Silence unless you have significant intel to pass. Teams Alpha and Gamma, slowly make your presence known. All others remain behind cover awaiting orders."

A shorter figure, her shape decidedly feminine, led the group of newcomers. Rose counted six of them, including the female whom she took for Alice McAleese, though Rose figured the chances Alice had brought so few guards along for this negotiation hovered somewhere around the zero percent mark.

The newcomers approached the parking area slowly though they all walked as if they owned the world. None of them carried a firearm so far as Rose could see. That, like their numbers, was probably a bluff. Rose doubted Alice's people went anywhere without weapons. The five men at Alice's back wore cheap suits with ties and broad lapels. They reminded Rose of slum lords come to collect back rent.

Determined to hide her surprise at the newcomers' ability to slip through her defenses, Rose stepped forward, keenly aware of the Kimber pistol resting in a concealed hip holster at her side. Her draw on calm kept her heart out of her throat but could do little to dry her palms. She resolutely did not wipe them on her jeans.

Alice stopped short of the asphalt, her blond hair rendered white by the distant glare of streetlights. "Do you know how I found success taking over societies in my home country and beyond?"

Rose stopped as well, taken aback by the abrupt question. She shook her head, nonplussed.

"By doing exactly what you have done here." Alice spread her arms. "I empowered the lowborn. I gave them a voice—even better, I gave them guns. A thousand years of pent-up anger and resentment boiled in their breasts, and I set it loose. The upper class in Ireland and England didn't know what hit them. They had never imagined an uprising like the one we brought to their doors. Yes, they were powerful, but we had the numbers."

"Then you understand what you're facing here in the States." Matt kept his voice even, but Rose could hear the fervor beneath it.

"I do that, Matthew Snow. Otherwise, I wouldn't have come here tonight—I wouldn't have agreed to meet you at all."

"Are we negotiating here?" Rose had no problem talking in the open—she'd take that over some stuffy office anytime—but these weren't the environs she had imagined for peace talks with a foreign invader.

"Negotiating?" Alice's accent rang heavy on the word. "Is that what you think we're doing here?"

"What would you call it?"

Alice turned aside slightly, her gaze darting to a group of shadowy figures heading their way from the park.

"What the hell?" Tanner's voice rang over the shared channel broadcast into Rose's ear. She had rarely heard the usually jovial man sound this frustrated. "Where are they all coming from? How'd we miss them in our sweeps?"

"Charm." Chibueze pointed in the general direction of the newcomers. "One, perhaps more, of the Irish are powerful charmers—strong enough to hide themselves and their soldiers from us."

"Just now figuring that out, are you?" Alice asked, her pretty lips drawn to one side in a smirk.

Rose frowned. She hadn't felt a thing. Though she excelled at drawing physical traits like dexterity, speed, and strength, she was no slouch when it came to charm, and yet she hadn't felt even the smallest amount of it affecting her thoughts.

But that was the giveaway, wasn't it? Always amongst succubi, she could feel the tingle of charm brushing her awareness. Most of her kind couldn't suppress their charm if they tried. It boiled out of them like sweat in a sauna. Except now, that constant susurration was gone. Somehow one, or perhaps dozens, of Alice's people were suppressing the natural charm Rose should be feeling. Instead of the reassuring tingle she expected to find amongst other succubi, she felt an absolute void—a nothingness like the silence of an empty house.

Rose clenched, a technique that allowed her to shut herself off from outside influence. Instantly, her vision cleared, though she hadn't realized it was cloudy. She couldn't draw her own powers while clenching against outsiders, but she could at least feel certain no one was manipulating her. She glanced at Matt and saw, to her satisfaction, that he too appeared suddenly more aware, his expression morphing from a near stupor to sudden rage.

"You were charming us?" Matt rounded on Alice, which prompted her two nearest bodyguards, incubi of considerable height and girth, to start forward.

Alice raised a lazy hand to ward them off. "You can't blame a girl for trying."

"I wouldn't exactly call that acting in good faith," Matt said.

"I don't particularly care about your faith, Matthew."

With her mind cleared, Rose took a second look at the group headed their way. She didn't recognize any of them, especially in the dark. There were eleven by her count. And...she blinked and sucked in a sharp breath. Upon closer inspection, she realized she did recognize one of them, a handsome older man dressed in jeans and a bulletproof vest. She couldn't remember his name, but she had seen him on television the last several months as her interest in politics grew during Torres' campaign. A senator of some renown, he was a fixture on the evening news opinion shows so popular these days. Him, and the woman next to him—a young succubus senator on the rise inside the Beltway. God, were they all DC elites?.

Olivia, Preston, and Satterfield kept pace with the new group, careful to keep them surrounded though at an acceptable distance. Satterfield carried a subgun on one shoulder while the other two appeared empty-handed. Not that guns mattered much to vampires.

Rose didn't know how she felt about revealing the vampires' presence this early in the talks. Alice might take it as a threat, but Tanner must have deemed it a sound idea given the circumstances. If Alice and her people could sneak past them this easily—and charm the hell out of them in the offing—perhaps a show of force was a good idea.

"Senator Leeds," Thandiwe said to the young woman at the head of the group. "What an interesting surprise."

"Director." Leeds dipped her head fractionally as she and the others assumed positions adjacent to Alice and her bodyguards.

"Some of my friends decided to show their support," Alice said with a nod to Leeds. She turned back to Rose and Matt, grinning. "This, you see, is not a negotiation. Let us be clear on that from the outset. It is an unconditional surrender on your part."

"Call it what you like," Rose said, struggling to keep her composure, "we're here to talk terms."

"Terms for your ruffians, yes?"

"For the Order."

Alice rolled her eyes. "You and your clan names, how gang-like you are. I'm surprised you don't have a common tattoo and an initiation ritual. Exactly what terms are you demanding of me?"

Alice knew what Rose wanted on behalf of her people: freedom, the chance at representation in whatever government Alice forged on Society's glowing ashes, and the ability to live unmolested by anyone in power. If she wanted Rose to say all that aloud, fine.

"We want freedom. We want—"

"You want what every terrorist organization wants from a legitimate government: a share of the power."

"Legitimate, my ass," Matt said.

Ignoring him, Alice stepped forward to face Rose, close enough to touch though she made no move to do so. "I'm going to give you the same deal I've given your sort everywhere I've found you. My lads and I will allow you to live."

Rose ground her teeth for a moment before she trusted her voice. "How generous."

"I thought so."

"Question is, will we let you live?"

Alice's grin spread into a full smile, her teeth white in the wan light.

"You aren't facing the Order alone here, Alice." Thandiwe made no move to confront the smaller woman, yet somehow she seemed to grow taller, as if she had enlarged like a pool of light magnified. "The Consortium has thwarted you elsewhere."

Alice looked her up and down before nodding at her. "Yes, you make quite the coalition. The ragtag vagabonds, the slinkers, and—" Alice turned her gaze on Olivia and Preston. "The blood merchants of fear. Tell me, where is Piper? I see her babies, but not the queen herself."

Though Alice's tone remained conversational, Rose needed no draw on discernment to feel the anger boiling beneath her calm exterior. Piper's attacks on Alice's people had left the Irish succubus in a rage.

"We've cut our ties with her." Rose hoped the truth might go some way to winning Alice's favor. Better to admit the break than make it seem like Rose had Piper hidden away somewhere nearby waiting to strike. "What she did, killing your people, that was wrong."

"That was war." Alice shrugged one shoulder. "I had hoped she would show tonight, but perhaps that's for the best. Less distraction, eh?"

"I'm glad you see it that way," Rose said. "I had hoped we might start anew. I didn't come here to make threats or—"

"Of course, you didn't. You can offer me no threat. You came here to plead for my indulgence."

Rose's throat clogged with rage, her eyes opened wide.

"Tell me I'm wrong." Alice leaned forward, so their noses almost touched. "You tried attacking me once before. As the youngsters say these days, how did that go for you?"

"I want peace, Alice. I want the chance for my people to live without fear."

Alice shook her head slowly, a look of utter sadness and pity creasing her features. "Darling, you lost that chance the night you crossed me. The best you'll get now is the ability to go on living, unlike your vampire friends."

She made a gesture, an offhanded flick of her wrist, and Olivia's head exploded. Blood sprayed across the grass and onto the asphalt at Rose's feet, followed immediately by the concussion of distant gunfire.

Someone screamed, Rose thought it might have been herself, and Olivia's lifeless body hit the ground.

22

ENGAGEMENT

Rose couldn't say when she switched from clenching to drawing. It happened instantly, the way her shock and fear gave way before her rage. She could only hope that whatever supercharged charmer Alice employed either couldn't break through her raging emotions or else suddenly found herself too overwhelmed to control anyone.

The decision to attack came in like manner to Rose's towering anger. One moment she stood frozen, her body cold with shock and anguish. And in the next, her limbs unfolded like weapons of war. She momentarily forgot the pistol at her side, settling instead for a whip-cracking punch to Alice's jaw. If she had been human, the blow would have broken Alice's neck on impact. Maybe it did. It certainly sent the smaller succubus reeling backward on her heels, her face contorted in pain and not a little surprise. She must have supposed herself so much faster than Rose; she saw no danger in standing close.

Big mistake.

That answered at least one question: Alice's charmer hadn't stopped Rose from delivering that punch, which meant she was free to exact revenge. Rose showed her teeth and drew every trait she could manage.

Alice fetched up against one of her thugs, who dutifully helped her find her balance while his peers drew concealed weapons to defend their leader. Rose half expected Alice to call them off as she had earlier, but not this time. Alice smiled, blood staining her white teeth, and with a bestial growl, launched herself at Rose, her limbs a blur of speed.

Gunfire filled the air, loud enough to damage hearing with its relentless barking. Rose didn't notice. She was too busy fending for her life. Alice moved with a supernatural swiftness, grace, and accuracy Rose had only ever managed to match once in her life. The fear draw had given her that sort of sublime animation—a kind of mechanical precision no physical body should be able to obtain. And like a machine, it robbed her of all emotion, all care except that directly associated with the moment. She recognized the fear draw in Alice, but Rose refused to reach for it herself. Its passionless drive struck fear in her—fear of what she might become if ever again she sought its cold, raw power.

However, relying on her on regular abilities left Rose at an appreciable disadvantage, one she could feel the instant Alice attacked.

Though Rose managed to duck two of the other woman's first punches, a swift kick to the gut doubled her over. Pain shot through her like a bullet. For an instant, she feared Alice had managed to shoot her, but she had no gun, only an immense draw on speed and strength, two traits she put to work again when she followed up the kick with a resounding left hook that spun Rose to the asphalt in a heap.

It took a deep draw on healing and wakefulness for Rose to remain conscious. Even so, the world spun for a few seconds as she scrambled to gain her feet. Such a delay would have proven deadly had Chibueze and Matt not intervened. Matt, who knew the fear draw well and wasn't afraid to employ it from time to time when necessary, interposed his body between Alice and Rose while Chibueze attempted to punch the Irish succubus in the jaw.

The blow missed by inches as Alice jerked out of its path, dropped one shoulder, and delivered an uppercut to his jaw that sounded like someone flat-handing a ripe pumpkin. Chibueze slammed into one of the parked cars, stumbled sideways in a desperate attempt to keep his balance, and sprawled on the ground.

Before Alice's blow had connected with Chibueze's jaw, Matt attempted to strike her in the ribs. The punch landed, but she rolled with it, sapping much of its impact, while simultaneously twisting to land a horrifyingly powerful counter to Matt's jaw. His head rocked, his face seemingly folded in on itself for a moment like a boxer caught on super slow-motion playback.

Even with his own draw on fear, Matt was no match for Alice. Neither was Rose, and she knew it, but that didn't mean she would give up. Suppressing her urge to catch Matt before he could hit the pavement like Chibueze before him, she drew speed and charged Alice in hopes of catching her off guard.

Screaming, almost entirely unaware of the bullets whizzing past her or the brawl raging all around, Rose barreled into the other woman with outraged abandon. She threw a left-right-left combination that should have floored Alice, but though one of the punches grazed her shoulder, Alice slipped and rolled away from them with the agility of a ballerina. Rose screamed in rage, fists and feet awhirl with deadly intent, but no amount of anger, speed, or even discernment appeared adequate to the task.

Alice, almost playfully, struck Rose across the face with an open hand followed by a blow to her throat that left her gasping for air. It was all she could do to remain on her feet as purple blotches burst in her vision. She drew healing to clear it and just had time to right herself before Alice slammed her against Thandiwe's car. The door bit painfully into her back. She tried to free herself, but Alice held her pinned, one arm across her throat. Rose threw a knee in an attempt to catch Alice unprepared, but she deftly evaded it and pressed closer.

"Your people are dying." Alice spoke into Rose's ear like a lover, her voice frustratingly calm despite Rose's struggles. With a grip like a thousand-ton glacier, Alice turned Rose's head to face the abandoned park.

In the chaos of her own fight, Rose had lost track of the larger battle. She saw now that many of her people hadn't engaged. The same was true for Thandiwe and nearly a dozen of her forces. A handful of their combined crew had left their positions in the park to take on the enemy, but most stood in place, unmoving. Preston, the only vampire left with Olivia dead, fought on, but despite his best efforts, and the seemingly limitless powers of an enraged vampire, he was no match for Alice's lads combined with nearly thirty more succubi allied with her. Though he remained dangerous to any five of them, they were, at this point, playing with him—pummeling him slowly into submission. Not that he would ever stop fighting. From the look of manic rage on his face, Preston would die seeking revenge for his slain sister.

"Charmed," Rose said, the realization coming with the word. Alice's powerful charmers hadn't bothered keeping Rose, Matt, and Chibueze in check. Instead, they had focused on the bigger threat: Tanner and his guard units.

"It's one of the most undervalued of our gifts, don't you think?" Alice gazed on the frozen slinkers arrayed before them. "We all have it, which I suppose makes us take it for granted. But it's a most deadly sort of power in the hands of a master."

Try as she might, Rose couldn't tell who amongst Alice's people might be the charmer turning her forces into mannequins. Not that fingering the perpetrator would do her much good. With her impossible strength, Alice didn't need mind tricks to neutralize Rose. Fighting her was like trying to swim against a whirlpool. Rose had as much chance of breaking free to stop the charming as a puppy had of jumping a chain-link fence.

"What do you want?" Rose grumbled past Alice's arm across her throat. She was keenly aware of the gun still holstered at her hip but knew she could never draw it faster than Alice could react.

"The first thing I want is your vampire friends dead. The lads are having their fun with that one," Alice cocked her head at Preston, his face a blood-streaked mess. "But I think playtime is over. Lads, kill that monster already."

No creature Rose knew of could soak up damage like a vampire or one of their misbegotten cousins, the wight. But though their capacity for healing outstripped even the most powerful of succubi, all things had limits. Unlike movie vampires—fanciful creatures possessed of life beyond life—real vampires were living creatures. Their bodies, while resilient, functioned according to the dictates of their peculiar biology. Therefore, when one of Alice's lads caught Preston about the middle with both arms, and two others set about ripping his head from his shoulders, the dictates of life demanded their due. Preston's screaming cut off abruptly as his skull separated from his body. One of the lads, smiling like an imbecile child, held it aloft while the others cheered.

Rose's gorge tried to rise. She struggled to look away, but Alice kept her head turned to the gruesome scene.

Satterfield, frozen in place like everyone else, showed no sign of emotion, but Rose got the feeling she knew exactly what had happened and was undoubtedly screaming inside the silent prison of her body.

"We don't abide vampires in our lands." Alice relaxed her grip on Rose's jaw. "That is the first law of Irish rule. Simple, eh? The second is even easier: you do as you're told, and we let you live. I know you think you can make life hard for us here, but you're wrong. In fact, I'd wager you're starting to understand that better tonight, aren't you? You see, I don't fight limited wars, Rose. I don't leave enemies to stab me in the spine. That is why I win. Do you understand?"

Rose swallowed and nodded. She did understand. And though she raged inside for the loss of Olivia and Preston, and maybe the Order itself, she knew her best chance at saving the remainder of her people rested solely on her willingness to submit. She glanced at Matt. He had regained his feet but appeared charmed like the others.

"You will quell your people," Alice said. "You'll tell them not to fight. Otherwise, I kill them. All of them. Everyone who has ever associated with you or your Order will die."

"Everyone?" The male voice spoke so close to Rose's back, she momentarily thought he must be inside the car behind her.

Alice's eyes went wide. "Who the devil are you?"

"I'm not the devil, *señora,* just his son."

Rose knew that voice. "Rubio?"

"*Si*. How are you, Rose Carver? Not so good, I think. You remember, *Señior* Kraft and I offered our help for you all that time ago? Perhaps now you want to take it?"

"Yes! God in heaven, yes."

"I thought you might reconsider." Rubio's voice had moved. He sauntered into view around the backside of Thandiwe's car to lean on the trunk. "If I'm telling the truth, *señiorita,* I was going to help you anyhow. I've been meaning to run down this Irish *puta* for months, and now seems as good a time as any."

"Lads!" Alice shouted without taking her gaze off Rubio.

Rose expected to hear running feet headed their way. Instead came the sound of renewed gunfire and the unmistakable wail of vampires going to battle. Shoving hard at the now distracted Alice, Rose managed to turn her head enough to view the park. The sight made her smile.

Dozens of vampires boiled out of the trees like living shadows. The bewildered succubi, both the Irish and their American counterparts, struggled to face the onslaught, but the numbers were quickly overwhelming their ranks. Pound for pound, a vampire outstripped a succubus in strength, speed, and power in almost every case. Even a relatively weak vampire tended to possess more votaries than the average succubus, since blood ties created bonds for them not only with their victim but with that victim's family as well. Because of their relatively low population compared to their succubus cousins, vampires could rarely front large enough numbers to pose any significant threat. From the look of things, however, Rubio had solved that problem.

"Stop this!" Alice's drawn-enhanced voice boomed across the lot with so much force, Rose felt it reverberate in her chest.

Rubio nodded as he stood up from the car. "*Si,* let's stop this."

The words had barely escaped his lips before Rubio had his hands wrapped tightly about Alice's throat. He slung her to one side like a sack of dirt and slammed her against Rose's van. Her back dented the door, and her head cracked the window in a spray of tiny glass fragments. Giving her no time to recover, Rubio reversed directions and pounded her into Thandiwe's car. Her arm went through the driver's side window and came out bloody.

"What happened? Why are there vampires?" Thandiwe, who had only a moment before been standing like a department store dummy behind the car, grasped Rose's arm and pulled her away from the fray. "I lost time, I think."

"Charm." Rose didn't have time to say more. She wrested her hand free and dashed after Rubio and Alice, who had progressed almost to the edge of the lot.

The vampire no longer had things all his own way. While he had managed to get the upper hand via surprise, she was without question the strongest succubus Rose had ever faced. Rubio's strength and speed might outclass hers—it was hard to tell—but if so, not by much.

Alice slipped from his grasp, side-stepped like a seasoned boxer, and punched him three times, two in the ribs, once in the face. He stumbled sideways, off-balance, and would have received another, likely more damaging blow from Alice if Rose hadn't slammed into her from behind at speed. She took the other succubus to the ground. They slid in the overgrown grass, Alice struggling to throw Rose off her, but her angles were wrong.

Knowing she couldn't maintain the dominant position for long against a far stronger opponent, Rose punched Alice twice in the face while she had the chance and then rolled quickly away.

Alice jumped to her feet in the wet grass, her jeans and designer shirt covered in muck. She looked ready to tear Rose apart with her nails. Unfortunately for her, she no longer faced Rose alone. Rubio stood like a stone monolith facing her, and so did Thandiwe, who had taken up a position next to Rose, and Matt, and Chibueze.

Rose could see Alice calculating her odds at taking them all and coming up short. Powerful she might be, with her draw on fear, but even she had her limits, and the fear draw tended to give its succubus a clear mind for logic. A short glance over one shoulder made that estimation even worse. Two of her lads were down, along with most of the extra muscle she had brought along. Leeds and the male senator whose name Rose couldn't remember both lay still in the grass.

Alice cursed and started to turn, obviously intending to run for the trees. With her level of votaries and pure drawing power, Rose knew she would never catch the woman. One of the vampires might have better luck, but given the tumult of battle behind her, Alice stood a good chance of escaping.

Despite her doubts, Rose nonetheless drew speed in anticipation of chasing after Alice, but the Irish succubus never got the chance. Without warning, a gunshot flared in the night, and Alice jerked suddenly, her shirt turning dark with irregular splotches of blood. The gun fired three more times, and Alice collapsed.

Jason Kraft stepped out of the darkness wearing a gray trench coat and a vintage 1940s style hat, a large caliber revolver smoking at his side. "God, that felt good."

"You came," Matt said, his voice flat.

"You invited me."

Rose stared between them, her heart hammering, her mouth hanging open. "You called your father?"

"I never trusted Alice for one second."

"But you said—"

"I said I didn't trust my father." Matt's lopsided grin looked forced. "But better him than her."

"Sounds like my stock is on the rise." Jason turned to survey the last of the fighting. A handful of Alice's people still battled the circling vampires who had mixed liberally with Rose's force while the Consortium members stood watch. The tables had turned.

"What shall we do with them?" Rubio asked.

"This." Jason marched to the edge of the circle. "Stop playing with your food, people. Kill them!"

"No, wait!" Rose started forward, her heart in her throat. She wasn't opposed to using lethal force when attacked, but she would never condone siccing vampires on an already defeated group of succubi.

Unfortunately, her voice went unheard, or at least unheeded. The vampires made short work of the remnants, some feeding, most settling for beating their victims to death.

Rose swore and buried her face in Matt's shoulder until the sounds of ripping and tearing ceased. The sight, sound, and smell of the fight left her feeling sick.

"They would have done the same to us," Jason said without the least bit of sympathy or regret in his tone.

"They did exactly the same to Preston." Rubio, not one given to moving unless forced, actually inclined his chin toward the young vampire's remains, his face a blank slate.

Rose followed the gesture, and her breath caught. "Valerie."

Satterfield sat on her knees, both hands folded over Preston's headless body. At some point, part of her long hair had escaped her bun. It hung in her face, unnoticed. To Rose's surprise, the super-model-level beauty wasn't crying. She sat in silence.

Seeing her that way brought back the gravity of all that had happened. Rose sank to her own knees, her chest tight, her eyes stinging with tears. First Olivia, whom Rose had grown closer to than she had ever imagined possible, and now Preston, who had clearly loved Satterfield. Sadness like a smothering weight flooded over her. She wrapped her arms around her friend, and the two of them sat rocking, taking what solace they could from one another under the glare of magnified loss.

Rose wasn't sure how long they remained that way. Eventually, Matt and Tanner helped her and Satterfield to a car. The police were coming, or so Rose gleaned from the stream of talk that fluttered around her without ever quite entering her skull. She might have slept, she couldn't say, but Matt's voice eventually penetrated through to her consciousness.

"What do you think?" he asked.

"About what?" Rose sat in the front seat of their van. She twisted around, momentarily frightened they had separated her from Satterfield, but no, Valerie lay asleep across the van's backbench.

"I said, Piper's going to find out what happened tonight one way or another. We should probably be the ones to tell her."

Rose swallowed. Her throat felt parched. "Yeah, we probably should."

"She's not going to take it well."

"She's going to go insane. More insane than I feel right now."

"What do you think she'll do?"

Rose looked at him, her blood running cold at the thoughts his question raised. "I don't know for sure, but it's going to be bad."

They drove in silence for several minutes before Matt spoke again, his tone inquisitive. "You know, something odd struck me just now."

"What's that?"

He turned to face her, his brows furrowed. "Where was your sister tonight?"

23

CATALYST

A twinge of guilt washed over Rose as she stood in the wings of the auditorium. How could she go on with business as usual a mere three days after losing Olivia and Preston? It shouldn't have been like this. They deserved to be mourned. Problem was, Rose didn't have time for that. None of them did.

She and Matt had organized a short notice confab at the offices of Run Time Error, Inc. for their allies. What the building's auditorium lacked in size—it could accommodate little more than a hundred people—it made up for in amenities. The flat-screen hanging over the stage appeared larger than a jumbotron to her unpracticed eye.

Rose had worried Moss might get upset at so many people invading his private domain, but the slim incubus had appeared excited by the prospect. He said he liked the idea of bringing so many different factions together. That didn't mean he enjoyed the sight of Jason Kraft in his building, but the two hadn't interacted so far as Rose knew, and she doubted they would.

"I have hosted so many speaking engagements I've lost count of them all," Thandiwe said. "But for some reason, this one is making me more nervous than all the rest combined."

"I feel it too, but we'll get through it." Rose patted Thandiwe's shoulder.

"Well," Matt said, grinning, "either that, or we're doomed. Can't see order coming from all the chaos we've caused."

"Thank you for that piercing insight." Thandiwe gave him a sour look.

Rubio grunted. "He's right. If this doesn't work, I'm taking my people back to Mexico."

"And I'll go with you." Kraft nodded at the vampire, though his expression spoke reluctance at the prospect.

Gloria Torres, who had mounted the stage a moment before, stepped up to the lectern, the stage lights illuminating her silken black hair and gorgeous face. She had taken the end of her campaign bid as more of a blow than Rose would have expected, but like any true professional, she bounced back fast. She pulled the microphone down to speak.

"Ladies and gentlemen, thank you for coming here on such short notice. Your respective groups have convened this meeting to best decide how we all should proceed in the future. We are conducting it based on Consortium rules, which call for voting representatives to consider proposals and make decisions as they see fit, because haste is important right now."

Rose couldn't see the audience, but their utter silence made her worry. Did they mistrust their leaders? Or perhaps they hated the idea of siding with one or the other faction in the mishmash coalition she and the others were trying to form. She couldn't blame them. If the slinker she had been a few years ago happened upon this conclave, she doubted that Rose Carver would have stuck around five minutes. She would have figured the thing for a lost cause and gotten on with her life.

"We encourage audience participation in the upcoming meeting," Torres said. "But please wait until after the various speakers have presented their case. We will hold an open forum discussion first, then open the floor for questions and suggestions."

With that, she turned to face the wing and began calling out names, Thandiwe first. Part of the crowd cheered, but even that reception was tepid. They picked up a bit on the next, Matt, and then even more for Rose, followed by Rubio, but the cheering nearly died out when Torres called for Jason Kraft. A few succubi in the front row dutifully clapped, but no one else.

They sat in comfortable padded chairs arranged in a semi-circle facing the audience. Rose found the microphone pack on her back waistband uncomfortable but resisted the urge to adjust it. She wouldn't want to damage the thing.

She gazed at the crowd. With the house lights up, she could see them clearly. Part of her despaired at the clear lines of separation between them all.

The Africans, a smaller sample than the group Thandiwe had brought to evaluate the Order, sat in a cluster on the right side of the stage. They watched the various leaders take their seat with stoic expressions, but Rose thought they had a doubtful air about them.

Filling out the auditorium's middle section, Rose's own Order ops appeared attentive yet reserved. Most of them she could name on sight, though a few eluded her. No matter if she knew them or not, Rose was confident they would follow her and Matt so long as the two of them proved worthy of such devotion. Even with her heart aching, she felt determined to earn that loyalty.

Rubio's vampires, a gaggle of pale, unimpressed faces, and Jason Kraft's succubi occupied the remaining seats. Even amongst their group, the division between vampire and succubus jumped out. They sat together but separated by an invisible wall that wouldn't let them mix.

As moderator for the discussion, Torres launched into a quick recitation of the prevailing facts and events that had led up to their groups coming together to defeat Alice McAleese. It didn't take long since most of the crowd likely knew all the salient facts. Rose and Torres had cut those out, along with anything that might have hamstrung the meeting in endless questions. Better, she figured, to let their respective leaders cover that ground later. A few of the succubi in the crowd looked shocked at one fact or another, but as a whole, they appeared unruffled.

"At this point, I'd like to give the time over to Thandiwe Buhari, director of the Consortium, to explain our purpose here." Torres moved aside and gave Thandiwe a slight nod.

The African succubus, who had chosen a shiny green and silver gown with matching headdress for the evening, smiled at the crowd, most of whom applauded her even if only out of a sense of kindness. Rubio's vampires didn't move, but Rose figured that was more affectation than protest.

"Friends," Thandiwe said. "I have been asked to present a proposition for an alliance between our various peoples. Those of you who know me know I detest bureaucracy. I have no time for it. And thus, I shall address the matter straight on."

The Consortium group sparked applause led by Sammy Wolf, who stood up to whistle through his hands.

"Sit down, Sammy Wolf; you embarrass yourself." Thandiwe smiled despite the chiding remark.

"Oh, I wasn't cheering you, Thandiwe," called Sammy. "I was cheering for brevity!"

Everyone laughed, excluding the vampires, though Rose thought she saw one or two almost smile.

"Ayiee!" Thandiwe said. "Your mouth moves, old man, but nothing intelligent appears."

This brought a rousing cheer from the Africans, many of whom slapped Sammy's back or shook his shoulders. He laughed with them, taking the ribbing good-naturedly, and just like that, most of the tension in the room vanished. Rose still sensed doubt from the crowd, but the feeling of complete incompleteness had fled.

"As I was saying, we're here to discuss combining our forces." Thandiwe let the silence that followed the laughter hang for a moment, giving her words more weight. "I know many of you don't like the idea. In some respects, neither do we on this stage. For many years, my own Consortium has eschewed all contact with coven kingdoms of any sort. While we seldom had cause to fight them, we made no efforts to ally ourselves with them, and largely ignored their existence insomuch as we could.

"I'm afraid that ploy is no longer useful in this changing world, my friends. The vampire, Piper Ross, is building a powerful—as she names it —coven queendom. No one knows the full extent of her network. It could be hundreds, perhaps even thousands of loyal vampires. We in the Consortium can no longer afford to ignore these numbers. We do not know her plans, but we fear they may well involve the eventual usurpation of American Society. If that happens, she will control most of North America, because there will be no one to stand against her. What about the Irish, I hear you asking. Even with Alice McAleese dead, someone will surely take her place. Won't they attempt to stop a vampire takeover?"

Thandiwe shook her head, her lips pulled tight into a line. "Alice McAleese created a cult of personality. Someone may come along to replace her eventually, but when? From all that we see, with both American and Irish Society reeling, Piper Ross stands in the perfect position to assert her power here and defend it for centuries to come. If we fail to act, we may inadvertently forward her ambitions. I implore you all to help us avoid such an eventuality. Thank you."

Stronger applause followed Thandiwe than had preceded her. No matter the outcome, she had at least impressed some in the crowd. Torres approached the microphone.

"Now we shall hear from one of our Order leaders, Rose Carver."

The Order ops put up an impressive cheer, some of them drawing voice to bolster their calls or strength to turn their clapping into the sounds of gunfire. To Rose's astonishment, many of the Consortium members almost matched her own people's applause. Perhaps her fight with Alice had won her appreciation from the sector, which was nice considering so many voted against including the Order in their ranks during their admittance hearing.

"I feel the same as Thandiwe," Rose said into the mic. "I don't like long speeches. I want to know what's going on without any fluff, and I think you do as well. Brass tacks, as my father used to say. It's time someone takes the wheel in Society."

That brought a cheer, especially from the Order section, but even some of the vampires clapped.

"We in the Order have spent too long begging for a place at the table from elitists inside the Society machine. I thought, after we defeated the fear factory, they might see us as something more than mere slinkers. But if the last year has taught me anything, it's this: victory can't defeat bigotry." Rose felt immensely proud of that line. "Even if Alice McAleese and Piper Ross hadn't left American Society in disarray, I see now the Order would still remain outcast. In fact, showing them our might may well have made things worse for us. I and the others on this stage are proposing a coalition of our groups not only to protect ourselves in the coming days but with the eventual goal of asserting rule over Society."

She had more to say, but the crowd overrode her with cheers. She nodded and left it at that.

Rubio took the lectern next, moving in that staid, creepy way of his. He stared at the crowd for the better part of thirty seconds, an absolute eternity when it came to public speaking. Rose lifted an eyebrow at Matt, and he shrugged.

"Do vampires get stage fright?" Rose whispered.

"What should we do if he never speaks?" Matt looked on the verge of standing to approach the seemingly frozen vampire.

"I guess I could do his part," Rose said. "Maybe we can—"

"*Amigos*," Rubio said, his voice deeper and more resonant than Rose had ever heard it. He placed his hands on either side of the lectern, his face suddenly animated, his spine straight, his dark eyes sparkling under the stage lamps. "You and I have lived in one world our entire lives, a world of simple truths. Vampires are few; succubi are many. Vampires have little power. Succubi have much. This world stands on its rules—rules that may have seen my kind held down and held back, and yet those same rules also protected us and our succubus cousins from detection by humans. It was never perfect, but it was ours. That world, though, is coming to an end. Society is falling, and Piper Ross wants to control it."

The vampires in the room hissed in unison, startling many of the succubi, Rose included, who jumped in awkward surprise.

"We cannot let the upstart, Piper, take control. She doesn't respect tradition—she doesn't respect us. By joining with the Consortium and the Order, we cement our place in Society's future rule. We will make certain vampires are given the same rights and freedoms as any succubus so long as we obey the law."

Many of the succubi in the crowd appeared uncomfortable at those words, but the vampires, breaking all precedent to Rose's mind, stood from their chairs to cheer and applaud.

Rubio nodded once and then, resuming his statue-like mannerisms, marched swiftly back to his seat, all signs of his previous emoting gone.

"Thank you for that impassioned address," Torres said, seemingly uncertain whether to smile or frown. She settled on the former and adjusted the mic for her height. "There you have it, folks. You've heard from your various leaders what we're proposing. We'd like to form a new organization that encompasses all of our people worldwide based here in the States. Our immediate goal, meaning in three to five years, will be to establish control over American Society with the intention of reshaping it to become more equitable for us all. Now, I would like to open the floor to questions. Please approach one of the mics set up on either aisle to address the stage.

Fewer people than Rose expected offered up questions. Most involved how she and the others proposed to govern a large group of succubi and vampires, two factions that had never gotten along well in the past. Since this was a preliminary meeting to gauge the popular opinion of establishing the coalition in the first place, Rose and the others could provide few details.

"We don't know yet, I'm sorry," Rose said, addressing a young succubus in the fourth row. She looked maybe twenty and worried.

"Well, who would be the leader?" asked the woman. "Which one of you will be in ultimate control?"

Everyone on stage stared around at the others in silence. For a moment, Rose worried Jason Kraft might speak up. The group forbade him from addressing the crowd, leaving his faction's part up to Rubio. Most people hated the man, but he had motivated Rubio and his loyal vampires, along with no small number of succubi, to band together. Saving Rose and her crew from Alice hadn't hurt either. That was probably why she hadn't heard too many disparaging remarks about Jason's presence.

"I think it should be Rose Carver," said Rubio, stunning everyone not just with his outburst but his words.

Rose could tell by the expression on Thandiwe's face, the African woman fought some internal struggle before she nodded. "Yes, that is a good idea."

Rose held up both hands. "No, on two counts. First, this is premature. We haven't even voted on allying ourselves."

"That can be remedied," Thandiwe said.

"And second," Rose said, ignoring the interruption, "if anyone should lead, it's Thandiwe. She has more experience than me leading a much larger organization."

Truth told, Rose wanted to nominate Matt for the position, but when she suggested it the night before, he roundly vetoed the idea. Not only did he detest the very thought, but he also pointed out his former role as one of his father's top wranglers, commissioned to kidnap succubi for the fear factory. While he had proven himself to the slinkers within the Order, he didn't feel others, especially in foreign nations with whom their new coalition might one day seek alliances, would be willing to ignore his past sins.

Kraft and Rubio were out. Kraft for the same reasons as Matt only tenfold, and Rubio because the succubi in their group would never accept a vampire as their top leader. The mere fact they seemed okay with the idea of including vampires, especially the Consortium members, was already surprising enough. Rose figured pushing them further might introduce strain their new group couldn't yet absorb.

That left her and Thandiwe. Between them, Rose knew Thandiwe coveted the position more. In fact, Rose didn't want it at all. That left her wondering why the Consortium director had seconded the suggestion. She gave Thandiwe a quizzical expression.

"I know members of the Consortium may wonder why I shouldn't lead," Thandiwe said, projecting her voice with a draw. "And yes, I have had experience with this sort of thing. But the bulk of our members, both succubus and vampire will, at least for now, reside in the United States."

"That's right!" said an incubus in the Order section of the crowd.

"Perhaps in the future, we may elect a leader—and yes, I said elect —from outside this country, but I do not think that time is now."

The crowd cheered Thandiwe's words.

"We should choose Rose Carver because she knows what it's like to lead and to be led," Thandiwe went on. "The succubi here, while many of them may not respect her due to her upbringing, they at least know her name. To them, for the most part, I am no one. Better they should fight for a succubus they know, and one from their own country, than a complete outsider like me."

"How about it?" Matt said into Rose's ear over the applause that followed. "It looks like you've got a job offer, and it sounds a hell of a lot better than waiting tables."

"What about—" Rose glanced around, aware of how many gazes rested on her, how many super-powered ears could likely hear every word she was saying, especially once the clapping died off a bit. Then again, what did they matter when it came to her and Matt? "What about us, our plans? We were supposed to have that talk, but I didn't think that meant on a stage in front of a hundred people."

He flashed his lopsided grin. "So, we put it off a little while. We're still together. I wouldn't let you do this alone, and I think, right now, they need you more than me. Go for it."

Rose watched his eyes for a moment and saw reflected in them all the hope, love, and pride she felt in her own soul. She kissed him, and the crowd erupted in cheers. Drawing calm and strength, she approached the lectern. It took her a moment, even with votary-supplied calm, to find her voice.

"I'm willing to lead you if that's what you want, but maybe we should have that vote first?"

Succubi and a surprising number of vampires laughed. Chibueze appeared from the wings with a tablet. He proceeded to quickly explain the voting system. Everyone in attendance had already downloaded the Consortium's voting app, which they used to quickly make their desires known.

The results, a ninety-three percent victory in favor of forming a united coalition, appeared on the enormous flat-screen behind Rose, who hadn't left the lectern. She smiled up at it despite the overwhelming responsibility settling on her shoulders and the aching sadness over Olivia's death she had managed to suppress until now. For some reason, even as a wave of happy charm and adulation washed over her, those emotions returned. Part of her didn't deserve happiness, she knew, not with Leslie and now Olivia dead. She wanted to cry and held it back to mimic joy and pleasure at the vote.

"Shall we vote now for a leader?" Chibueze asked. "Is it necessary? Or do we all know it's Rose Carver?"

"I won't accept without a vote," Rose said, making sure her voice carried to the open mic.

"Fine, fine. Give me a moment to set up the next poll." Chibueze tapped away at his tablet, his handsome face focused hard on the screen.

A phone rang in the crowd. One of her people answered it, but he wasn't alone. More phones rang, the sounds accompanied by hundreds of new message alert chimes. Rose twisted around to the other leaders on stage, most of whom had already pulled out their phones to check their incoming alerts, even Matt.

Someone in the first two rows cursed loud enough to be heard across the silent auditorium, and a welter of moans and gasped followed.

"What the hell?" Rose asked as she resumed her seat next to Matt to peek at his phone. Her eyes went wide at the image on his screen, and all the breath left her.

Piper Ross, lounging in a comfortable chair, one foot tucked up under her opposite thigh, sat opposite a well-known reporter named Allen Mitchell, a man known for insightful interviews of people from the biggest Hollywood stars to everyday bus drivers.

"Do we have enough live viewers yet?" Allen asked someone off-camera.

"Up to three million," said a faint voice.

"That should be enough," Allen said. "Don't you think, Ms. Ross? I bet we'll get more as we go along."

"Three million should be plenty, hon." Piper's southern drawl sounded particularly deep juxtaposed to Allen's polished news speak.

Allen faced the camera, which zoomed in on his chiseled features. Rose had always thought the guy could have made it in the movies if had wanted. He flashed his trademark smile, the one that made all the stay-at-home-moms crush on him, and cleared his throat.

"Hello," he said with utmost confidence. "I'm Allen Mitchell, and this is an exclusive live event being simultaneously streamed on the internet and my mother network, CNN. We're interrupting our usual programming to bring you an exclusive story, one I'm not sure many of my viewers will at first believe. Sitting before me is Piper Ross. Ms. Ross is a vampire. Yes, friends, you heard me right. I'm not insane or drunk, nor is this April Fool's in July. Ms. Ross is an honest-to-God vampire. Is that right, Ms. Ross?"

The camera switched to Piper's exquisite face. She smiled, and her fangs slowly extended to cover her human teeth. "Yes, Allen, I am."

"You drink blood?"

Piper nodded. "I do indeed. But don't worry, I won't drink yours."

Allen grinned. "That does put me at ease. Now, Ms. Ross—"

"Piper."

"Piper, I understand you have something you'd like to share with our viewing audience, yes?"

Rose couldn't tell for sure if Allen was under Piper's charm or merely doing his job. Having experienced Piper's influence a couple of times in her life, she knew it could go either way. Piper could be subtle when she wanted to be.

"I do." The image zoomed in closer so that Piper's face filled Matt's phone screen. "I want the people of America to know they've been lied to for hundreds of years. Their government is a sham, one controlled by creatures much like me. And, yeah, I know that's hard to swallow coming from a woman on the internet—this could all be a hoax—but I think most people are going to realize the truth before the end of tonight."

"You believe you can convince them?" Allen sounded doubtful.

"Oh, I don't have to convince them; my daughters will do that."

24

FINAL DISCLOSURE

The first reports of congressional assassination began less than a minute later. Matt's phone received an alert from Reuters. The bulletin said Senator Becky Linden of Ohio had been shot in her car driving home from a party by an unknown suspect. By the time Rose finished scanning that report, a new one had posted. According to it, Congressman Michael Stroud out of Alabama had been shot at point-blank range while shopping in a DC-area mall.

More followed. Hundreds more.

On the live feed, which Chibueze had moved to the flat screen above the stage, Allen Mitchell's gaze went unfocused for a moment even though Piper was in the middle of answering one of his previous questions. He pressed a finger to the earpiece on the right side of his head.

"I'm very sorry, Piper, I'm getting an urgent message from my producers. It seems there have been a string of attacks throughout the metropolitan DC area over the last several minutes. These look like coordinated—for lack of a better word—assassinations." Allen swallowed, and his throat made a sound loud enough for his mic to pick up.

"My daughters," Piper spoke like an affluent southern matriarch presenting her marriageable age girls to an interested suitor.

Allen's gaze returned to her, his blue eyes rounded. "Your daughters are doing this?"

Piper nodded once.

A series of expressions passed over Allen's face, like an actor trying them out for a class. He settled at last for consternation—the ignorant but otherwise intelligent man finally recognizing a con. Except, this was no con. "You are what you say?"

"You put me on the air. You must have believed something I told you."

"You lifted those weights." Allen turned to the camera. "Folks, Piper lifted a six-hundred-pound barbell in front of me. There was no way I was tricked. This is all quite real—extraordinary, but real."

Rose, her heart in her throat, flicked her gaze between the huge screen and Matt's handheld. His phone buzzed—it had hardly stopped in the last few minutes—and Rose read the newest headline.

Shots fired at home of General Andrew Gormley, Chairman of the Joint Chiefs of Staff, the senior military officer in the United States. Preliminary reports indicated the general died en route to George Washington University Hospital.

"Why is she doing this?" Thandiwe asked. "Attacking Alice was one thing, but exposing us all to the world, to the humans, this way is suicide. She's starting a war between us."

"Maybe," Matt said. "But she's also setting a precedent. She isn't waiting for us to organize. She's going on the attack. She wants to control Society before we get the chance."

On the screen, a pale and visibly distraught Allen Mitchell looked as though he wanted to escape but lacked the courage to run. "Why are you doing this? Killing all these people."

New alerts sounded across the auditorium, including one on Matt's phone. Another senator was dead.

"I know this will be hard to grasp, Allen." Piper's expression told of her sympathy, her heartache at performing a grisly yet inescapable task. "But those people you keep hearing pronounced dead in your ear; they weren't human. They were succubi. A succubus is a type of vampire, only instead of feeding on blood as I do, they feed on human abilities and emotions. They are the ones who have been in control of the United States since its inception."

A new message, a new death. This one the head of the FBI.

Allen shook his head. "Ma'am, I was willing to go along with all this on a lark. The weight thing was impressive, and I wanted to catch you lifting something similar tonight, but this is insane. I think, perhaps, you and your cronies are likewise insane. Can you please call off your daughters? If you need someone to beg them, I'll do it. I'll beg for the lives of any other people you plan to execute."

"No, I can't stop them." Piper's face fell for a moment as if part of her knew the immorality of what she did. "What you take for assassination is nothing more than house cleaning, Allen. We are making way for a new regime, one that places vampires where they belong, at the top."

"What about the average citizen?"

"You mean the humans?"

Allen nodded.

"Frankly, Allen, they don't rate. I have no intention of harming any humans who stay out of my way. For those who seek to impose their will on me and mine, however, it's a different story."

"Do you drink blood?" Allen looked queasy, but he held it together.

"Yes, but very rarely do I kill anyone through blood-drinking."

"Why is that?"

"First, because I have little desire to harm anyone outside a very short list. And second, it's nearly impossible to drink that much at once. Now, I said I would give an interview if you put me on your show, but I find this line of questioning too personal. Ask me something else."

"What are these succubuses—"

"Succubi."

"Succubi doing that makes you want to assassinate them? What crimes have they committed against you and your daughters?

A new wave of phone updates echoed across the audience, more than twenty messages arriving one atop the next. Rose's stomach ached. She wanted the bad news to end, but it kept coming. Unlike the previous updates, which all centered around the DC area, these new ones came from across every state in the union. Governors, local mayors, even city council members weren't safe from Piper's executioners.

Matt keyed his earpiece. "Tanner, your perimeter guard notice any activity outside the building?"

"Nothing, boss," Tanner replied, his voice tinny over the security channel. "I've got everyone on high alert though and I'm outside walking the perimeter now."

Rose couldn't help but remember how Alice and her minions had ghosted past Tanner's crew less than four nights ago. She hated herself for thinking it, but who said an army of vampires led by one of Piper's daughters couldn't do the same thing? Then again, the Run Time Error facility was supposedly secure.

Piper was still answering the previous question when Rose turned back to the screen.

"—there hasn't been one fair election in the history of this country. You've been enthralled by these creatures forever."

"But what you're proposing, it's a takeover." Some of the color had returned to Allen's face. He sat forward in his chair, eyes intense, the epitome of professional journalist written in his very stature. "Aren't you simply picking up where this supposedly corrupt government left off? If you assume power without a fair election, what makes you any different from the succubi you would replace?"

"One simple thing, Allen. Honesty." Piper smiled slowly, revealing her fangs one by one. "The succubi have lied to you and manipulated you for time out of mind. They ruled in secret. I won't do that. I'm going to run this country in the open. You have a vampire queen now. No hiding. No misdirection. I am exactly what I say."

Allen sat back, watching Piper, nodding slowly. "And what if I say you're a fraud? Yes, I saw you lift an impossible amount of weight, but I've seen a circus dwarf do the same sort of thing. It may have been staged."

"And the succubi my daughters have been excising from the world?"

"You're a psychopath in league with psychopaths. It wouldn't be the first time the world has seen that sort of thing. You've got some sort of prosthetic in your mouth, and a fixation with vampires in your brain. It doesn't make you real."

"No?"

"Oh, God," Rose whispered.

A hush had fallen in the auditorium as all eyes turned to the big screen. Piper, seemingly demure, alluring, sensual, leaned toward Allen the tiniest bit. Her fangs shone in whatever lights his production crew used to brighten their set.

"No," Allen said more firmly as if he might convince himself of his theory. "I say you're crazy, and you've committed atrocities because of your untreated psychoses."

The digital refresh on the jumbotron television wasn't fast enough to catch the instant Piper left her chair and sank her fangs into Allen Mitchell's throat. One instant, she sat still as a dozing cat, the next, she held him pinned to his seat, her jaws locked on his neck. He tried to push her off with all the effectiveness of a chocolate-bladed knife. He screamed, as did someone off-camera, while the succubi in the audience gasped, and the vampires looked on like owls.

Someone dashed into view, a portly, balding man dressed in jeans and a ball cap. He tried to push Piper off Allen, but she punched him in the gut, and he went down gasping, all while her lips remained solidly locked on the reporter's throat.

After some seconds that felt like a week, Piper released Allen. He was still breathing, but his eyes had rolled back into his head. He collapsed, unable to support his own weight. Alice turned to the camera and smiled, her fangs pink with her victim's blood.

Rose couldn't believe the show hadn't cut to commercial during all that, or maybe one of those old test frames from way back, anything to hide what had just happened. It occurred to her then that she had seen no commercials at all throughout the program, a near impossibility in this day and age. That meant Piper had allies in the control booth. In fact, she must have had people helping her at every level of this production, or it would never have aired, not on network news or even the internet.

"America," Piper said. "In the coming days, you're going to face a new reality. I am your queen. You can fight it, or you can prosper from it. The choice is yours. I have no ill will toward you. I want us to thrive together." She drew closer to the camera, her eyes peering out of the screen like two pools of hot oil. "But Rose Carver, I know you'll hear this. For you, I have nothing but hatred. You got my children killed. My only son, Preston, my sweet Olivia—I trusted you to care for her like your own. They died because of you, Rose, and I promise you this, you're going to die because of me."

THE END

ABOUT THE AUTHOR

David Alan Jones is a veteran of the United States Air Force where he served as an Arabic linguist. A 2016 Writers of the Future silver honorable mention recipient, David's work spans the science fiction, military sci-fi, fantasy, and urban fantasy genres. He is a martial artist, a husband, and a father of three.

An eclectic reader, David counts Anne Tyler, Stephen King, Lois McMaster Bujold, Robert J. Sawyer, J.K. Rowling, and many others among his favorite, and most influential, authors.

You can find out more about David's writing, including his current projects, at his website: davidalanjones.net.

FRIENDS OF FALSTAFF

Thank You to All our Falstaff Books Patrons, who get extra digital content each month! To be featured here and see what other great rewards we offer, go to www.patreon.com/falstaffbooks.

PATRONS

Dino Hicks
John Hooks
John Kilgallon
Larissa Lichty
Travis & Casey Schilling
Staci-Leigh Santore
Sheryl R. Hayes
Scott Norris
Samuel Montgomery-Blinn
Junkle

www.ingramcontent.com/pod-product-compliance
Lightning Source LLC
Chambersburg PA
CBHW030534310726
48979CB00010B/1905/J
9781645541042